"The Seed of Corruption" Book One Reviewed

This book is an exploration of love, life, crime - everything that our lives are about.

– Benjamin Franklin Awards

Resonating with the hardships of the recent global pandemic, *The Seed of Corruption* explores a complex world of large corporations and state-sponsored entities who are able to operate in plain sight, no matter how questionable their intent, while average citizens are distracted by the greater implications of a viral pandemic.

– BookTrib

It is a very thought-provoking read, reflective of the strange, intimidating times that we find ourselves living in, written with aplomb and a wry tone which gives the book an undertone of humour despite the serious matters proposed.

– Discovery

This is a thought-provoking thriller, with fresh insights. An intriguing journey written with wit and keen insight into deep matters. For those who like intelligent espionage thrillers. The character voices are fresh and likable even when doubting themselves. They display a strong capacity for growth. There is excellent critical thinking and problem solving as they journey to find a solution. Not overly romantic, but the reader sees an adult relationship unfold.

– Benjamin Franklin Awards

A.I. Fabler's THE SEED OF CORRUPTION is a heady stew of influences, from the travel literature of John Le Carré and Graham Greene to the dark journeys of *Apocalypse Now* and *Heart of Darkness*. Fabler's beautifully evocative, clever writing, however, transcends pastiche to emerge as a hauntingly original work.

— IndieReader

Fabler's ability to draw on his own experiences to portray a struggle with no easy escapes makes for a compelling story. It ultimately catapults protagonist Faraday into the world with dangerous results that hold thought-provoking implications for modern pandemic scenarios, making for an especially timely and involving read that will attract interest on many different levels and from different types of readers.

— Midwest Book Review

The Seed of Corruption by A. I. Fabler is a fantastic story that will hold your attention all the way through. Set against a backdrop of Vietnamese history and culture, this story will draw you in from the start, taking you on a journey from the stifling Mekong Delta to the remote outreaches, from fishing for Snakehead fish to trying to survive an epidemic while facing down corruption of the highest order. With action on every page, this is about more than just a simple romance. This is about searching for the truth, whatever that may be, about morals and ethics and you will feel every emotion as it plays out on the pages in front of you.

— Readers Favorite

THE ANTIGEN

The **SEED** *of* **CORRUPTION PT2**

A NOVEL

A.I. Fabler

W&L

Wild & Lawless

Also by the author:
'AGENDA 2060 Book One: The Future as It Happens' 2021
'AGENDA 2060 Book Two: AI and The View from Space' 2023
'The SEED of CORRUPTION: A Novel' 2022
'A Song for Leonard' 2023

ISBN 978-1-7386031-5-2 (Paperback)
ISBN 978-1-7386031-6-9 (Epub)

W&L
Wild & Lawless

Creative Management and Licensing
E: wildandlawless@aifabler.com

This version designed and edited by:
Robin Fuller, Editing
David Prendergast, Book Design

History repeating

On 22 January 2020, *The New York Times* ran the headline *As New Virus Spreads from China, Scientists See Grim Reminders*. The new virus was initially named SARS-CoV-2 after being identified as genetically related to the coronavirus responsible for the bird flu SARS outbreak of 2003. For over a year, mainstream media, leading scientists, and health bureaucrats worldwide maintained the line that any suggestions that the virus had originated in China's Wuhan laboratory were 'conspiracy theories'. Social media sites deplatformed users who dared to even raise such suspicions.

To label a belief as a conspiracy theory is to imply that it's false. More than that, it implies that the people who accept that belief, or even those who want to investigate whether it's true, are irrational. The term is used to stigmatize and marginalize people whose beliefs conflict with the officially sanctioned or orthodox beliefs of the time (whether rightly or wrongly).

There were, however, parallels that emerged between the bird flu version of SARS and COVID-19. The 2022 novel *The Seed of Corruption* was set in Vietnam during 2004 against the backdrop of the former. It was not common knowledge then that both China and the United States were experimenting with the manipulation of SARS viruses in contravention of international protocols—***just underreported***. However, my research over the intervening years revealed that the behavior of Big Pharma, government agencies, and corporate media displayed similar patterns.

The Seed of Corruption 2: The Antigen picks up the story and focuses on those patterns of behavior. If the first book was seen as unusually prescient at the time it was published at the height of the COVID pandemic, *The Antigen* can be read as a warning to watch for the emerging signs of the patterns already being repeated in the reportage of the influenza A (H5N1) bird flu virus threat in 2024.

This story is told using fictional characters and entities, including the wildlife painter, Anton Faraday, and the investigative journalist, Caroline Brinkley, who were at the center of the first book. All characters and events in this publication are fictitious, and any resemblance to real persons, living or dead, is purely coincidental.

I am indebted to David Bell, senior scholar at Brownstone Institute, a public health physician and biotech consultant on global health and a former medical officer and scientist at the World Health Organization (WHO), for permission to reprint his paper titled *Bird Flu, Fear, and Perverse Incentives* (June 10, 2024), which you will find in the appendix.

This story is far from over. In mankind's competition between good and evil, I don't yet have the courage to declare a winner.

A. I. Fabler, 2024

(Updated from the preface of The SEED of CORRUPTION, *Book One, 2022)*

The Antigen

PREVIOUSLY

Anton Faraday is a successful painter of wildlife whose career was launched by the commission of a series of paintings depicting threatened animal species, commissioned by the Paladin Foundation for the Environment, based in Switzerland. When one of those paintings turns up at Christie's auction house in London twenty years later, submitted by a vendor based in Vietnam, Faraday recognizes it as a forgery and heads off to Vietnam to track down its source.

His journey in search of the painting's origin is also a journey of self-discovery as he examines the legitimacy of his commercial success, the part that the Paladin patronage has played in it, and the role that his London gallery owner, Ralph Lutyen, has had in his career.

In a deserted hotel in Can Tho on the Mekong River, he meets an American journalist, Caroline Brinkley, who has an adopted Vietnamese brother, now working as a microbiologist in Hanoi for a subsidiary of the international pharmaceutical group Anglo Swiss BioLab. Faraday and Caroline arrange to meet again in Hanoi, and on a whim, she invites him to join her for the weekend in Sapa, in the Northern Highlands, where she is meeting with a wealthy charity donor to help launch an initiative establishing clean drinking water wells for mountain villages.

Their arrival in Sapa coincides with an accelerating spread of bird flu in the mountains, resulting in many deaths and rising fears in the local population. But the tribal leader who is to spearhead the establishment of village wells cannot be located, having headed into the mountain forest, so Faraday employs Duc, a Dao mountain guide he had met earlier in his travels, to try and track him down. Together they stumble into a heavily guarded encampment run by the Paladin Foundation, headed by an American named Sam McAvoy. It seems that Paladin is protecting an area where they are harvesting a valuable seed used in pharmaceutical manufacturing.

Back in Hanoi, Faraday is struck down with the virus, and Caroline monitors his recovery while filing stories on the bird flu epidemic with the East Asia News Agency (EANA) headed by Sinclair Baines. Faraday has learned that the counterfeit painting was sold by Sam McAvoy, who works not for Paladin, but at the US Embassy. Meanwhile, Caroline's brother, Tuan, has alarming stories to tell about the work being undertaken at Nui BioLab, a subsidiary of Anglo Swiss BioLab, involving manipulation of viruses and unmonitored testing of vaccines on the population of the Highlands that seem to link with Paladin's secretive presence in the mountains on the Chinese border.

Sinclair Baines offers tickets to Caroline and Faraday, who have now become lovers, to spend a weekend on Cat Bar Island in Halong Bay, to enable her to write up a story for EANA outlining the suspicions they have about Paladin's activities, and those of Anglo Swiss/Nui BioLab, all of which are connected through their chairman, Charles Van Heeren in Switzerland. On hearing that the virus has spread into South China, and being told by Duc that village water wells are being deliberately infected, they elect to return to Hanoi and find Tuan, who is signaling that he needs to go into hiding on account of the information he has uncovered.

With the virus shutting down activities around Hanoi, the Halong Bay boat is empty apart from a German couple who claim to be traveling photographers, but are caught searching their cabin and Caroline's laptop. During the ensuing struggle, Faraday is shot, and the boat catches fire. They manage to escape in an inflatable dingy, but it is questionable whether they will be rescued in time for Faraday to survive…

ONE

At a touch before 4:00pm on a stinking hot day in late August, Bryan Liddell, the London bureau chief of the East Asia News Agency, received an email from a sender he'd been persuaded two days earlier to add to his jealously guarded private email account. The email was marked *CONFIDENTIAL* and was copied simultaneously to Sinclair Baines, the Hanoi bureau chief of EANA, and to Kate Manning of Heathcote Manning Partners, EANA's legal counsel. It was Sinclair Baines who'd asked Liddell to ensure that emails from this particular sender were not diverted to the agency's server or to spam.

The sender was Caroline Brinkley, a freelance journalist, commonly referred to as a 'stringer', whom Liddell had never met or corresponded with before. Though he'd been forewarned by Baines about the subject of the email, its contents caused Liddell's brow to furrow and his hand to reach for his cell phone. The number he instinctively wished to call was that of Baines in Hanoi, but his hand hovered for a moment before being withdrawn as he realized that not only was it five minutes shy of midnight in Vietnam, but the only thing he wanted to say at that moment was, 'Shit!' Beyond that, he needed to think.

The email was in the form of a draft news story. Smart stringers embedded their news copy in the body of emails, being aware that attachments could be easily deleted along the trail, whether by accident or by design, while the body of emails tended to remain intact. In that respect, at least, Caroline Brinkley appeared to be a smart stringer. Her story, however, did not immediately endear her to him. What he could see in it was a shitload of problems, hence his desire to pass on to Sinclair Baines a forceful expletive, for this was a story that he would have preferred to never be written. It had INJUNCTION invisibly stamped all over it.

* * * *

A brisk ten minutes' walk away in Chancery Lane, Kate Manning opened her email after recognizing the names of the two other addressees, but not the sender. She read quickly, as always, scrolling through the content at rapid speed, highlighting text as she went, her lips slightly pursed in concentration, but her face otherwise expressionless. The email was not long, and the decisiveness with which she identified elements needing her attention suggested that her field of interest was very specific.

In the corridor outside her office, a grandfather clock chimed four times on the hour. Though regarded as an aggressive young law firm with an abrasive reputation, Heathcote Manning Partners liked the evocative sound of the old clock as an ironic reminder for partners and associates to enter their clients' time charges in the folders on their screen savers, a quarter hour being the practice's minimum unit of charging.

A quarter of an hour was almost the exact time that Kate spent on the email before standing up and pouring herself a glass of water from the carafe on her office sideboard. She was a slightly built young woman with very short auburn hair, minimal makeup, and no jewelry. Her plainly cut two-piece suit and unadorned court shoes bore the hallmarks of the professional woman's uniform, not so much camouflage as protective armor. She was thirty-six years old with crystal-clear hazel eyes and unblemished skin, and she moved with the economy and purpose of a gymnast.

Of course, the chargeable time spent on a client's business could not be measured solely by the lawyer's attention to a screen. The time spent cogitating as a result of what was read on the screen was where the real (some would say 'inestimable') value lay, and behind Kate's hazel eyes, calculations were being made—not only as to the best interests of the East Asia News Agency, its shareholders, and the customers who took in its news feeds, but the best interests of Heathcote Manning Partners. There were things in this news story that had landed on Kate's desk that flowed well beyond the tidal stream occupied by EANA, and it was going to take some careful reflection on her part to ensure that she responded to them correctly.

* * * *

Over nine thousand kilometers away, on the seventeenth floor of one of Vincom's Royal City apartment buildings in Hanoi, despite it being midnight, Sinclair Baines was still typing busily on his laptop when an incoming message alert told him that he'd better save his work and switch his attention away from what the World Health Organization's spokesperson for 'avian flu and other epidemic diseases' had sent him and see what Caroline Brinkley had finally come up with.

If any one of the three recipients had cause to be anxious about the email's contents, it was him. It was his call that had initiated the idea of copying the story simultaneously to the London bureau chief and the agency's legal counsel, and it had been his decision to take the risk of not vetting its contents first. No, that was not exactly correct; he'd not had any choice in the matter of checking its contents first. It had been a condition of the writer that it be received by the three recipients at exactly the same time, unabridged and unedited. She'd been adamant that her story be delivered in its entirety, or not at all. Sinclair Baines's only decision had been whether to accede to that demand, or tell her to get fucked, so it had better be worth it.

Well, she had a story alright. She had one hell of a story, if it was true, and he knew from the first line of her email that his decision to accede to her demands for simultaneous distribution had been correct. What he didn't know was whether Bryan Liddell and Heathcote Manning Partners would have the courage to handle the bombshell she was dropping, and whether associating his name with it would be a career-enhancing move or a dangerous mistake.

Despite the hour, he felt certain that Liddell would call him and make his views known, whether good or bad. Either way, an empty stomach was poor preparation for the conversation that would follow, so he printed out a copy of Caroline's story, then left his apartment in search of food.

The underground food hall beneath the Royal City apartments was Hanoi's largest and most diverse, but after him living above it for three years, there was only one tiny corner of it that stirred Sinclair Baines's gastric juices into life, and that was the late-night pho and congee stall run by Mrs Qui and her daughter, Miss Anh. Mrs Qui told him about the weather and the hopelessness of mankind, and Miss Anh stirred his fantasies of love, smiling shyly at his poor attempts at flattery.

This evening, however, as with every evening for the last two months, the weather reports and awkward charm would be muted. Across the whole of Hanoi, everyone wore cotton face masks—it was considered an offense not to do so, except when eating—and there was only one topic of conversation, and it was not a happy one. On the back wall of Mrs Qui's stall was a picture of a chicken and a duck with a red cross painted corner to corner. Next to it was a picture of a pig with a large green tick of approval. That said it all.

Baines ordered some congee with ground pork and corn, then sat down and contemplated the email he'd printed out. There were many things to like about it. It was a story with legs. Far from being a story about slant-eyed people dying far away in Asia (which was how most of the newsrooms in Europe and North America viewed his stories about the avian flu epidemic currently raging), this was a round-eyed, pale-skinned scandal that sheeted back to the cold, moneyed heart of the Western establishment.

It was a story that would grab the testicles of North America and Europe, the new imperialists and the old, and squeeze them until they took notice. *The New York Times*, *The Washington Post*, *The Times* of London, *Le Monde*, *Der Spiegel*—these were the stages where this drama would play out if it was allowed to run. And Sinclair Baines, if he was smart enough, could be credited as both the writer and director.

Miss Anh brought out his steaming bowl of congee, flip-flopping delicately across the stone floor and laying out his bowl, ceramic spoon, and cold rolled napkin with the elaborate care of an emperor's courtesan, then waited for him to take his first mouthful. Silky and comforting, congee was not just rice and water; it was a delicately flavored blend of different grains of rice, brewed precisely in the amount of liquid and cooking time needed before the addition of the subtly flavored minced pork, garlic, ginger, and Shaoxing wine, and the final sprinkling of steamed corn kernels. Baines blew softly on the hot spoon, raised it to his lips, and sucked the contents noisily into his mouth, then laid the spoon down, placed the palms of his hands together as in prayer, and smiled. It was superb. Miss Anh smiled shyly in return, bowed her head, and flip-flopped back to her mother's food stall, not knowing that his eyes were following her. Or perhaps she did.

TWO

It was 5:30pm when Bryan Liddell got up from his desk and took the lift down to Wine Office Court, where the sun had long ceased to shine and the air was stale and thick. He walked through to Fleet Street, exiting by the Cheshire Cheese pub, which was starting to fill up with law clerks and secretaries who had the luxury of quitting work for the day. (Well, they weren't technically 'secretaries' anymore, because that was now considered a sexist term; they were 'administrative assistants,' and not to be taken for granted.) He turned right and ambled towards Chancery Lane, swinging a blue plastic document file in one hand as if it were a tennis racket. The file contained a printed copy of the email he'd received not quite two hours earlier.

Fleet Street, once the haunt of journalists, was now home to Goldman Sachs and the burgeoning law firms of the surrounding Inns of Court. Like companion plants, he thought, they helped each other to grow. The Fourth Estate had flown, scattered to the wind by rationalization, the dismantling of unionism, and digital typesetting: *The Daily Express* to London Bridge, *The Mirror* to Canary Wharf, *The Telegraph* to Victoria Station, and *The Times* and *Sun* to Southwark. For their proprietors, the real estate had become more valuable than the mastheads. So, where did that leave the news agencies, like EANA, who supplied them? That was a conversation that his private equity shareholders must be continually having, surely. He was certain that Kate Manning would be party to such talks, but they hadn't included him yet. Was that a good sign, or a bad one?

At Chancery Lane, he paused. He'd said he'd be there at six, and he was running early. In another life, this is where he would have stopped for a refreshing ice-cold lager. For him to go to young Kate's office rather than have her come to his was not unusual. Her time cost money; his was free. On this account alone, meetings at Heathcote Manning tended to go quickly. Neither party was inclined to be discursive. He knew the red flags he had to raise on this story out of Vietnam, and he was sure that Kate would have more than a few of her own. It was a story that he would be loath to see run by a rival agency, but he'd be a fool to take it on himself to release it in any form without a cast-iron endorsement from legal. And that meant a sign-off from Wilton McGwyer Private Equity, his masters.

*　*　*　*

As Kate Manning waited for the arrival of Bryan Liddell, she considered calling Sophie Cunningham at Wilton's and warning her that there was a potentially explosive story sitting in EANA's inbox, and that Wilton's media investment boss, Karim Farzan, might need to be brought into the loop. Why would she be calling Sophie and not Karim directly? Because Sophie was a member of the sisterhood, she assured herself, and getting her compass properly set before striking off on a dangerous journey, like the one proposed in this email, was always handy when deciding on the direction she should take.

Well, that's what she told herself.

But no, after a moment's hesitation, she decided that if she needed to spread liability for her decisions, she'd start by getting Andrew Heathcote to sit in. Andrew, who had started Heathcote Manning with her father, Gerald (now Judge Manning), knew libel law better than anyone, and he was a good listener. But when she dialed his extension, his voice message announced that he'd gone for the day.

Alright, no problem; she'd cover the issues in a briefing note to all parties once she'd had her meeting with Bryan. The issues were, in her opinion, so obvious that an intern could spot them.

* * * *

'I seem to recall you don't drink, Bryan?' she greeted him. 'So, I won't offer you a glass of wine. Is that a health thing, or did you just get sick of it? Because it was always my impression that journos felt an obligation to drink Britain dry.' She smiled, just in case he might be offended.

Truth was, he *was* offended. He'd stopped drinking eleven years ago, after it killed his marriage and almost killed his job prospects, as he was damn sure she knew.

'I retired,' he replied curtly, 'but don't let me stop you.'

'Actually, I'm training for the next marathon,' she said, spreading her arms to display her fat-free limbs before doing a brief jogging demonstration. 'No alcohol, no bread, and no potatoes for three months.'

'Good for you.' He sat down and pulled the copy of Caroline Brinkley's email out of its plastic folder, waved it in the air, and slapped it on her desk. 'I'd like to run this story in some form before someone else gets it,' he stated, cutting to the chase, 'but I want your assurance that we can defend it.'

Kate poured herself a glass of water and returned to her desk. 'Well,' she replied, 'in my opinion, there's no question that we couldn't possibly defend it as written.'

She flipped open a records management file on the desk in front of her. Ominously, it already had a file number and a color-coded title ready for lateral filing. From where he sat, Liddell was unable to read the handwritten title, but the contents of the file, already punched and bound, included a heavily highlighted copy of the email and a yellow-lined sheet headed *Briefing Notes*, with a set of neatly written bullet-point paragraphs that filled the page.

'Starting with…' she muttered, running her finger over her notes. She stopped and looked up. ' …the very first word: "CLAIMS." Whose claims? Are those the anonymous parties mentioned in paragraph six, or are they just anonymous sources, and it's your reporter making the claims? What's her name—Caroline Brinkley? Because if it's an employee or agent of the news agency making the claims, then that's who they'll go for.'

'"Sources,"' Bryan replied taciturnly. 'Journalists are entitled by law to protect their sources. Article Ten of the European Convention on Human Rights.'

'Which, arguably, no longer applies in Britain since Brexit.'

'Then we'll continue to rely on Section Ten of the 1981 Contempt of Court Act.'

Christ, this was bog-standard stuff; she'd better not have started her time clock.

'Alright,' Kate conceded, 'I'll move on—though your news editor clients would prefer it, I'm sure, if you could get a named party to stand by the claim in question. It comes down to credibility, and your correspondent doesn't address that issue until her sixth paragraph, in which she mentions "a senior microbiologist at Nui BioLab." I presume this is some sort of whistleblower, right? Who she's choosing not to name, even though his employers are bound to be able to work out who it is. So, why not come out and say it?'

'Read on. They're in hiding. She says their lives are at risk.'

'They'll be less at risk if we name them. Who else has she got? "A mountain guide recruited by Paladin"—how reliable will he be? And "a third party with high-level connections"… I'll admit, Bryan, that none of that would normally disturb me—it's pretty standard kite-flying journalism— if it weren't for the parties who stand accused.'

'You mean Anglo Swiss BioLab?'

'All of that. You don't go after one of the biggest drug companies in the world with accusations like this and not expect to get a barrage of lawsuits in return. And the Paladin Foundation for the Environment? She sure does pick some big targets.'

Bryan grunted. She was only confirming the obvious. 'Too big for EANA, Kate?' he asked. 'Too big for you?'

Kate bit her lip and swatted the question away. 'You need to have those sworn statements on file,' she asserted. 'It's a big risk to go anywhere near this without them. Can you do it?'

'I don't know. As you see, they're incognito and in hiding, supposedly on account of threats to their lives. Understand that I haven't spoken at any length with our Hanoi desk yet, nor this Brinkley woman, but I'm well aware that there's a great deal of legwork to be done before we put this on the wires. Having said that, it's the sort of story we can make money from, so long as we control it.'

Kate closed her folder. 'It's also the sort of story you could lose your shirt on, Bryan. I'm not worried about the British or American governments kicking back; you know how to play them for good copy. But if the Paladin Foundation and Anglo Swiss go for us, we may not have deep enough pockets. And the WHO—well, that's another thing altogether.'

'Is that your advice?'

'My advice is, don't publish anything until you can assure Karim Farzan that your sources are rock-solid. Then it's his decision.'

Liddell shrugged, picked up his folder, and headed out the door with nothing more than an ironic wave. Kate waited until she heard the elevator doors close, then she picked up her phone and dialed Karim Farzan's direct line.

THREE

When low clouds hang over Asia, and there is no wind or monsoonal rain, the air is filled with a dense distillate of gasoline, carbon particles, and heavy gasses. With the oxygen removed, breathing becomes an act of faith. There was a band of heavy pollutants circling the earth from Indonesia in the south to Mongolia in the north, and all the hand-wringing in Europe and the more enlightened parts of North America wasn't going to change it. Globalization had shifted industrial production to cheap labor economies so that corporate profits could soar, and those at the top couldn't give a rat's ass about pollution.

Baines was sick of the subject. After thirteen years in Asia, his lungs had learned to adjust. It was the speed of deterioration of his freshly laundered shirts each day that he resented.

He paid off his xe om taxi on Cau Go in the Old Quarter, then headed into the chaos of Cho Cau Go lane, looking for the hotel where he'd had the Halong Bay boat tickets delivered to Caroline Brinkley. That was nearly three weeks ago, when they'd agreed for her to go away for a day or two to write up her story the way she'd told it to him over the phone. Luckily, he'd kept the hotel's address.

He'd thought at the time that she might be peddling a conspiracy theory, but the earlier stories she'd filed about the flu epidemic in the Northern Highlands had been concise and professional, suggesting she had potential as a regular stringer, so he'd wanted her to have the chance to work up this new angle. Free overnight boat tickets and accommodation on Cat Ba island was one of the perks EANA got in return for running travel pieces, so there was no cost to him in letting her have them. But instead of coming back to him after the weekend, as arranged, she'd gone off air. until ten days later, she got on the phone, read him her headline and opening paragraph, and told him her conditions for sending the rest. No explanation offered, other than the enjoinder that he just read her story, and everything would become clear.

Since her email came in, he'd tried calling her cell phone twice, and he'd gone online with an urgent request for her to call him back, but her Skype address had stubbornly showed her as away, and he'd heard nothing in return. This was not something he'd wanted to admit to Bryan Liddell when he rang after midnight, and not something he'd normally accept from any member of his reporting team. If she wanted to stay on his payroll, that was the first thing he'd tell her once he tracked her down. The rule was very clear: there was an umbilical cord that attached every correspondent, be they staff or freelance, directly to his phone twenty-four hours a day, whatever the story they were working on. They were in the news business, for fuck's sake, and news did not take vacations or leaves of absence.

The footpath on Cho Cau Go was filled with fruit and vegetable stalls, trestle tables covered with slabs of raw meat, bowls of orange and red powdered spices, and racks of canvas shoes and knockoff baseball caps. Any space not occupied by vendors' stalls was crammed with parked scooters and bicycles, leaving the middle of the lane as the only place for him to walk. It was also crammed with scooters and bicycles, ridden at high speed, all with horns shrieking as though there were an ambulance coming through and they were the outriders. There were, of course, no numbers above the doorways, so he had no clue as to which end of the lane he'd find the hotel on. All he had was the name: Chau Hoa.

Hoa. What the hell was that? Wasn't it a flower? And *chau*—that was some sort of bucket. Was it a pot, maybe? Flowerpot Hotel? As a coach came towards him, flashing its lights and forcing everyone to squeeze themselves into gaps where there weren't any, he took an apple from a basket that was blocking his path, then stepped back into the road and kept walking.

Liddell hadn't been nearly as excited as he should have been, but that was par for the course. London was the fee-gathering center of the business, where financial officers, license fee auditors, and shareholders dictated the agenda. For old-school journalists like Liddell, that was bound to kill enthusiasm. Even a worldwide scoop (like this one could be, if only they could get it running) was not the jackpot that it used to be. The moment it hit the wires, every online outlet would rip it off for free, leaving the paid subscribers wondering why they'd bothered. So, it wasn't the story that Liddell would be focused on; it was the added value they could create before anyone else picked it up.

'You know how it works, Sinclair,' he'd explained with a sigh. 'We have to get our sources locked up so tight that nobody else can get within sniffing distance of them, and you need to have their stories written and witnessed before News Corp and the rest of our Top Twenty have even agreed to terms—all of which presupposes that legal counsel signs off on it, which is not a foregone conclusion at this stage.'

'You mean…?'

'I mean that Wilton McGwyer Private Equity invests in order to *make* money, not to lose it on humongous fucking libel suits. And this one smells libelous—very fucking libelous.'

How many times had Baines heard this throughout his career?

'Bryan,' he protested. 'I told you this would be circulated raw. I didn't even know what was in it. Well, I got the general drift, but I saw it at the exact same moment as you, so I've had no chance to edit it or quiz her on it. Those were the terms under which we were getting it. She didn't want one person to be in a position to kill it, because she had to make promises to her sources. I hope you've made that clear to Wilton McGwyer and Kate Manning. I know full well that there's work to be done, but what I need from you is clearance to do that work.'

'What promises did she make to her sources?'

'That there'd be a paper trail in case someone came after them.'

Liddell was skeptical. 'If they didn't want someone coming after them, why did they agree to be part of the story?'

'Caroline's explanation is that they've already been threatened, and the story going public is probably the only way to discourage whoever it is from following through. Think Edward Snowden. Think Assange.'

Liddell sighed. 'Christ, let's hope they're not anything like those two… Look, on social media, you can make any outrageous accusation you like, and there'll be people willing to believe you. That's what we're up against every day. We have to work doubly hard to sell the truth, even when the evidence is overwhelming. So, overwhelm me, Sinclair.'

Baines knew he couldn't do that. He also had a sudden fear that once they started, truth or otherwise might not matter.

'You know what worries me about this, Bryan? When I first saw it, I had no trouble at all believing it. What the hell does that tell us about the state of the world—or is it just the work we do that's made us this way?'

'I'm not your psychiatrist, Sinclair. You'll have to figure that one out for yourself,' Liddell replied. 'Nothing surprises me about anyone anymore. The only thing I'm focused on is that these people have very deep pockets. That's why we won't be rushing into print, and that's why you need to get that girl in and handcuff her to your wrist until you know everything there is to know. The last thing we want is to give a platform to self-deluding evangelists. And while you're at it, teach her the meaning and value of the word "alleged." "Claims" are for gold miners.'

Baines chuckled and decided that was a good place to end the conversation, particularly as he didn't want to have to explain that not only did he not know Caroline Brinkley's current whereabouts, he had never even met her.

* * * *

The Flowerpot was easy to spot when he finally reached it. It sold flowers. It was also (in small letters) a hotel—the kind he thought was probably suited to medium-term accommodation of the type that a freelance journalist might take. So, his hopes were high as he stepped into the air-conditioned lobby, made his way through the fragrant flower display, and found the reception desk, staffed by a middle-aged woman in a gold dress who was engrossed in a gossip magazine.

She looked up and smiled, sensibly assuming that he spoke English. 'Welcome, sir. Welcome to The Flowerpot.'

Though his Vietnamese was good, he encouraged her assumption. 'Good morning, ma'am. I'm looking for one of your guests: Miss Caroline Brinkley. Is she still staying here?'

The woman shook her head thoughtfully, eyeing him up and down while taking out a guest register, which her manner suggested she had no need to consult. 'No, not guest now. They leave long time. I tell other man. You American? You from embassy, too?'

Baines smiled and shrugged casually. 'Someone forgot to tell me. It sure would be a help if you could show me the dates when she was here.'

She flicked back through her pages, then turned her register towards him. 'There: Miss Caroline, and Mr. Anthony. They leave together. I already tell.'

'Ah!' He took out his smartphone and photographed the page. 'I'm sorry.' He smiled again. 'I didn't realize a colleague had already asked this question. Do you remember his name? We seem to be doubling up.'

She opened her desk drawer and held out a card for him to see, but not to take. Peering at it from a distance, Sinclair struggled to fix the details in his mind.

'Black man,' the woman said. 'You know?'

'Oh, him! Do you mind…?'

He held out his hand, and she reluctantly laid the card on the reception desk.

'He asks me to say when she return.' From the same drawer, she took out half a torn US fifty-dollar bill and waved it in the air suggestively. 'Fifty dollar!' she proclaimed. 'He give me other half when I tell him they return. But they not return now. Police say boat catch fire.'

Baines took out his smartphone again and removed a fifty dollar bill from its money pocket. Then he graciously handed it to her. While she was absorbing this sudden windfall, he quickly photographed the business card lying on the counter.

'Tell me that again. The police tell you what?'

'They go cruise Halong Bay. I tell your other man, like he ask. They no return. But police come later, say tourist boat missing, catch fire. They say my customer drown, not return. Very sad.'

'Is that all they told you?'

'No bodies. Nothing. You can tell this to your man.' She tapped the card. 'So, now you give him back his money. Half is no good to me.' She laughed briefly, before remembering why she would not be claiming the other half.

Baines took it and slipped it into his phone cover. 'I'm sorry,' he said, trying for an appropriately serious tone, while knowing that her assumption about Caroline having drowned was incorrect. 'But there's just one other thing. You will have copied their passports when they checked in. Do you still have those copies?'

She looked at him suspiciously, taking back the business card lying on the counter, while he quickly opened his phone cover again. This time he took out two twenty-dollar bills.

'Our government has a duty to properly identify missing citizens,' he stated formally. 'If I could pay you to make photocopies, it would help us tell their next of kin —*gia dinh. That dang buon.*'

As his expression showed, it was very sad, but next of kin needed to be informed. Apparently reassured, she pressed her palms together before turning and retreating into a back office, taking the business card with her.

He decided to follow. If she was calling someone, he wanted to know who. Then he heard the sound of a photocopier, and he tiptoed back to the reception counter.

'*Ho chieu,*' she proclaimed a minute later, offering the copies to him while deftly palming the twenty-dollar bills into the sleeve of her dress.

'*Cam on chi,*' he acknowledged, glancing at them quickly and reading aloud. '"Caroline Alana Brinkley, and … Anthony John Faraday." Thank you.'

'Mr. Anthony leave package,' she announced. 'Will you take?'

Before he could answer, she disappeared into the back office, reappearing some minutes later, struggling with a large flat package in a corrugated shipping carton, together with a somewhat battered black suitcase.

'He leave picture. You give to family?'

FOUR

Midday in Hanoi: 5:00am in London. Baines had no more than four hours in which to track down Caroline Brinkley before Bryan Liddell called him again. He'd returned to his office in Hanoi Towers on Hai Ba Trung, disturbed by what he'd learned. The hotel manager's claim that the Halong Bay cruise boat, for which he'd supplied complimentary tickets, had sunk with no trace of its occupants made no sense; he knew that Caroline was alive. Yet, for whatever reason, the police had assumed she was dead—and she and her companion, this Faraday guy, had chosen not to return to the hotel to pick up their belongings. So, what the hell was that about?

The picture, now removed from its corrugated shipping carton, was propped up on a chair beside his desk. It was a painting of a panda bear seen through the bars of a cage, presumably in a zoo. In the foreground was a sea of people's heads, observing it. It was pretty good, if you liked that sort of thing, and it had an inscription in the margin that made no sense, but gave it an air of gravitas:

Peel back the mask of my allure
and you will find the morning of my life
has killed the seed within.

It was signed, *A. J. Faraday.*

A quick Google search established that the Anthony John Faraday whose passport details lay on Baines's desk, noting his occupation as 'artist,' was a well-known painter of wildlife, represented by Lutyens Gallery in London, and brought to prominence by his 1998 exhibition of *'twelve of the world's rarest and most beautiful animals on the verge of extinction, captured by an artist with a rare talent, bringing Expressionism to a subject too often rendered with hyper-realism and overt sentimentality'* (*The Guardian*). Baines clicked on the gallery link, then whistled softly. They weren't cheap: eighteen hundred dollars just for a print, and sixty thousand for an original. That made the painting on the chair too valuable to casually leave behind.

He picked up the passport photocopy and tried to get a feel for him. A British citizen born in Bulawayo, Zimbabwe, he was a young-looking forty-five-year-old with shoulder-length brown hair and dark eyes that looked ready to smile. From what could be seen of his upper body, he was not a man of action, Baines guessed, but he was well built and over six feet tall—Baines's height.

The hotel's register showed that he and Caroline had initially booked separate rooms, before checking out again three days later. Then there was a gap of five days before Caroline returned for three-and-a-half weeks, before checking out the day after Baines had arranged for two Halong Bay cruise tickets to be delivered to her by Cat Ba Perfect Time Tours. There was nothing to show that Faraday had checked in again during that time, yet the hotel manager had them leaving together and putting luggage into storage. (Were they lovers? Had to be.)

The five days away coincided with the dates when she'd filed her first story on the epidemic from Sapa in the highlands, and that was the area where she was now alleging that the Paladin Foundation was up to no good. Presumably, Faraday had been with her at that time, so was he the man referred to in the sixth paragraph of her story as *'a third party with high level connections within the NGO'*?

Next, he focused on Caroline's passport. At last, he had a face he could give to the voice. She was thirty-five, dark-haired and olive-skinned, slim and erect, with a very direct gaze from eyes which were noted in the passport details as green. Born in Jackson Township, New Jersey. She wore no makeup in the photograph, but he had a feeling she didn't need it. She looked like she sounded: a no-nonsense female who shouldn't be underestimated. The suitcase he'd brought back from the hotel was unlocked and contained only women's clothes. The name tag on it was hers, with no address, just her Vietnam cell phone number.

How the hell had she stumbled onto this story, and what had caused her to go missing again?

FIVE

The hybrid culture that had developed in the offices of EANA in Hanoi Towers was a reflection, on the one hand, of Sinclair Baines's desire to immerse himself in the customs and manners of a people whose appeal for him was their impenetrable view of life, and on the other hand, of his local employees' desire to show willingness in matters involving Western language and culture, without buying into them for one minute. Like all hybrids, it was a culture that had inherited qualities from both parents, but in exaggerated forms.

On one wall of the reception area was a photograph of the flagpoles at the United Nations building in New York, and on the other was a garish painting of an overexcited dragon rising from the waters of Halong Bay. America saw itself as 'The Land of the Free,' while attempting to impose itself on a reluctant world; and Vietnam described itself as 'The Land of the Ascending Dragon,' without ever having attacked anybody, to Baines's knowledge. This sort of contradiction seemed to sum the place up.

EANA's reception desk was controlled by a fearsome thirty-year-old woman whose given name was Kim-Ly, but who was called Cai Tho by everyone in the office, 'Cai Tho' being an approximation of 'Boss Girl.' As it was midday, Cai Tho brought lunch to Baines's desk and laid it out for him: cold prawn dumplings and hot pho. He pressed his hands together in acknowledgement, then took out his cell phone and tried once more to call Caroline Brinkley. As with each of the previous times he'd called, the message delivered in Vietnamese said that the phone was either turned off or out of range. He pushed the dumplings aside and took two or three quick mouthfuls of the hot pho, then swiveled his chair around and stared out the window.

Of all the information he had gleaned from the manager of The Flowerpot Hotel, it was the report that the cruise boat had sunk with no survivors that puzzled him the most. Clearly, Caroline had survived. But that information, linked with her story's claim that her witnesses had received threats to their lives and were in hiding, made him wonder whether the same threats and need for hiding applied to her as well. That would explain her silence for three weeks, her insistence on communicating solely through Skype, and now, her cell phone being turned off.

He turned back to his desk, took another two spoonfuls of pho, and opened his phone photos to look at the business card he'd been given for the man the hotel manager had described as a black American, sending the image to his computer, where he could read it better.

Sam McAvoy
Information Officer
Office of the Consulate General of the United States of America
US Embassy
7 Lang Ha Street
Hanoi

The name wasn't known to him, though his job title was all too familiar. He wasn't there to stamp passports or help citizens in distress, that much was certain. So, why his close interest in Caroline? Or was it her companion, Anton Faraday, that he was trying to locate? And if the threats that Caroline described were so real that they'd opted not to return to the hotel to collect their belongings, would they have gone into hiding in Vietnam, or might they have left the country?

Faraday had given a London address in the hotel register. Hazarding a guess, Baines sent another email to her, as the one he'd sent earlier that morning, urgently demanding that she call him, had been ignored.

Are you in London? Is Anton Faraday one of your informants? What happened on the boat? Who the hell is Sam McAvoy? You said in your story that the United Kingdom and United States Embassies in Hanoi were informed of these activities and cooperated in them. How so? What's your proof?

The story needs more specifics. The background you sent me is all stuff that's in the public domain.

Christ, this wasn't good enough. You couldn't drop accusations like this on someone's desk and then play hard to get. She needed a firm boot up her ass.

Bottom line is, we'll need those signed statements from your sources, and if I don't hear from you within four hours, we'll presume you can't supply them, and we'll have to drop the story.

SIX

The simple goal in the game of squash is to command the center of the court, known as the T. Whoever commands the T wins.

Being small, agile, and fit, Kate Manning could retrieve from almost anywhere on the court without difficulty, so allowing her opponent, Sophie Cunningham, to occupy the T was a deliberate ploy on her part to increase her own aerobic workload. Sophie's longer arms and legs gave her a reach advantage, but less speed off the mark, so whenever she felt inclined to win another point, Kate would deftly play a drop shot into the front nick, or (her killer shot) a high lob that clung to the side wall and died in the back corner.

Though Sophie had no idea of her opponent's calculations, Kate had determined that she had time for a thirty-minute workout, and a score of 9-6 9-6 would provide it, while also persuading Sophie to believe that her playing skills were more than adequate, encouraging her to keep to their Wednesday morning routine.

At 7:30 sharp, they came off the court as Kate had planned, and that gave them thirty minutes to shower and change before picking up a Greek yoghurt and granola bowl and a green vegetable smoothie with ginger before proceeding to their respective offices: Kate to Heathcote Manning Partners off Chancery Lane, and Sophie to Wilton McGwyer Private Equity on Fenchurch Street.

Did four games in four weeks constitute a routine? It felt like it to Kate. Sophie was four years younger, lighter of spirit and manner than her more

disciplined and serious partner, but she seemed flattered—excited, even—
to be falling into the friendship that this regular exchange of physical effort,
sweat, and shower room intimacy provided. Kate's body was slim and
athletic when she stripped and stepped into the shower stall. Her nakedness
could never be considered confronting. Sophie, by comparison, was full-
breasted and statuesque in a way that had caused Kate to shake her head
and look away when she first saw her wet and naked. Yet Sophie's lack of
self-awareness had quickly dampened the effect of her body. They were
beginning to feel natural with each other—natural enough to share secrets.

'Your phone call to Karim last night stirred up a hornet's nest.' Sophie
laughed as she sprayed perfume on her neck and wrists. 'God knows who
he was phoning, but his door was closed, and I could see a lot of arm waving
going on when I left. It must have been something important.'

'You have no idea who he was calling?'

'Nope. When Karim closes his office door and gets on his cell phone,
it's either one of his partners in crime, or a go-to for instructions.' She held
out her wrist for Kate to smell. 'Here, what do you think? Too strong?'

Kate took Sophie's wrist and lowered her nose to it. She couldn't say
what she thought. Perfumes were not in her vocabulary. 'It's fine.'

She turned away and checked herself in the mirror: neat, well cut, fit for
purpose. Every day had a purpose, and every conversation during the day
served that purpose.

'What's a go-to?' she asked.

Sophie turned to her and opened her eyes wide like an anime character.
She'd painted her lips in a high-gloss liquid strawberry color that was so
wet, it looked as though it might drip on the floor. 'A go-to is someone so
important that we mortals are not allowed to know. They're where the
money comes from, I guess.'

'You mean, the investors,' Kate confirmed. 'But you must all know who
they are. The FCA would see to that.'

'Tilbury 901, Lift-off 2012, Bedouin Road Plc, Martha and Rubin's

Trust 2009, The Harbinger Fund… Need I go on? Wilton's investors are not people, Kate. They're faceless. Only directors, like Karim, know who they really are.'

'And the partners in crime?'

'Private equity is a dirty business. Wilton McGwyer doesn't invest in hunches. It waits until it knows what others don't know.'

'It doesn't sound like you have much admiration for your employer's secrecy.' Kate reached out and took Sophie's wrist again, sniffing softly. 'No, actually, it's just right.' She continued holding it while smiling up into her eyes. 'Except that the important names are obviously all on Karim's cell phone. How tantalizing.'

* * * *

Bryan Liddell was firmly installed behind his desk at 8:00am, as usual, well into his second cup of coffee and his toasted egg-and-bacon sandwich. Three stories had been filed overnight that needed his attention, two of which he dealt with in his trademark fashion by copying everyone in the organization on his liverish reply. *No Trump. No Brexit. And no fucking Meaghan and Harry. Got it?* Those were subjects that clogged the wires twenty-four hours a day. EANA got paid for the stories that others missed.

The third story was closer to the mark. Steve Roche ('Cock' Roche, to all who knew him) had stumbled upon a secretive religious cult whose members believed that their leader was a reincarnation of Muhammed. What made this story different from the usual whacko piece was that the guru in question actually denied that he was Muhammed—a very wise move, Bryan would have thought—and the cult members weren't breakaway Muslims, but predominantly white middle-class academics and high achievers.

Cock Roche, an Australian from the good old days when Rupert Murdoch had dragged the British press down into the gutter, where he believed most readers resided, was famous for his stories that defied belief. But there was invariably a kernel of truth in everything he filed, which made it dangerous to take him too lightly. Liddell decided to run with it, after applying the usual Salman Rushdie caution.

Then he turned his attention to a background piece filed by Caroline Brinkley, which Sinclair Baines had sent in overnight. It had been addressed to Baines prior to her circulation of the bombshell accusations she was now making, and it was presumably designed to set the scene prior to laying out those accusations.

```
BACKGROUNDER: The Vietnam Epidemic's Rapid Rise
Vietnamese health authorities first notified the
public of the existence of the A-virus in poultry
sold in the Sapa Market on May 12th of this year
and ordered destruction of all domestic and
commercial poultry within a thirty-kilometre
radius. On May 20, two patients presented at the
Sapa General Hospital with influenza symptoms, and
within one week, that number had risen to twenty-
eight.
    By late June, the epidemic had spread through the
Northern Highlands, affecting all but the most
remote villages from Lao Cai west to the Laos border
and north to the Yunnan Chinese border area. The
World Health Organization reported on July 30th that
the number of patients presenting with symptoms of
the disease had risen to fifteen thousand. No
reliable estimates of death tolls have been given.
In early August, the Chinese government reported
that the virus had spread into the Yunnan and
Guangxi regions, which were immediately quarantined.
```

While no confirmed reports of human-to-human transmission have been provided, neither has any explanation been offered for the rapid spread of the virus, with the WHO and the Chinese and Vietnamese governments remaining silent on the issue.

On August 9th, Nui BioLab issued a press release to the world's media. It was headed "FDA Fast-Tracks Avian Flu Treatment: Govt and Defense Prioritized," and it contained the following:

"The Food and Drug Administration has approved a new antiviral medication in response to the alarming spread of new strains of the avian flu virus now infecting people in South China and the Vietnam Highlands.

CD8Magna has been developed by Nui BioLab, a wholly owned subsidiary of the Swiss pharmaceutical giant Anglo Swiss BioLab, for early-stage treatment of infection. Using a unique fast-track modelling system that overcomes the extended time delay of conventional human testing, Nui BioLab, based in Hanoi, has persuaded the FDA that the seriousness of the current epidemic warrants speedy release of the new product, which works by blocking the neuraminidase (NA) enzyme from escaping a host cell and replicating, thereby inhibiting the virus's ability to spread through the body."

The FDA's Centre for Drug Evaluation and Research (CDER) has confirmed that the average time for a new pharmaceutical drug to be approved for use is twelve years. Neither CDER nor Nui BioLab will

confirm how long CD8Magna has been under evaluation
in human trials, or when application for licensing
of the new drug was first lodged. It is understood,
however, that Nui BioLab has a contract with the
Vietnam Ministry of Health for the collection and
analysis of patient data and the conduct of
treatment trials. Those trials are believed to have
included CD8Magna.
<< ENDS

At ten minutes before nine, Sinclair Baines came on the line from Hanoi. He was uncharacteristically circumspect.

'Did you get the background piece?' he asked.

'Yes, but it's just desktop journalism, Sinclair. You were right to sit on it. The internet is overflowing with so-called investigative journalists trying to capture the market for news. We need to offer our subscribers stuff that has value—stuff they can't get for themselves. We're up against it, if you want to know. The News Agency model is buggered. Which brings us to this girl's latest allegations. Has she got something or not?'

'So far,' Baines began carefully, 'I'm leaning towards the belief that her story is not exaggerated. But we're going to have to be damn cautious putting all the pieces together, because her sources have every reason to believe they're in danger.'

'You have proof of that?'

'I'm satisfied of that, yes.'

Then he went silent. That was not his style; Sinclair Baines was a talker, not a thinker.

'So, give me more,' Liddell demanded. 'Is this Brinkley person reliable, or is she just playing connect the dots? It's a hell of a leap from this background information—which everyone has—to making the accusations she's sent us. What's she like?'

'I'd say professional,' Baines replied, though he didn't sound fully convinced. 'She's filed stories with us before, which I've sold locally, and then this background piece three weeks ago. She followed up, saying she had information that we weren't likely to get from anywhere else, including accusations about the WHO. I told her to work it up, and then she went missing. I presumed the story wasn't checking out, but then…'

Baines's voice dropped, as if he'd turned away from the phone, or someone had entered the room.

'What?'

'When I said that her sources have every reason to believe they're in danger, that extends to her as well.' He paused. 'Apart from her email address, she's presently untraceable.'

'Oh, for fuck's sake!' Liddell exclaimed. 'How am I meant to handle that? You don't make accusations like she's making and then go missing. Does she really believe we'd run up against people like Anglo Swiss BioLab without cast-iron proof? Jesus Christ, Sinclair, find her, or I'll kill the story. In fact, if you can't deliver her, I'm going to pretend the whole thing was a hoax. Eight hours, no longer.'

He threw down his phone and went in search of another coffee.

* * * *

The reason Baines turned aside and momentarily went silent was because at that moment, he caught sight of an incoming email from Caroline Brinkley, and rather than fight her corner with Bryan Liddell, he opted to hang up and engage with her while she was still online.

Without reading her email, he immediately replied, *Go to Skype*, then called her up using her email address. It timed out without connecting. Cursing, he left himself online and parked it in the dock while he read her email. Like the previous one, it was copied to Liddell and Kate Manning.

Sinclair,

No, I'm not in London, and not in Vietnam. Where did you pick up Anton Faraday's name? Your question about the boat suggests you know what happened there. As you yourself organized the damn tickets, you'll understand that makes you suspect in my eyes. Right? Rather than ask me who Sam McAvoy is, perhaps you could explain why you know his name in connection with these events. What else do you know?

Your threat to drop the story makes sweet all sense. If you're complicit in the Anglo Swiss fraud, then you'll want to keep me close for as long as you can and try and learn all that I know. If you're not complicit, then you'll be damn alarmed by what I'm alleging and keen to see proof. See my point?

Either way, you'll have to accept that my whereabouts, and the identity of my sources, will be protected throughout.

So, if EANA has a specific list of questions it needs answered in order to gain some comfort before going public, send them to me. All communications between us must be copied to your legal counsel and London desk, as we agreed.

If I don't hear from you within eight hours, I'll cease contact. Once this story goes out on an online news aggregator, it'll take on a life of its own. It's over to you.

Caroline

Baines didn't have to check who it was that was calling on his cell phone as he finished reading the email for a second time, nor was he surprised by the tone of Liddell's voice.

SEVEN

Ngo Nam Koi was a smiley man with a habit of tilting his head to one side before speaking, as if trying to loosen a seized neck vertebra. The tilt was accompanied by a disconcertingly loud click. Friends and colleagues knew that Koi had in fact suffered from a broken neck at some stage, and this habit of his was a constant reminder of his past, just like his rolling gait, which was the product of having had both his kneecaps shot out.

Koi, known around the EANA office as Tham Tu (which loosely translated as 'detective'), was well known by two levels of society in Hanoi: the notorious branch of the Intelligence Agency known as TC2, and the equally notorious Halong City and Haiphong gangs known as Top. He had worked for both at some time in the past, if not also in the present, as was the Vietnamese way. His value to Sinclair Baines and EANA was too obvious to be stated. Though his investigative methods were unusual for an accredited journalist, they were highly effective in a city like Hanoi, where the truth was so often hidden within a maze of cultural inhibitions that a Westerner could never begin to penetrate them.

When Koi rolled into the office of Cat Ba Perfect Time Tours, the receptionist quickly saw past his smile and ushered him straight into her boss's office, closing the door behind him. The conversation was polite, but direct. Cat Ba Perfect Time Tours had received valuable exposure in travel features produced by EANA, and in return, they had provided hotel vouchers and complimentary cruise tickets from time to time. The last one was for August fifth, for two nights on Cat Ba island and one night in Halong Bay, in the name of Ms Caroline Brinkley.

Did the manager recall the booking? Yes, indeed.

Well then, he would know that the boat returning Ms Brinkley and her companion to Haiphong was reported to have caught fire and sunk.

He was not sure.

Not sure of what?

That he knew they were on the boat that sank.

Well then, Koi suggested, with his trademark smile, he would wait while the manager made himself sure, however long that took—and he would like to speak to each person in turn that the manager of Cat Ba Perfect Time Tours chose to telephone in order to confirm what had happened to the boat that night in Halong Bay, and more importantly, to Ms Caroline Brinkley and her male companion.

It took an hour for Koi to be satisfied, during which he made one or two additional calls of his own, which led him first to the captain of a fishing vessel that had picked up two Westerners from a drifting inflatable dinghy on the night of August seventh, and then to the hospital in Haiphong where a man giving the name of Tony Armstrong had been treated for a gunshot wound, before disappearing without being discharged.

The look on the face of the receptionist as Koi left the office suggested that he was not the first person to have come calling with questions about the recipients of those complimentary tickets.

* * * *

'Do you believe him?' Baines asked two hours later.

'Mostly.'

'Which parts?'

'I believe they catch boat from Haiphong and stay in Cat Ba hotel. I believe they check out after one day, and they were on boat that catch fire and sink, but I don't know who operate that boat.'

'Explain it to me.'

They were sitting in the food hall beneath the Royal City apartments. It was now early evening. Baines had ordered *beef pho bo* from Mrs Qui, and Koi had ordered *mam kho*, the salted fish stew, from an adjoining stall. Their white cotton face masks hung down around their necks, like they were two hospital surgeons taking a break, for everyone in public was now wearing them—a reminder, as if it were needed, of the hysteria raging around the epidemic.

'Travel agencies do not own boats,' Koi explained. 'Each boat has owner-skipper, and they compete for business. The boat operator for Perfect Time Tours onsell the booking to another boat. Business is very bad since the epidemic arrive, so operators choose to stay in port and not lose money.'

'So…?'

'So, that boat owner say yes, his boat sink, but he cannot say more about it.'

'Why?'

'Before it sail for Cat Ba, his crew, he says, replace by Halong City mafia. That all he can say.'

'Why?'

Koi laughed. 'Because he want to live.'

'No, I mean, why were they replaced by mafia? Do you believe him?'

'Probably. Somebody deliver money to him to pay for the boat after it sinks, and they tell him ask nothing more. Even if they mafia, that not say who they work for or why.'

Baines leaned back as his soup arrived, feeling the rustle of Miss Anh's rayon sleeve against his bare arm, and he inhaled in the hope of catching her light floral scent. Koi watched him with that damn smile, bending his head from side to side in a click routine that spoke louder than words. What Koi knew was always far more than he told.

'Okay, so, what's your guess, Koi? We know that the girl and Faraday—assuming it was Faraday—are alive, and you're saying the boat sank without a trace, so what are your friends in the police saying?'

Koi stood up abruptly and went in search of his fish, and probably also in search of an answer. When he returned, he'd found one.

'Mr Sinclair, when people say 'mafia,' they sometimes mean Bo Cong An or TC2. And when people say Bo Cong An or TC2, they sometimes mean mafia.'

'You mean, the Ministry of Public Security and the gangs are the same thing?'

'That girl,' Koi said, tucking into his fish, 'she like you. I can tell.'

* * * *

Once Koi had left, Baines went to the Royal City gym and pounded on a treadmill until his heart rate broke a hundred and fifty beats per minute. Then he swam twenty lengths of the pool, thinking only of his breathing and the timing and grace of his turns, for swimming was a metaphor for life, he believed: the greater the turbulence, the less effective the result.

Returning to his apartment, physically relaxed and mentally recharged, he scanned the satellite news channels, listened to an Al Jazeera interview with the WHO's Hanoi spokesman, Richard Dibble (making a note to call him the following day), and then switched to ESPN to watch the Yankees playing the Red Sox, before realizing that he no longer had any emotional commitment to being a partisan Red Sox fan.

An increasingly familiar feeling left him torn between making a cup of green tea or hitting the bourbon—the ex-pat syndrome. He'd lived and worked outside the United States for so long now that he'd ceased to identify with it as home. But as familiar as it had now become, he had not identified with Vietnam as home either. He had no home. He was an ex-patriot, and that was the view that shaped his life.

He finally made a cup of tea, then sat down at his laptop.

Caroline's last email had jolted him. He hadn't expected the girl in the passport photograph, now displayed on his computer screen, to speak so forthrightly. Her language had the crude directness that he would normally associate with a pugnacious male, not an attractive thirty-five-year old female. He'd misjudged her. His concentration had been on the implications she'd made about the fraudulent behavior of one of the world's largest pharmaceutical groups, and the scale of corruption it would expose. He'd forgotten completely that she was writing from the position of outrage, fear, and determination felt by a person who had survived a murderous attack. Unless he could assure her that she had his protection, he was certain she would take flight and be gone.

So, he wrote a reply to her, this time deliberately not copying it to Liddell or Kate Manning.

```
Caroline,


I  checked  out  the  Flowerpot  Hotel,  where  we
delivered  the  boat  tickets  to  you.  We  also  checked
out  the  tour  operator.  Your  boat  was  taken  over  by
a  crew  that  was  hired,  POSSIBLY  by  the  local
intelligence  agency  (that's  speculation,  but  we'll
try  and  find  out).  Vietnam  is  still  a  communist
country,  and  all  foreigners  should  expect  that
their  hotel  rooms  will  be  routinely  searched,  so
your  tickets  revealing  where  you  were  going  were
probably  found  also.  That  doesn't  tell  us  who  found
them.  I  do  know  that  the  US  "information  officer"
going  by  the  name  of  Sam  McAvoy  had  been  tracking
your  movements  at  the  hotel.  Who  is  he,  and  what's
his  interest?  You  need  to  tell  me.  If  you're  still
```

with him, tell Anton Faraday that I have recovered his painting of the panda from the hotel.

I guess what I'm saying is that right now, I'm more concerned with your safety than cracking the great scandal of our times. Okay? So, if you decide to go ahead, tell me what you need from this end, how I can help, and what kind of communication will make you feel secure.

As you can see, I've taken this off the EANA server and used TAILS to send it on TOR, where it leaves no trace. If you want to do the same (you should), here's the <u>link</u>.

Or call me. As far as I know, my cell is secure!

Sinclair

EIGHT

At 12:30, Kate Manning applied some lipstick, changed into high heels, and caught a cab to 20 Fenchurch Street. The director's floor at Wilton McGwyer Private Equity was serviced by one of the better executive kitchens in the city of London, and she could never be sure whether an invitation to lunch was going to involve a private room for meaningful discourse with Karim Farzan and in-house counsel, or a long table with twenty or so men behaving as if they were the horsemen of the Apocalypse. Lipstick and high heels were the only weapons with which she deigned to arm herself.

Today, it seemed, the pleasure was to be Karim Farzan's alone, and he was waiting for her in a private room with the table set just for two, rising to his feet to greet her with the grace of a Persian cat and the purring Iranian tones of a well-heeled old Etonian. But he didn't extend his hand, and he certainly didn't attempt to kiss her cheek.

'Kate, thank you so much for coming, and for calling to alert me about this matter. I've ordered a light lunch, as Sophie Cunningham tells me you're in training for another marathon.'

'When I have the time.'

'Well, I've ordered a smoked salmon salad with devilled eggs, so hopefully that will be to your liking.'

'Very much, thank you.'

'And I might ask Sophie to join us for coffee.'

Small talk always bookended meetings with Karim. On this day, the bookends were going to be short.

'As you so rightly identified,' he conceded gracefully, 'this story that has been dropped on EANA's desk has the potential, in its present form, to upset a number of people. I take your point that we don't have any control over the accusations reaching the internet headlines eventually, even should Bryan Liddell choose *not* to run with them, because we have no control over the people behind them. But it seems extraordinary that the author's whereabouts are unknown to us, even though she is one of EANA's employees.'

'She's not an employee,' Kate cut in. 'She's a freelancer, I gather. And the issue seems to be her belief that she and her sources are in danger.'

'For which we can only take her word, I suppose.'

How much did Karim know? Was someone copying him on the email exchanges taking place? It wouldn't be difficult for someone to hack into every device within EANA's offices, presumably, so the prudent course would be to assume he was privy to everything.

'The Hanoi Bureau seems convinced,' she stated firmly. 'They're in no doubt at all that the danger is real, according to their report overnight. Unless she can be tracked down, EANA is going to have to accept that communication will be on her terms.'

The food served was exactly as Karim described it, except the devilled eggs seemed to be sprinkled with caviar (Iranian, no doubt), and the smoked salmon was not of the thinly sliced packet variety, but a whole salmon, cold-smoked, lying on a sideboard platter, served by the waiter with a cucumber-and-yoghurt dressing. Kate looked at her plate and concluded that she would have to increase her training mileage to compensate.

'So, Kate,' Karim proceeded, satisfied that they were now past the preliminaries, 'what is Heathcote Manning's advice?'

She took a first bite, chewed it thoughtfully, then laid down her knife and fork. 'Get affidavits from each of the witness-informants, and do due diligence on them. Then, if we're completely satisfied, give Anglo Swiss and Paladin prior notice and a right of reply before publishing.'

Karim smiled. 'And the WHO also. And if all that proves too difficult?'

'Don't publish. Let it be known to Anglo Swiss that we were offered the story and rejected it.'

Karim nodded thoughtfully. It was the sort of sound, cautious advice he would expect from her, designed to protect EANA's legal position while still retaining the possibility, however slight, that there was a saleable story here that could carry a profitable by-line.

Karim ate for a moment in silence, focusing on the little black caviar dotted throughout the salad, picking them up delicately on the back of his fork, ignoring everything else on his plate. He was, Kate realized, almost hypnotically flawless in his precise movement, manner, and speech, and she wondered whether Sophie might be sleeping with him.

'What I really need to know from you, Karim, is EANA's financial capacity to defend itself in the event that it chooses to go ahead and publish. This isn't so much a question of whether the story is libelous as it is whether the accused are willing to out-muscle you, no matter the cost. Do you have contingency funds? Would Wilton McGwyer stand as guarantor?'

Karim smiled knowingly. 'Are you asking whether Heathcote Manning could be at risk of not being paid?'

'I'm asking whether EANA has the resources to take on an adversary like Charles Van Heeren of Anglo Swiss.'

He thought for a while. Being cautious likely appealed to a part of him, but that was not how he made his money.

'I wonder whether there might not be another option,' he mused quietly.

'What did you have in mind?'

'Well, putting on my private equity cap rather than my news media hat, I'd have to say that we are in possession of some information—provided it checks out—that could seriously impact the equity value of a number of substantial entities.' Here he held up his hand, as if to stop the traffic at an intersection. 'But before I go on, I need to caution that I'm leading you into territory where libel suits are the least of it. Where I'm heading is the far more dangerous area of insider trading. You need to understand that once I take you there, you'll be responsible for how you negotiate it. Shall I go on?'

'I'm well beyond the insider trading rules. They don't alarm me,' she replied.

'Good. Let's start, then, with the name Charles Van Heeren, chairman of Anglo Swiss BioLab, the third-largest pharmaceutical company in the world, up there with Johnson & Johnson, Pfizer, Roche, Glaxo, and Merck, in a sector where the top ten listed companies alone have a market capitalization in excess of two *trillion* dollars. The cross-shareholdings, patent agreements, and boardroom connections among them are more complex than a bacterial gene. An attack on Anglo Swiss is an attack on all of them, so my responsibility as a director of Wilton McGwyer is to ask whether such an attack is in our best interests.'

Kate laid down her knife and fork and picked up her glass of water. 'But this is about EANA and the freedom of the press, not about investment decisions, surely?'

She could do clipped English tones better than anyone. After all, her father was a high court judge.

'Are you saying that EANA's freedom to publish news is not based on whether that news is fairly reported and framed in a manner that protects the news gatherers from legal action,' she continued, 'but is, in the end, about how it affects Wilton McGwyer's "best interests," by which I presume you mean your existing investments?'

Karim stretched his body out like a Persian cat seeking a hand to mollify it with a gentle stroke. 'Oh, Kate, I'm not suggesting that at all.'

He reached his hand out to touch hers, but she was not having that. Her hand disappeared into her lap before he had finished the thought.

'No,' he purred, 'what I'm suggesting is that there are some stories that inevitably bring more harm to the storyteller than to the intended subject of attack. The reason I raise the issue of Wilton McGwyer's best interests is because we are, unavoidably, where the buck stops when it comes to EANA's choice as to what to publish.'

Kate decided that the salmon was, after all, too rich for her tastes, as was the conversation. Though he was backtracking from the subject of insider trading, she knew damn well that it was a revealing slip on his part. Her father had often said to her that there would be moments when clients might presume that engaging her as a lawyer meant that she was obliged to give guidance and protection on all matters that arose. His advice was to quickly disabuse them of that belief. If she hadn't been engaged to handle the specific issue, then she should say so, and insist that the new brief be accurately defined.

'Karim,' she said, wiping her mouth on her napkin and removing the lipstick with it, 'my brief is to provide advice to EANA in respect to potential grounds for exposure to libel. If you are wanting to engage Heathcote Manning on matters related to Wilton McGwyer and its investments, then I need to talk with Andrew Heathcote, who, I'm sure, would be happy to accept a brief.'

And with that, they changed the subject to the next London marathon, and whether or not it was a suitable event for serious runners, or just a mass demonstration by people addicted to taking selfies (Karim's view). Kate declined the offer of coffee, pleading an urgent caseload, and left, barely forty minutes after arriving, with the uneasy feeling that Karim had an agenda to which she wasn't necessarily going to be a party.

'I'll tell them to get ironclad affidavits before we talk again,' she said upon leaving.

NINE

Three weeks earlier, Caroline Brinkley had borne no resemblance to the person revealed in the hard-line emails received by EANA's bureau chief. Her focus had been solely on survival, particularly that of her wounded lover.

She and Anton Faraday had caught a bus from Hai Phong that went inland towards Bac Giang, avoiding the main route to Hanoi, which anyone pursuing them would assume they'd take. It had been a slow, tortuous ride for his damaged thigh and broken ribs, the seats and aisle crammed with so many of the other passengers' possessions that the bus was more a cartage business than a passenger service. What should have taken two hours took three, but when it ended, dropping them at a crossroads near the destination she'd chosen, their relief had as much to do with the absence of police or unwelcome enquiry as it did with the journey's end.

The house stood on its own on a rural road surrounded by cropping land and smallholdings, enclosed by wattle-and-daub walls topped with Vietnam's ubiquitous barrel clay tiles. Inside the compound were three standalone living quarters, surrounded by informal plantings of vegetables and herbs fussed over by free-range hens. It was a feudal hamlet, immune to the centuries of invaders who had tried to subsume the land. This was the house where Tuan, her adoptive brother, had brought her to meet his uncle when she'd first arrived in Vietnam a year ago, and if he was in danger, it was to this house that she was sure Tuan would retreat.

For Anton, on crutches taken from the hospital where their fishing boat rescuers had dropped them, every step was agony, and Caroline knew from the changing color of his skin and the gin-trap tightness of his jaw that they were risking his life by leaving the hospital.

After their experience on the boat, they had no doubt that the people looking for them had both resources and ruthless determination. They'd been able to take over a cruise boat and man it with their own crew at short notice, and they'd put trained killers in position to monitor their activities, alert to their every move. While news of the fire and the sinking of the stricken junk would have quickly got back to them, so, too, would news of the fishermen's rescue of two Westerners. They had to presume that those resources were already being directed to tracking them down, so Anton's insistence that they had no choice but to get away from the hospital quickly had been impossible for her to refute.

Though unannounced, their sudden appearance at the rural hamlet was accepted without question. She'd led her crippled companion in to meet Tuan's uncle—a man of few words, and all of them in Vietnamese—before a woman of the house emerged from the shadows and led them to another room, where she'd removed Anton's pants and dressed his wound, politely and incuriously, without a single word spoken, before laying him down to sleep, then giving Caroline a bowl of green tea and leading her to a seat in the garden.

There she'd sat, on a metal chair with a wooden back and an old cushion on the seat, the rain cascading in sheets off the iron roof above her, trying not to think about the next steps they needed to take. She wondered how much to tell Uncle, and how many other people lived in the shadows of this compound, and what they were thinking of them at that moment— for strangers in trouble bring trouble with them, according to the saying in Vietnam.

For Caroline Brinkley, an urbanized product of a New Jersey upbringing, well travelled and quick to adapt to foreign cultures wherever she encountered them, the brick-walled hamlet on the quiet, dusty road outside the hamlet of Canh Thuy was an unlikely sanctuary. But it was the only place she could think of where they might be safer than in the world from which they'd run.

*   *   *   *

When the rain falls in Vietnam, it is to wash away the stain of death, to dilute the pain of sadness, to pause the rushing mind, and to give primacy to the soil over man. The Southwest monsoon sweeps up moisture-laden air from the Indian Ocean and the Gulf of Thailand until the sky, so heavy that it can't hold it anymore, releases it onto the long-suffering country that has learned from time immemorial to channel it away in millions of little drains, down tiled roofs, across brick paths, under pavement, into streams, and out through the perimeter of the precious land into the Gulf of Tonkin, where it stains the sea a nut-colored brown.

The Gulf of Tonkin, where the Americans contrived an excuse to invade Vietnam in 1964. The Gulf of Tonkin, where the Chinese see the protection of their sea lanes as so vital that they ship millions of cubic meters of soil and concrete into it to create artificial islands they can then claim as their own territory. God help Vietnam; no wonder the skies weep.

'So, this is all about China,' Anton Faraday said the day he'd gone to the British Embassy in Hanoi to try to get them to admit what he'd discovered in the highlands.

'Vietnam has always been about China,' they replied. 'It has never been about Vietnam.'

And behind that calm, matter-of-fact response lay a lie that took his breath away—a lie that Caroline Brinkley, sitting under the shelter of a tiled pergola in the garden outside Canh Thuy, could not bring herself at first to put into words, so enormous was its shameless immorality and deceit.

For days, she'd watched her lover fight the infection from the bullet wound in his groin, burying her grief and anxiety under a mounting pile of anger, before deciding she had no choice but to act. But as Anton's strength had slowly returned, so had her clarity of mind, until the idea to use EANA slowly began to form.

While Sinclair Baines had known about the story she wanted to write, and knew the details of their planned boat trip, he'd had no reason to send people to intercept them and prevent them from revealing what they knew, because he was the person to whom she would have delivered that information upon her return. Provided she could get it into the right hands, she believed their story would partially protect them—so long as it couldn't be buried. And more importantly, it was a story that *had* to be told, no matter what the risks, because outrage at injustice was imprinted in her DNA.

But how long could she afford to sit in a Vietnamese garden before they were tracked down?

* * * *

After five days, Anton was able to leave his bed. The fever had subsided, and the wound was healing. Of all his injuries, the broken ribs gave him the most pain, but only time, as the doctor at the hospital had told her, would mend them—time and rest.

She'd walked with him in the garden as he regained his strength, and she'd fed him soup that she helped prepare in Uncle's family kitchen. But she hadn't told him her thoughts, or what she had planned, because she sensed that in his weakened state, his preference was to lay low and not antagonize an enemy for whom they were no match.

While he slept, she wrote up her story and sent it to Baines. When Baines and Liddell responded, she kept it to herself. So, when she emerged from the house one morning, nearly two weeks after their arrival, and interrupted Anton's daily walk to lead him indoors, offering no explanation, he had no idea what she was about to tell him.

'Come,' she said, smiling. 'It's teatime.'

She led him into a shuttered room with a formal table and chairs and the dry, musty smell of disuse. The furniture was heavy and dark. A bright red wall hanging with gold symbols hung alongside a black-and-white photograph of Ho Chi Minh. Caroline continued to hold his hand.

'I've told Uncle some of what we know,' she began. 'I told him Tuan is possibly in danger because of what we believe he was trying to tell us about his work. I told him that we need to warn Tuan, and that we need to escape from these people, and that we need to get across the border to Laos.'

Anton looked at the photograph on the wall, pointed to it deliberately, and shook his head. 'I wish you hadn't said any of that,' he replied. 'We can't afford to trust anyone.'

'I trust Uncle.'

'Well, I trust no one. And what's happening now? Why are we sitting here?'

'He told us to wait.'

'For what? So he can alert someone?'

Then a woman they hadn't seen before came into the room, older, carrying a tray with a teapot and three cups. She put them down and left without speaking.

'Three cups?' he asked.

The scar on Caroline's cheek was raw, and he reached out, touching it lightly, wondering perhaps if love had the strength to make skin tissue heal, wondering how long love lasted, how much of it was need, and how much a self-induced illusion, filling the space vacated by his departed faith in life, a branch to cling to in a swollen torrent of disenchantment and despair. These were thoughts that she'd already had.

'Symbols are more important than words,' she answered quietly. 'Three cups is a comforting message. How is your wound today?'

'Clean.'

'How are your ribs?'

'Broken.'

'Uncle is arranging for a man to drive us to Dien Bien Phu.'

'What? What on earth are you saying?! What man? Why didn't you tell me?'

He withdrew his hand and stood up, but his ribs cut into him so sharply that he had to quickly sit down again.

'For Christ's sake, Caroline, you're not Vietnamese, you're American. Could you please just tell me what's going on?'

But she wasn't listening to him. Her eyes were focused on the doorway behind his head, and when he turned to follow her gaze, Tuan took a step out of the shadows and into the room.

'I know why I'm in danger,' her brother challenged, 'but why are you? Why did you come here?'

Caroline decided to pour the tea. 'You may be a *Viet Kien*, Tuan, but Mom and Dad spent twenty years trying to teach you manners, so fucking well start again. Try, "Hiya, sis, how's tricks? Good to see you." Then sit down and behave like a proper Nam.'

She pushed a teacup towards a vacant chair at the head of the table and waited.

'*American* manners,' Tuan muttered derisively, but he took the chair and sat down.

'They gave you life, love, and education, in case you've forgotten. They didn't have to do that. You were a homeless refugee kid, and they gave you a safe haven. You don't have to like pumpkin pie or the Super Bowl, but you do have to like someone who raised you as their own and gave you a decent chance at life.'

'Why are you making this about them?' Tuan complained.

'Because, buster, you haven't even written to them, let alone called them, in over five years. You choose to pretend you're a poor abandoned orphan, because that suits your need to justify your anger and self-pity, and your pathetic attempt to play the martyr—just as you're doing now—when the truth is you're not alone, you're not a victim, and it's time to step up and be a man.'

Anton blew on his tea unnecessarily, keeping his eyes down, waiting. She knew he'd never had a sister, never really had a mother, but he must have known who held the power in the room at that moment, and it certainly wasn't him or Tuan.

'You don't know anything,' Tuan protested feebly. 'If you knew, you wouldn't speak to me like this.'

Then, having decided that the picador had done her work and it was now safe for the matador to enter the ring, Anton had finally put his teacup down.

'We know why we're in danger, Tuan,' he declared. 'We can prove that the bird flu virus was deliberately spread in the highlands and in South China. We know who organized that, and we know who's profited from it. You work for them.'

Caroline had then reached out and taken Tuan's hand, which, much to her surprise, he didn't try to withdraw.

'So, now you tell us why you're in danger,' she demanded. 'What do you know, and what can you prove?'

TEN

The car that Uncle had organized to drive them to the border with Laos was actually a 1960s Fourgonnette Citroen panel van, with a *deux chevaux* engine only slightly more powerful than a lawn mower, and with canvas seats and suspension that caused the chassis to bounce upwards at the slightest variation in the road's surface. Caroline and Anton sat in the back, Tuan in the front. Uncle's friend, the driver, had no teeth, but smiled a lot. He thought they were avoiding public transport to the border because everyone crossing was now being subjected to bird flu temperature testing, and Uncle had confided in the man that Anton had been treated in hospital and was now well, but wanted to avoid the risk of being turned back. If Caroline had been hoping for some stimulating conversation on the way, Tuan's taciturnity and Anton's inability to understand Vietnamese quickly disabused her of that notion, and she decided she was not in the mood for making up the deficit.

They set off as night fell on a drive that was destined to take eleven hours, sustained by fresh oranges and cold spring rolls filled with sticky rice and sliced cucumber, courtesy of Tuan's aunt, who'd dressed Anton's leg. The men pissed by the roadside, and Caroline went behind bushes. At Son La, they stopped to buy mineral water and grilled meat from a street vendor. The mountain mist was damp and clinging, the forests dark and forbidding.

Anton had run out of painkillers, becoming deeply absorbed in a battle between the relentless bouncing of the suspension system and his determined stoicism, until, finally exhausted, he fell asleep, waking just as the dawn was breaking to find they'd stopped at an intersection.

'Dien Bien Phu is only a short distance away,' Caroline said, pointing to the signpost. 'We need to look for the side road where Duc told us to meet. It won't be safe for us to hang around in public places.'

She'd been doing the thinking for them. After what Tuan had told them at Uncle's house, there was no time for second thoughts or wishful thinking. They had to get out of the country, and Duc, the Montagnard guide whom Anton had relied upon during their time in the highlands, was their only option.

From Dien Bien Phu, they were to keep driving on the QL279 until they came to the railway station at Tay Trang. Before the border crossing, they were to look for a road on the left with a yellow plastic sack tied to the sign post. Four hundred meters up that road, Duc would meet them in a green-and-yellow truck.

'You will need money,' he'd stressed to Anton. 'You have dollars?'

'Yes. How much?'

'Three hundred this side. Two hundred in Laos.'

'We have it. There are three of us. Okay?'

'Okay.'

So, they'd proceeded in silence, but as the border grew closer, there was no sign of the road or the yellow plastic bag.

'Why should we trust him?' Tuan asked, as if reading Caroline's thoughts. 'How will he get us through the border post? They'll want our passports. What if Laos isn't letting anybody in?'

Caroline had asked herself similar questions.

'All I can say is that Anton trusted this man with his life once before, and I'm willing to do the same again. If you decide you're not willing, then I'm sure Uncle's friend will drop you off anywhere you choose. For my part, I already know there are people who want us dead, and Duc isn't one of them.'

But who were the people who wanted them dead? German had been the first language of their two attackers on the Halong Bay junk. German was also the first language of Switzerland. Switzerland was the home of Anglo Swiss BioLab, which had deliberately engineered a viral epidemic and designed its antidote, a product that the American and British governments were preparing to recommend, without proper testing, for wide-scale public sale.

Who was it that wanted them dead: the drug company, or the government agencies?

Were there pathological minds who were prepared to sacrifice untold lives by manufacturing a disease in order to sell its cure? And would government agencies be a party to that? If so, there must be any number of people who'd not want someone talking—especially someone like Tuan, who'd worked on the reassortment of the virus and identified its mutations, before being suddenly transferred to work on the clinical trials of the antiviral medication, CD8Magna, finding—by chance, or by deliberate investigation? —that the results had been falsified, and the drug had been put into production with the side effects redacted from the trial reports. Now, that was a man they would definitely not want running around with a wagging tongue.

'Your risk is greater than ours, Tuan,' Anton observed quietly. 'Maybe Vietnamese border security has not been alerted, and we can cross openly, but I'm not inclined to take that risk. What do the Vietnamese call the Montagnard people in the highlands?'

'Moi.'

'A term of abuse?'

'Less than human. Successive governments have been trying to eliminate them for centuries.'

'Well then, in this situation, I prefer to trust a Moi.'

There, at last, was the yellow rubbish sack on the signpost, and there was a green-and-yellow truck with a man behind the wheel, whom Anton said wasn't Duc. They stopped alongside it, and Caroline opened the car door and got out so that Anton could gingerly unwind himself from his canvas seat. The man behind the wheel looked at them and nodded.

'Where is Duc?' Caroline asked.

The man wound down his window. 'Duc?'

'*Da*. Where is he?'

'*Dang sau.*' He pointed to the back of the truck, then climbed down from the cab, waddled around to the tailgate, and banged on the closed roller door, which was opened from the inside to reveal the familiar figure of the guide who had led Anton on his trek through the mountains north of Sapa, just as he'd described him: same safari jacket with its bulging pockets, same boots, same rucksack, same bright eyes.

'Look!' Duc said proudly by way of greeting. The truck was filled with large washing machine cartons, which he pushed aside with one hand. They were empty. Behind the cartons was a narrow space with a rug on the floor.

'Plenty big for three,' he announced confidently.

'That's it?' Caroline asked.

Duc jumped down, and the driver went back to his cab.

'He is from my people. He do this many times. When he get the signal, he cross the border and drive you to Muang Xay. It take four hours. There, you get Laos Airlines at Oudomsay Airport to fly you to Thailand or Singapore. You got water?'

'What about the border control in Laos?'

'No problem. He pay. You give me the money now.'

'Does he know we can't risk being checked by the border police?'

'Of course. That is why he pay.'

'But…' This was not filling her or Anton with confidence.

'Is he a people smuggler?' Anton asked.

Duc laughed. 'No, he do television and video. Much cheaper in Laos. When he get the signal, he cross the border, no trouble.'

'What signal?'

"The flag on the border post fly upside down. Two stars at the top, and one at the bottom. That say everything is okay. Only friendly guards.'

'Do the other guards not realize that?' she asked.

'Oh, yes, they do. It means for them to stay away also.'

'Why?'

'They get paid later.'

'Holy shit!' Anton exclaimed.

Their lives depended on the reliability of endemic corruption? Was this what it had come down to in the end?

Caroline looked long into the eyes of the little man, searching for signs of doubt. There were none. So, she and Tuan unloaded their bags, then she helped Anton climb up into the back of the truck.

'Can your people stay safe from what is happening in the mountains?' Anton asked.

'The ancestors are unhappy,' Duc confided, 'and the shamans have no cure for the disease. We are used to being hunted, but the mountains protect us.'

'Like those elephants you told me about,' Anton said enigmatically.

'"When elephants hide, it is not from the tiger—" '

'"… it is from man." I know, you told me. And you're sure it's the wells that have been poisoned?'

'The wells bring the sickness.'

Duc took his rucksack from the cab of the truck, gave the money to the driver with firm instructions, and then climbed into the Citroen with Uncle's friend. Caroline watched them drive away, then clambered up into the back of the truck herself, closed the roller door, and joined the others behind the empty cartons to sit and wait until the signal came from the border police that the flag was flying upside down—the flag with the yellow star on the vivid red background that symbolized the bloodshed in the revolution and wars that had left Vietnam pushed to the edge of the ocean.

ELEVEN

As usual, Bryan Liddell was starting the day with a toasted egg-and-bacon sandwich, washed down with coffee from a paper cup. He was in a good mood. Cock Roche's story about the risen Muhammed was taking on the tone of an urban myth almost before it was published. Roche had that talent for skating on the thin ice of truth while executing breathtaking pirouettes, and Liddell always approached his copy with a mixture of fear and exhilaration.

It was in this mood that he turned again to the story out of Vietnam. Under normal circumstances, Caroline's latest email might have been expected to put his nose out of joint. It was the best example of 'get fucked' that he'd read in a long time, and rather than angering him, it had helped make his day, reminding him of his daughter when she started cutting her teeth on women's rights issues at university. Of course, he didn't admit this to Sinclair Baines, in case it sounded too much like an endorsement of insubordination, but it did confirm to him that they weren't dealing with a flake who was likely to roll over and recant once her accusations were challenged.

His gut feel now was that her story was very likely going to stand up. The decision he needed to make was in respect to their timing. There was no question that they needed to have signed witness statements in their pockets first. Kate's preference was that they be notarized affidavits. Whether they took them to Anglo Swiss, the WHO, or Paladin for comment before publication would depend on the strength of the accusations, and on what

Sinclair Baines was able to glean on the ground in Hanoi, where he seemed to have very quickly picked up a trail worth following.

It was time to commit to this woman. Three watertight witness statements, and he would press the launch button; that's what he'd tell her. But first, he needed to clear his desk of his morning coffee cups and the wrapper from his bacon-and-egg sandwich, because coming towards him across the newsroom floor was the saturnine figure of Karim Farzan. What the hell was he doing here at this hour of the morning?

Liddell rose to greet him, looking about for his jacket, then abandoning that futile thought as a hangover from days when management bothered to dress up for work. Nobody dressed up for work anymore, unless they were merchant bankers or lawyers. He rolled his shoulders and cleared his throat, ready for a hearty welcome—just as Karim turned into the side office of the agency's financial officer, Megan Hastel. Had they caught each other's eye, and had Karim deliberately chosen not to acknowledge him first? Perhaps he was reading too much into it.

He returned to his desk and called Sinclair Baines to let him know his decision to proceed with the Anglo Swiss story, subject to the quality of the witness statements. For his part, Baines had lined up an interview with his contact at the WHO in Hanoi.

'You've got a feisty little bitch there, Sinclair,' Liddell commented admiringly. 'Are you confident she'll come through for you?'

'Everything's checked out so far. Do you want me to continue running this out in the open between the three of us, or shall I try and persuade her to move onto TAILS, where we'd have encrypted access? It's not a story we want accidently leaked before we're ready.'

Liddell took time to consider.

'Normally, I'd say that's a good idea. But she asked for it to be done this way because she wants a trail that we can't deny at a later date. I like the idea of Kate Manning being in the loop, so it comes down to whether or not we feel watertight. In the end, she's your source, and you need to decide how to get her across the line. I'm going to confirm to her now that we'll run with her story if we're satisfied with the witnesses, and then I suggest we sit back and wait. What you do in the background, and how you communicate with her, I leave to your discretion. Just make sure you keep me informed.'

On that note, he hung up, just as Karim Farzan came out of Megan Hastel's office and headed to the elevators without even looking in his direction.

* * * *

As a one-time foreign correspondent for a national daily, Liddell had a warm spot for journalists in general, and stringers in particular. But at the age of fifty-eight, answerable now to shareholders and monthly financial reporting, he found that warmth had long since ceased to be fueled by sentimentality.

The business of collecting and distributing news had changed so rapidly in the digital age that traditional journalists like Liddell were regularly being forced to evaluate their roles. Social media had stolen their role everywhere. Free of ethical and moral restraints, it operated as a lawless society of bloggers and trolls, with mixed motives and hidden agendas that demanded neither accuracy nor truth, let alone discretion. With more than half the world's population now carrying a news delivery mechanism in the palm of their hand in the form of a smartphone, the primacy of old-school print media and television news was long gone. The internet now ruled, and the internet was primarily an entertainment medium. Fake news and clickbait trivia had more dietary appeal to its followers than did real news. In fact, real news without the texture and flavor of fake news and trivia had no dietary appeal at all.

Despite his title as London bureau chief, he had no illusions about his importance in the EANA hierarchy. The top position belonged to the financial controller, Megan Hastel. She'd been appointed by Wilson

McGwyer, and she reported to them directly. He had no beef with that—if anything, it made his life easier—but it did beg the question: if and when the collection and distribution of news became unprofitable, at whose door would the blame be laid? Megan Hastel's, or Bryan Liddell's? And if, as she sometimes hinted, it was already unprofitable, why was a major private equity firm like Wilton McGwyer invested in it?

The reason he'd never asked this question directly was because he didn't want to know the answer. Lord Beaverbrook had owned *The Daily Express*, the daily newspaper with the world's largest circulation at the time, because he wanted to influence the politics of the nation. Rupert Murdoch controlled News Corp because he wanted to accumulate cross-media holdings through news channels—and influence politics. But a news agency?

One night, after a torrid day filing stories from all over Europe on reactions to the Brexit votes, Liddell had impetuously invited Megan to join him after work for a quick bite. She'd been given her position by Karim Farzan barely three months prior, and their conversations to that point had been restricted to explanations as to subscription models and licensing fees, topics that he knew were important, but on which he failed to fire. She was also the office's IT administrator, an area of expertise for which he had great admiration when something went wrong, but which he secretly despised as being the last refuge of geeks and nerds.

Of course, he'd couched the dinner invitation in terms that classified it as an employer's obligation to provide staff refreshments during an overtime shift, and he'd ensured that another staff member was present (Steve Roche, as it happened).

It was late when they arrived in Covent Garden, and they'd opted for a seafood hangout that didn't try too hard for celebrity, and as a result, had no queue. Then Cock Roche decided halfway through his first drink that he needed a flat iron steak, and some proper drinking company (Megan having opted to join Liddell, the teetotaler, in drinking sparkling water), and he almost immediately excused himself. This left Liddell sitting across the table from a woman he'd only ever spoken to about royalty income and internet viruses. She was in her early fifties, he guessed, and without a wedding ring, pleasant-looking and soft-spoken. He decided to talk about Brexit and the food. She had views about both, which was a relief, because silences over dinner brought back bad memories for him.

She said, 'If we leave Europe, the need for reporting from Brussels will decline, I believe, and we could afford to do with one less correspondent there.'

Making a joke, he replied, 'If we did away with both correspondents, we could pretend that Brussels was nothing more than a bad dream.'

'So, you'd support my recommendation for downsizing?' she asked.

Having his words taken literally when he was trying to be flippant was another thing that brought back bad memories for him. It was a moment that called for a drink, but he was no longer a drinker.

'No,' he replied bluntly. 'I'd try and retain our resources—but not in Brussels.'

She smiled in a way that he didn't like. Cost accountants thought the way to achieve success was to eliminate costs. News editors thought the way to achieve success was to hunt down the news. This was a conversation that needed to be held, but he hadn't planned for it.

'And where would you see them going?' she asked.

'One to Istanbul, and one to New Delhi.'

She tilted her head to one side pensively and considered the implications. Their food started to arrive. They both looked for fresh-cut lemons, refusing to start until they had them. She liked the look of his tin can filled with thin French fries, so he graciously passed it to her and ordered another, because he knew that he'd want a full one for himself.

Once they were settled, she began again.

'Why Istanbul?'

'Because they have the Middle East at their mercy, and they want to restore the Ottoman Empire.'

She nodded. 'And why New Delhi?'

'Because they are America's chosen proxy for the containment of China.'

It was at this point that he noticed something disturbing. She had picked up her glass of water and was directing it at him as she spoke, making her points without drinking from it. That was what people did with wine glasses, not water glasses. And that realization convinced him that she was a regular drinker who had chosen to abstain because she was conscious that he was a recovering alcoholic. He was weak. He couldn't be trusted. He was talked about behind his back. Clearly, the message was, 'Stay off the booze, in case he's tempted and falls off the wagon.'

Fuck them. Fuck them all, he thought.

'Sixty percent of our costs come from geopolitical news,' she said, 'but only twenty percent of our revenue—'

'Is that so?' he muttered, looking for a waiter.

'… while eighty percent of our revenue comes from celebrity gossip, lifestyle, and entertainment.' She frowned. 'But only forty percent of our costs.'

'I'm sure you're one hundred percent right, on both scores,' he conceded graciously. 'Now, this fish calls for white wine. Which variety do you prefer?'

She put down her water glass quickly, as if it were about to answer for her.

'How about a dry Riesling?' he suggested, not waiting for a response.

When it came, he let the waiter fill their glasses, and then he proposed a toast to Brexit. She drank thankfully, not noticing that he failed to take a single sip from his own glass. By the end of the evening, he'd managed to empty the bottle entirely in her direction, and she'd told him the story of her life, which, like most such life stories, was more interesting to the person who had lived it than to the person hearing it. There were, however, elements in it that he recognized might one day prove useful.

Now, almost a year later, he was thinking. If Karim Farzan was going to make a point of avoiding the titular head of EANA, insinuating himself into the agency's affairs through the portal provided by Megan Hastel instead, then the time was approaching when another bottle of dry Riesling might need to be uncorked.

TWELVE

In the Lotte Hotel in Hanoi, it was 5:00pm, and the temperature was still in the high thirties. On the hotel's indoor golf driving range, Sinclair Baines had already used up his fifty-ball bucket, while his companion, Richard Dibble, still had fifteen more to go, on account of the fact that he insisted on taking at least three practice swings between each shot, a habit that would have infuriated Baines if they were on a proper golf course.

Dibble, the Canadian-born spokesman for the World Health Organization's team in Vietnam, was a native of Toronto, and Baines was from Boston. Both were single men in their late thirties who had quickly sorted out a couple of North American sports around which they could bond. Obviously, ice hockey was not an option in the heat of Vietnam, but golf and basketball were both catered to at the five-star Lotte, where guests staying on the Club Floor had free access to indoor practice facilities. Dibble had earlier wiped the floor with Baines in their free throw and bank shot shoot-out at the basketball hoop, a competition that exposed the latter's inability to judge distance, on account of him having lost sight in one eye. Slam-dunking was his only strength.

'A quick swim, and then a drink in the Club Lounge?' Dibble suggested as he sliced his final drive into the practice net.

The Club Lounge provided free drinks and canapes to Club Floor patrons between 5:30 and 7:30 each evening, and Dibble, being a bureaucrat, wasn't ever going to miss out on that perk, rushing through the pool and the shower so that they made sure to get there on the half hour sharp. There was no need for face masks inside the hotel, but the presence of the avian flu epidemic hung over the place nonetheless, and they had the lounge to themselves. No one who could afford a five-star hotel was going to come to Hanoi while this disease was front and center, unless absolutely necessary.

'For a guy with the nearest thing to a pandemic on his hands,' Baines teased, 'you sure seem pretty relaxed. Do I take it this thing has peaked?'

'Peaked? Who told you that?'

'Your press releases. For three weeks, they've been touting the same figure: the perfectly round number of fifteen thousand infections.'

Dibble pulled a face. 'Everything comes out of the New Delhi office now. That's their headline number.'

'Well, it might be a good idea to put a word in their ear, because the message that sends to me is that either people have stopped getting infected, or the number was always made up. Either way, there's a story there if I want to make one. Which is it?'

Dibble flagged down a waiter for two more beers.

'We have to take the word of the health ministries on both sides of the border. It's impossible for them to give us accurate counts in the environment of the Northern Highlands. Whether it's fifteen thousand or sixteen thousand isn't material. All we know is that it's a damn big figure.'

'And you still won't tell us how many have actually died. Are hospitals being overwhelmed? That'll tell you whether it's growing or not. Surely they can count.'

'Possibly. Probably. We don't know for sure. Between the Chinese and the Vietnamese, you can't trust what they report. Sometimes you have to guess.'

Baines drained his glass so that the waiter could take it away, and then he started laughing, causing the beer to go down the wrong way, so that the laughter turned into a coughing fit. He wasn't going to die, but he kept it going longer than necessary because it had Dibble looking nice and worried.

'I love it,' Baines gasped.

'Love what?'

'That you cocksuckers are such whores with the truth. You haven't got a clue how many victims there've been—five thousand, fifteen thousand, who the hell's counting? Even if you put people in every hospital and every village checking the numbers, in the end, you'll decide what sounds like a good round figure, right?'

'What else can we do? It's not that the local authorities lie; they just lack the competency.'

'No, they're competent enough when they want to be. There's a game being played here. The WHO isn't going to say or do anything the Chinese don't like, because they have you in their pocket. And the Vietnamese are going to calculate how much money you're good for if you can be persuaded to declare a pandemic. Jesus, Richard, do you think we haven't seen this before? The World Bank's Pandemic Financing Facility is one good reason for a country to lie. How much moolah does that drag in? It becomes a pandemic when enough people are sick and dying and it's spread to another country, and you're the guys that sign off on that.'

Dibble stiffened and adopted a pinched expression. Was he pushing too hard, Baines wondered, and was it the other man's pride he was pricking, or his conscience?

'You'll have to ask the World Bank hierarchy about that, Sinclair. My sphere of financial influence stops at laboratory capacities and alert-and-response systems. It's chicken shit compared to what the World Bank doles out. The pun is intentional.'

They laughed. Baines was sure that after six beers, Dibble would want him to go to the Gia Lam District and keep him company while they looked at the girls, until Dibble found one he liked. This was a trap he'd fallen into before, and he wasn't going to fall for it again. Not tonight. Nevertheless, he allowed him to talk about his derring-do with the opposite sex, like the red-blooded buddy that Dibble supposed him to be. Before the fourth and fifth beers, however, he needed to slip in the question that had brought him here.

'I hear Nui BioLab is the biggest lab in town. Are they coping with the volume of tests, or are there other companies involved?'

'Nui's a research and development company, not a testing laboratory. We've helped the health ministry with ten pop-up testing labs in the last three months. That's our job. We're on top of it.'

'That's great,' Baines enthused, 'but Nui got its new drug through the FDA on account of the trials it had run with the cooperation of the Vietnam Health Ministry, so they must know more about the virus than anybody. Are you working with them?'

'There are things happening there involving vaccine development that I can't talk about.'

'Because…?'

'Commercial sensitivity, Sinclair. You can't quote me on any of it.'

'And I suppose you can't tell me when you're declaring a pandemic.'

Dibble shook his head, but couldn't suppress a faint smile. 'Soon, I'd guess. It's up to Geneva.'

'Ah, Geneva! So, tell me, does CD8Magna help recovery rates?'

The fifth beer arrived.

'Of *course* it does.'

'By how much? What are the figures? We need a good news story.'

Dibble's attention was beginning to waver. 'Christ, I don't know. It's too soon; we don't have any firm figures yet.'

'But I thought the FDA had approved it, and you guys were persuading governments to stock up big. Now you're telling me you don't know whether it works or not. Am I missing something? Because I thought a new drug had to prove itself over years of intensive trials if it's to get FDA and WHO approval. Surely you must know if it works or not.'

'Look, I'm a public health officer. These high-level things are decided by people at the WHO in Geneva. If you want to ask questions about CD8Magna, you should go see Louis Rey at Nui BioLab.'

'Great. Can you introduce me?'

THIRTEEN

They'd got to Heathrow at 9:00pm the night before, exhausted, bedraggled, and too shell-shocked to speak. Eight hours on the wooden floor of an airless truck to Muang Xay (of which four hours were spent waiting for corrupt border guards to signal them through—four hours when their anxiety levels squeezed their bladders and bowels with sadistic delight, knowing they couldn't be relieved) had then been followed by twelve hours at Oudomsay Airport, waiting on standby for any flight out of the country. Tuan had been the first to go, being the one in the greatest danger. Anton and Caroline had followed seven hours later, meeting him in Bangkok, where they got on a Thai Airways flight and fell asleep immediately, only to be woken nine hours later and sent into a transit lounge in Frankfurt, where everyone looked and sounded like the people who'd attacked them on the boat. After traveling for three days, they had the look and feel of refugees.

Tuan had been undecided about whether he would go on to New York from London, or find a safe house somewhere while he considered the severity of the threat he faced. So, they caught a minicab at Heathrow and dropped him at an Ibis hotel, before directing the Iranian cab driver to the M4 and heading on into London. Though neither of them had expressed it in so many words, they had adopted a somewhat fatalistic attitude towards the severity of the threat, unwilling to accept the idea that nowhere would be safe. It wasn't until they'd reached Cromwell Road, and Anton was about to give directions to his house in Kensington, that they realized the inadvisability of turning up on his doorstep.

'Let's go to a hotel and get a decent night's sleep,' Caroline suggested, knowing what he was thinking without having to be told, 'and make a fresh start tomorrow. If they're still looking for us, they'll assume we're in Vietnam. What I want to do is make love, sleep, have hash browns with scrambled eggs for breakfast, and then spend the day writing down everything I know and putting it up on my iCloud dropbox. If anything happens to us, at least Mom and Dad know that it holds all my secrets.'

In his damaged state, making love was never going to happen, but it was a nice idea.

When Caroline received Bryan Liddell's email the next morning, it didn't really change anything for her. She'd known EANA wouldn't act on the story without evidence, and she'd already begun writing drafts for Anton, Tuan, and Duc. Anton was not convinced that their story would see the light of day, but she stuck to the line that it was the only way they could end this thing and get on with their lives again.

'We need to tell our story in public, as soon as possible,' she insisted.

'And make ourselves targets again? Who the hell's going to protect us?'

'Don't you get it?' she argued. 'If they were stupid enough to harm us once the story's gone public, that would absolutely underscore its truth. They'd be crazy to attack us.' She prayed that she was right, and that their enemies would agree with her, even if Anton didn't.

When she'd first sat down to write her draft story to send to EANA, it had poured out of her like a perfectly blended sauce, all the ingredients coming together to provide a concoction of flavors that combined to taste and smell unmistakably like a corrupt conspiracy. Now, a week later, the flavors were starting to unlock, and missing ingredients were needed to hold them together. There were things that she and Anton believed they knew, but could they provide proof?

It was the call they'd tried to make on the phone, which Anton had recovered from one of their attackers before they escaped the burning boat, that weighed most heavily on her mind. That phone call was meant to have answered all the questions they'd harbored since the night they were attacked. Instead, it had triggered in Anton a conviction that what they were doing was futile.

They'd delayed ringing the number until after they left the hospital and reached Uncle's house. As they listened to the phone ringing, all the fear and horror of that episode on the burning junk on Halong Bay came back to her—the incandescent terror that had driven both of them to kill in order to save their own lives; the knowledge that this number, which they'd found on their attackers' phone, could reveal who was behind it all; the need to suppress their desire to call it until they were safe. And then, finally: *'This number has been disconnected. Ce numéro est discontinué. Diện thoại bị ngắt kết nối.'*

They'd left it too long. Professionals leave no traces.

But Anton seemed convinced that the voice they would have heard on the other end would have been recognizable to him, the centrality to whom all this evil was tethered, the one person in the world who could provide the answers to everything. Yet, significantly, he'd refused to share with her who he thought that might be.

* * * *

Of course, there was no question that it would be unsafe to go back to his London house. Using the Cash Passport card that he always kept in his cell phone cover, they checked out of the Cromwell Road hotel and hired a car in Earls Court. At no stage of their journey so far had he needed to use a credit card that could be traced, but their passports had been registered too many times for comfort. He had a friend from his school days, now living in New York, he said, who had a small cottage in East Suffolk on the edge of the marshes.

'I use it whenever I want to paint outdoors. The bird life is extraordinary. He uses it to shoot them; I use it to paint them.' He laughed.

'This man is your friend?' Caroline questioned in disbelief.

'One of my oldest friends. He only shoots game birds: ducks and geese, not the protected ones. It's one of the dichotomies that defines us humans: one half kills animals; the other half saves them. We're strange creatures is all you can say.'

They drove most of the way in silence. The traffic was heavy and required his attention. He shouldn't really have been driving with his ribs and leg still unhealed, but he insisted. While Caroline laid her head back and closed her eyes, she suspected that he, like her, was lost in thought. They'd been through a lot in the last few weeks, after being thrown together at a time when they barely knew each other. They'd come close to dying (twice, in his case), and now they were struggling to accept that they had unwittingly become the enemies of people whose identities and motives were obscure. But while these crises in their lives had undoubtedly driven them closer, she couldn't help wondering whether her passion to be the messenger of truth might not begin to drive them apart. It was clear that they didn't share that passion equally. Truth had to be clear and unequivocal if it was to be fought for with passion, and the truth she believed she saw didn't yet fit that description. It was one thing to abhor greed, deceit, and mendacity, but quite another to mount a crusade against them. Besides, truth had never proved a strong enough weapon to change the world.

At a small village outside Woodbridge, Anton pulled in at a service station to buy groceries. But then, spotting a CCTV camera, he quickly drove on, stopping instead at a small supermarket tended by a young Asian woman engrossed in a soap opera with East End accents that Caroline couldn't understand.

'What will we need?' she asked, not knowing what their destination held for them.

'Leave it to me,' he insisted. 'I've done this before.'

Back on the road again, she wanted to know what they should tell his friend if he happened to turn up.

'He won't,' Anton replied confidently. 'I doubt if he's been there once in the last five years. Its primitive charms no longer appeal to him, so I have it to myself. The downside is that the loo is a long drop outside. Great ventilation, but no place to linger in winter.'

'Does it have running water?' she asked skeptically.

'Oh, sure.'

'But not internet, I'm guessing.'

He laughed. 'Now, that's where you've guessed wrong. David is a hedge fund manager. He'd rather go naked in public than be without internet. It comes in through a satellite dish.'

'And cell service?'

'FaceTime or Skype. What do they call it…?'

'Voice over Internet Protocol.'

'There you go. Every comfort. I've bought some supplies to get us through the next few days. Who knows how long we'll be there?'

They arrived at Marsh Cottage just as it was getting dark, turning through an unmarked gateway ten minutes outside the nearest town and bumping down a gravel track alongside an open field that eventually led through dense woodland, before emerging at the head of a deserted steel-grey estuary that lay calmly breathing in the moonlight. The two-storied cottage was tucked into the edge of the trees.

While Anton searched for the key and opened up the house, Caroline looked out at the dark horizon and shivered. The only sound was the far cry of a seabird echoing across the mudflats. Then Anton turned on the lights and came out clapping his hands and stamping his feet.

'All is good,' he assured her.

From the minute they entered it, the house seemed to welcome them as if it had been waiting for their arrival. Their spirits lifted, and their numbed, inanimate souls awakened, rubbed the sleepy dust of five traumatic days out of their eyes, and sprang to life. At last, their expressions acknowledged to each other that they could safely relax. He let her go ahead while he unloaded the car, then closed and bolted the door behind them, looking for her reaction to an environment filled with markedly male possessions, which he felt might give his bachelor status away.

'It's a bit bare of creature comforts,' he apologized. 'Neither David nor I ever felt the need to bring a woman here.'

'God, I love it!' she exclaimed. 'A few books, some old music—anything to get away from that feeling of being hunted. And does your friend keep guns?'

'A side-by-side shotgun under the kitchen floorboards. Why?'

'In case we need it,' she said, surprised at herself.

The kitchen was not designed for cooking, but he'd had the good sense to buy a cooked chicken and a cold bottle of wine, for which Caroline unerringly found wine glasses. They turned towards each other, two survivors of a holocaust, raised their glasses silently to survival, and kissed each other's lips with the exquisite softness that lovers reserve for those moments when words are not enough.

He searched her face. The scar on her cheek was healing. The long sleep at the hotel had restored brightness to both their eyes.

'While you were sleeping last night,' she confessed, 'I went online with Sinclair Baines.'

He blinked. 'Was that wise?'

'He'd been trying to reach me to find out whether I was back in Hanoi. I didn't say where I was, but he seems to have some idea about what happened on the boat. The guy from the US Embassy had been to the hotel, looking for us. It must have been the hotel that gave away the details of our travel plans. He stressed that the agency needs signed statements if they're to break the story, particularly from Tuan.'

'Do they believe what you told them about how the virus was spread?'

'I can't be sure. We need Duc's affidavit.'

She turned away and began pacing the room with the restless energy of a caged zoo animal. He knew what was coming.

'Anton, I want to see this story given maximum coverage. I want to do whatever is necessary to see these people exposed. I have to.'

'You know the risk.'

'I know… We'll both be at risk. That's why I need your agreement.'

'Tell me more about Baines. He's the bureau chief for this agency I've never heard of. How can you be sure it doesn't have links to the CIA or whatever? What do we know about this world?'

'It's EANA—the East Asia News Agency. You know that. There isn't a news agency anywhere that doesn't have journalists on government payrolls. That's a reality. I've got to work out a way of stopping them from discrediting what I file and shutting the story down.'

'And how will you do that?'

'By doing what I've already done: filing simultaneously with the London bureau chief, the Asian bureau chief, and the editorial legal department. It was Sinclair's idea.'

'And will Tuan back you up, or will he go to ground for good?'

'He's scared, but he's willing to come forward if they print my story.'

Anton turned away. 'Are you sure you want to do this?' he asked quietly. 'The spin they'll put on it will see your claims disappear into the ether, to be instantly dismissed and forgotten—the unsubstantiated and biased assertions of just another wild-eyed, anti-business, anti-government activist suckered into her own conspiracy theories. By the time they've finished, even you will be doubting your own story. Are you prepared for that?'

She didn't have to reply for him to know the answer. Her eyes were as black as coal, glaring at him with angry determination.

He shrugged. 'Well, I'd better clear a space for you to work. You're going to be busy.'

FOURTEEN

Anton rose just as the sun rose, dressed, and left the cottage as the morning light brightened. He was well across the woody heath and skirting the saltwater reed beds when the sun finally exposed itself above the grey horizon of Europe, shining its light on the gunmetal-grey expanse that separated the Netherlands from the English coast.

The North Sea was windless and flat, slipping away before him towards low tide, drawing back down into itself and leaving the intertidal zone to trap and bind the sediments it left behind. On this part of the East Suffolk coast, the tidal range was four meters, the land so flat that it took half a mile for the incoming ocean to reach its upper tidal limit, washing over gravel beds, mudflats, marshes, and reedbeds, feeding the vast garden of saltwater delicacies upon which the abundant bird life waited to dine: snails, worms, bivalve mollusks, aquatic insects, tiny crustaceans, and small fish with nowhere to hide.

He and Caroline had come out the day before to watch the marsh harriers in the late afternoon sun, and the black-and-white avocets with their long, curved bills stepping gracefully through the undrained mud pools. The two of them had been tense, building towards a disagreement that had no way of draining away of its own accord, despite their wish for it to do so.

After weeks that seemed like years of a rising tide of mutual attraction between them on the road in Vietnam, a king tide of love had swept over them, driven by the aligning forces of danger and the shared exhilaration of knife-edge survival. They had faced death together, been spared by chance alone, and had retreated, damaged, frightened, and baffled, to recover in each other's arms in this remote anonymous landscape, aware that they were not safe, only hidden.

But standing here alone now, he realized that the low tide of the previous day had brought with it a sense of ebbing hope. As they'd argued, he'd felt their love begin to splinter as if a hidden fault line had been revealed. No one was to blame; they simply didn't know each other well enough. Yet he felt that the fault line had left them standing on opposite sides. They'd returned to the cottage, each locked in their separate thoughts, and they'd gone to bed at separate times. It was not a proper row; it was a difference in attitudes, and he feared that it ran deep.

As he gingerly stepped down off a shale bank onto the mudflats, he winced and involuntarily clutched his side. It had been three weeks since that bastard Kraut with the steel-capped boots had caved his chest in on the Halong Bay boat, and the little doctor in Haiphong had said his ribs would take six weeks to mend if he rested. Escaping the burning boat with a bullet in his thigh, riding for twenty-four hours in the back of a truck over the mountains into Laos, and flying across the world to go into hiding in a remote marshland cottage with no septic tank was probably not the sort of rest the doctor had had in mind. And now, with what Caroline planned, he couldn't imagine much rest in the weeks to come either.

He walked out onto the mudflats, surprised at how firm they were. Ahead of him, a family of red-breasted stonechats was wading in a pool, oblivious to him, and oystercatchers were flitting from place to place, following some sort of secret radar embedded in their feet or beaks.

He'd been coming here for fifteen years, ostensibly for the light and the variety of wildlife, but the truth was that he'd done very little painting here. In the beginning, he'd come to keep his old school friend David Goode company. They'd smoked dope, played loud music, and told each other bullshit stories about how they saw life. David liked to shoot geese (the Canadian sort that were considered a pest) and any quail, partridge, or pheasant that made the mistake of straying from the surrounding farmland. Though he'd told Caroline otherwise the night they arrived, they'd also brought women here—the sort who liked to smoke dope and play loud music, like them. But since David had moved to New York and become a piratical hedge fund manager, those days were now gone.

Half a mile south from where he was standing were the remains of an old breakwater. He decided to head for it and test his damaged leg. Half a mile there meant a full mile there and back. Was he risking it too soon? Dammit! He decided to strengthen his muscles, no matter how much they hurt. Pain would give him focus.

Concentrating on the ground, so as not to stub his foot, he failed to notice a dead skua until he was right on top of it. Dun-colored, it blended into the sand and would have been hard to spot even when alive. This one was very dead, and if his memory was correct, it should have been further north than the Suffolk coast. He stirred it with his foot, half wondering whether it had been shot, but found no evidence of a wound. Looking up, his eyes fell on another corpse barely twenty meters away. Skua were monogamous, so these two were likely mates.

Anton knew this shoreline well. He was a naturalist, so he could read it, and it was sending him a message. The normally busy sky was quieter than he remembered. Was it his imagination, and was he losing the instinct for simple explanations, which characterized the onset of paranoia?

* * * *

Caroline had heard Anton leave the house at dawn. She'd been in the room that he'd set up for her as a place to work, but he didn't look in on her, and that hurt. She was aware of the tension between them the night before, but because she was so focused on the path that she was following, she didn't dwell on what had been said, taking the attitude that it would work itself out once he realized that she had no option but to see this thing through.

But now, on reflection, she realized that they needed to go back over what had happened, and see where they had begun to diverge. This wasn't just about protecting their love; this was about protecting their lives. The journalist in her wanted to pore over every detail in search of the truth she was sure would be revealed. But the artist in him was content with the broad-brush strokes of an expressionist's picture. Questioning him too closely had become counter-productive, elevating the tension between them, so she'd turned to Google.

Her searches on Anglo Swiss and its subsidiary, Nui BioLab, revealed nothing more than confirming that she was dealing with Big Pharma. A large and vocal tribe on the internet regarded Big Pharma as the source of all evil. A significant and countervailing volume of voices in government, mainstream media, and globalist think tanks saw it as the savior of mankind in a world where disease, morbidity, and pandemics would otherwise be the natural order.

The link between Van Heeren, the billionaire head of Anglo Swiss, and the discreetly influential but strangely low-profile environmental group, The Paladin Foundation, led her nowhere. It had taken her less than half an hour to find a link mentioning Paladin's sponsorship of Anton's series of paintings of threatened wildlife species, and that link was to his agent's gallery, Lutyen's. For an NGO, they were remarkably publicity-shy. Yet there they were, operating with impunity on the Chinese border with Vietnam in what she, Anton, Tuan, and Duc were alleging was a cover operation for the deliberate spread of a virus concocted in the laboratory of an Anglo Swiss subsidiary.

No wonder Anton had been hesitant.

But not Caroline. The message she'd received from Sinclair Baines about his visit to the hotel, and to the cruise boat charter owner, had galvanized her. The fact that Sinclair had taken the initiative to find out who was behind the attack on the boat proved to her that he believed her claim about being in danger, and he was willing to report anything he learned. If he had been at all compromised, he could have chosen not to reveal what he'd discovered about the boat's crew, about what happened on Halong Bay, or about Sam McAvoy's enquiries. His decision to use private, encrypted email encouraged her even further. It made her feel that there was someone on her side who could help search out answers that were missing. Who else was involved? Who was it that wanted them dead, and what part of what they knew was such a threat to them?

Anton was convinced that the longer they waited for more to be revealed, the more easily a counter to their claims could be devised.

'Every day that the news agency fluffs around, seeking proof of what you're saying,' he'd protested the night before, 'is just another day for these bastards to make sure they're ready for you. They're pros, Caroline. They've been running rings around the truth forever. Just look at the size of the settlements they've made over the years for lawsuits involving clinical trials and patient safety. They shrug and move on. And have a look at their list of shareholders. Do you think they'll be affected by our allegations? Do what you threatened to do: send out your story on a viral news feed, and make the bastards sweat a little. Only do it *now*, or not at all.'

'If it comes through EANA,' she argued, 'it'll have more weight. If *they* are satisfied, then others will be, too.'

'Have you asked yourself why you're doing this?' he demanded.

'In order to expose them,' she replied. Surely that was obvious? 'To expose the fact that people's lives have been deliberately squandered in order for a powerful corporation to massively enrich itself, and it's been done with the full co-operation of the US and British governments. People need to know.'

'Really? People need to know?' He was not being sarcastic. He seemed genuinely bemused. 'People will have forgotten by the time the football results come on. How many Big Pharma frauds have you forgotten in your lifetime?'

She flushed. Yes, he was right; she couldn't remember.

'It isn't because people need to know; people don't give a rat's arse. It's because we need the people who want to kill us to know that we've told them everything we have to tell, and there's no point anymore in them killing us.' He threw up his arms in frustration. 'That's the only reason for telling your story, Caroline.'

With that, he'd stormed out—the first time since they met that she'd seen him so impassioned. She'd followed, of course, catching up with him down by the estuary, trying to make the point that as a journalist, she had to go the final yard to uncover the truth, whether the public cared or not. But it hadn't changed his view, and she wondered whether that was partly down to the feeling that he personally had been treated with contempt by the parties involved, and his self-esteem had been irreparably damaged.

That was something she should have given him the time and encouragement to talk through with her, but with danger and survival constantly on their minds, they'd neglected each other. So now, the following morning, she waited until he returned two hours later, looking more relaxed, reporting that the fresh air had given him a monstrous appetite, and he intended to cook up a large breakfast for them both, during which he would tell her a story he'd once heard about a migrating goose that got lost.

*　*　*　*

'The light-bellied brent goose is a small bird by the standards of most geese, and it has a limited number of habitats for its winter migration, travelling in October each year from its home in the upper Arctic reaches of Canada to spend the winter feeding and breeding on the estuarine coasts of Ireland. Because its migration path and chosen habitat are so limited and predictable, it has been a reasonably easy species to monitor, and like most of the world's bird populations, its numbers have been declining. So, the

Wildfowl and Wetlands Trust established a program some years ago to track its migration path by fitting ten-thousand-dollar satellite tracking transponders to a number of birds and seeing whether they made it safely back to their homes in the Arctic circle.

'One of those birds, they christened Kerry, because it had overwintered at Lough Gill in County Kerry. Well, much to the excitement of Canadian conservationists on remote Cornwallis Island, Kerry's signal was picked up loud and clear during their summer, and they set off eagerly to track it down.

'As they got closer to the signal, they stumbled across an Eskimo hunter's home—not an igloo, but a permanent house with electricity, albeit remote by any standards. Confusingly, the signal from Kerry's transponder was loudest as they approached the house, and weakened when they walked away. So, they knocked on the door and spoke to the Eskimo hunter, explaining their mission. As they were talking in the kitchen, one of them noticed that the signal appeared to be coming from the freezer.

'Sure enough, there was Kerry, fully intact with all its feathers and the miniature transponder, dead as a dodo. The hunter was somewhat put out that his traditional food supply had been fitted with electronics, and the researchers were excited by the success of their technology and tracking ability. They recovered the transponder, and the Eskimo kept his catch.'

Caroline's mouth opened as she waited for a punchline before responding. There wasn't one. That was the end of the story.

She laughed. 'I don't know whether that's funny or sad,' she protested. 'That poor bird. That greedy damned Eskimo… Did you see some of those geese down at the estuary just now?'

'No.' He went into the fridge and started pulling out supplies for breakfast. The tension of the night before had gone, but she wasn't quite sure what had replaced it. Eggs, bacon, toast, baked beans; he was cooking up a full British breakfast. This was way out of character.

'So, what made you think of the story?' she asked.

'When did you last use your cell phone? Did you call Sinclair Baines on it?'

'No, I called him using Skype. I haven't called anyone on it. There's no signal here. I purchased roaming data before we left Vietnam, and I've only used it twice since then, both times to call Tuan when we were in London. Why?'

'We're almost out of supplies,' he said, cracking the last of the eggs into a frying pan. 'I'm going to have to go back to that supermarket.'

'Why do you want to know about my cell phone?' she persisted. 'I'm not so stupid that I'd use it with anyone who could trace me, but it was the only way I had of communicating with Tuan. I needed to understand his story.'

'And where were you when you last spoke to him?'

She turned away and started laying out plates and cutlery. 'I called him the night we drove here, while you were in the supermarket. But…' She put the crockery down forcefully on the wooden table. 'I told him from then on, I'd only contact him by email, and he should use an internet café. Then I switched off my phone and haven't used it since. Okay?'

He smiled reassuringly, flipping the eggs before sliding them out of the pan together with the bacon, the smell of which was clearly inflaming his appetite. 'The village where we stopped at the supermarket is five miles from here,' he replied calmly. 'So, that's the closest point for identifying your location, which can easily be done through analyzing cell phone tower traffic, even when you haven't been talking.'

'Well, who the hell's going to do that?' she demanded impatiently. 'Anglo Swiss?'

He pulled out a chair and sat down. 'Let's eat before it gets cold. I'm ravenous.'

Sure that she was being criticized, she wanted an answer. 'Are you really suggesting that Anglo Swiss has that kind of reach?'

He put up his arms in mock surrender. 'Anglo Swiss is the least of it. Sinclair Baines has already confirmed that Sam McAvoy is looking for us—

which means American intelligence—and that Vietnamese intelligence is very likely involved, too. And that's without taking into account the Brits. It seems to me if we don't recognize what we're up against, and move on from there, we're going to end up like Kerry, dead in a freezer.'

'What about *your* phone?' she protested. 'It's British, so it must be a lot easier to trace.'

'You're right. So, let's remove the SIM cards and batteries from our phones and get prepaid burners when we need them.'

She decided she wasn't hungry. Coffee was what she needed, and a chance to think this through.

'Alright,' she said finally, 'I agree about the phones, just to be safe. But I think you're over-dramatizing our importance to whoever it is we're dealing with. They don't know for certain that we're still alive, let alone that we're hiding somewhere in East Suffolk, and unless Sinclair or his London boss has told them, they don't know what we're planning to publish. I vote that we stay here until the story airs. We agreed that's when we'd be safe to show our faces.'

'Okay,' he announced, 'but I'm going to go and get your brother. He's too important to be left out there on his own.'

FIFTEEN

As the center of the depression that was bringing the storm clouds from the west moved over East Anglia, it slipped south towards the channel, so that the narrowing of the isobars whipped up wind from the North Sea, lashing the windscreen wipers of his hire car as Faraday turned off the gravel farm track that led to their cottage hideout and headed towards Woodbridge.

He was glad to be out of the house. He liked the rain. He liked the traffic. He liked the sound of the windscreen wipers, and the babble of voices on the car radio. Perhaps, above all else, he liked the feeling of moving again. Wild game was harder to shoot when it was on the run.

From Woodbridge, he'd pick up the A12 for London. The urge to return to his house in Kensington was overwhelming. It was a part of the urge to forget everything that had happened and return to normal life, putting the bad dream behind him. Closing and bolting the heavy oak door of his solid terraced house (a house that had stood for three hundred years), he could live again in the peaceful world of his imagination, denying the implication that reality was making that he was unfit for living in a world of lies, greed, and corruption.

That he was unfit was not in question. Comparing himself to Caroline proved the point. She had a will to resist and conquer that was made of tempered steel. Her anger and indignation were a furnace whose heat would vaporize any obstacle that had the temerity to appear in her path. If the

Devil was the serpent, and Eve had been Caroline Brinkley, the Bible could have stopped at Genesis, for the Devil would have stood no chance. So long as she stayed alive, he was certain she would triumph. But what had made him unfit for this task? Why did he lack her determination to put the world right? Had he been born this way, or had he chosen it? At no stage had he felt the urge to put the world to rights. Only when he was faced with imminent death on the Halong Bay boat had he fought, and that was for his own life. Now, his responsibility was not exposing the truth; his responsibility was keeping Caroline alive.

From Ipswich to Chelmsford, the traffic started to require his attention, and by the time he reached Brentwood, he had begun to hate it. A part of him was fatalistic about being tracked through his phone, or the hire car. Did any of the people who felt threatened really have the capability or will to locate them by those avenues, or was that the stuff of action movies? There was no hard evidence that anyone was the slightest bit interested in them. Every anxious move on their part might be simply a product of their own paranoia.

At Hounslow, he stopped at a second-hand car yard and picked out a high-mileage, ten-year-old Peugeot SUV, negotiating the price down by fifteen percent for a cash sale, telling the Armenian yard owner that he'd be back in an hour with the money. Then he returned his hire car to the Europcar depot on Northern Perimeter Road at Heathrow before jumping on the shuttle and getting off at Terminal 3. Using a mixture of ATM machines, he withdrew four thousand pounds in cash, bought three burners from a terminal shop, and then caught a cab back to the car yard, where he promised he would take responsibility for filling out the change-of-ownership papers.

Caroline had emailed Tuan, telling him to be ready to be picked up at his hotel, but there was no way for Faraday to be sure he'd got the message, as he'd left the cottage before a reply arrived. The hotel where they'd dropped him off the day they returned from Vietnam was the Ibis on Cherry Lane, and he decided to head there and hope that Tuan had not gone out. It was three o'clock when he arrived, and he was keen to get back to East Suffolk before sundown.

After parking in the hotel car park, well away from the entrance, he approached cautiously, looking out for anyone who seemed out of place. When his enquiry at the front desk elicited the response that there was no one named Tran Minh Tuan registered as a guest in the last week, he knew he had a problem. A casual walk through the bars and restaurants, the outdoor patio, and even the swimming pool area failed to solve the problem. There was no point in waiting. The only solution he could think of was to find an internet café at the airport and hope that Caroline was online and monitoring her emails.

As he approached his car, he opened the doors from a distance using the key fob. In doing so, he was aware of a crouched figure running between the parked rows ahead of him, and as he reached the driver's side, his passenger door was wrenched open, and the frightened figure of Caroline's adopted brother Tuan jumped in.

'Go, go, go!' he pleaded urgently. 'Foot to the floor.'

Faraday, whose heart was already pumping, fumbled for the ignition and hand brake, then sped out of the car park onto the airport ring road towards the M4.

'What the hell is happening?' he demanded.

'My room was broken into. I came back, and two men were waiting for me, but I ran and hid in the garbage chute. I've been waiting for you in the car park.'

'But they said you weren't staying there. No one of your name has checked in all week.'

'I gave the name Nguyen Van Thanh. It's kinda like "John Smith" in my country.'

'What was the name on the credit card you gave them?'

'I didn't think they'd check it.'

'Right! If you wanted a pseudonym, John Smith might have been safer,' Faraday observed dryly.

He cursed silently as he headed for the motorway on-ramp, checking his rearview mirrors. His belief that there was no hard evidence that anyone was interested in them was now exposed as wishful thinking.

'Well, the first thing you need is a shower,' he complained. 'That garbage chute smells of rotten fish.'

SIXTEEN

The house creaked in the wind, and rain could be heard leaking through the roof onto the bare wooden floorboards of the attic.

Tuan was proving difficult. The isolated cottage on the edge of the dark moor frightened him. Their assurance that they were safe ran counter to his Asian agoraphobia. How could they escape, he wanted to know? How would they know who might be approaching them in the dark?

Anton retrieved his friend's shotgun from beneath the kitchen floor and propped it up beside the front door. He placed a box of cartridges next to it. Tuan was not appeased.

The problem was, as Caroline well knew, that he had too much knowledge. Without him, the story would fall over. He'd worked on the development of CD8Magna, knew the research that had been done at Nui BioLab on virus mutations, and was fully engaged in the collection of patients' blood trials under the secret agreement with the Vietnamese Ministry of Health. He was the star witness, but following the attack at the Heathrow hotel, he was a very scared one. If he refused to stand by the story Caroline had drafted for him, then critical elements of her allegations would fall into the category of hearsay. It was going to take all her emotional skills to overcome his cold intellect, and his legitimate fear.

Though there was no reception at the cottage, she gave one of Anton's burner phones to Tuan, wondering who he would try to call in the event that he wanted to use it. She knew nothing of his personal life, assuming that he didn't have one, yet he'd gone to Uncle's house the minute he realized he was in danger in Hanoi. Was Uncle the sheet anchor that would help stabilize him throughout this storm?

As usual, Anton did the cooking, having restocked their supplies in Woodbridge on the way back from Heathrow. In an inspired move, he decided to make a fish soup with noodles, and Tuan devoured it voraciously, finishing his bowl without even looking up to speak, giving the impression that he had not eaten since he'd arrived in England. In another inspired move, Anton had also purchased a bottle of brandy, three glasses of which he poured at the end of their meal, insisting that they formally drink a toast to their survival, and to Uncle and his family for ensuring their safe escape from Vietnam.

Time was Caroline's enemy. Anton's statement was complete. She needed Tuan's before the morning. He was, she remembered, dismissive of laypeople's ignorance, and she could imagine him balking at her attempt to put words in his mouth.

Anton poured a second round of drinks and raised his glass. 'To the brother and sister who fight for truth,' he proposed.

'What is the truth?' Tuan asked.

Anton thought hard. 'That good science must defend itself against bad intentions.'

Tuan emptied his glass. 'And how does it do that?' he asked scathingly.

'You would know better than anyone,' Caroline assured him. 'If I make you a guest on my laptop, will you write for us about how your work was corrupted by your employers, and why your life has been endangered by what they've done? Tell us in your own words, Tuan.'

Without waiting for a reply, she retrieved her laptop from the other room, gave him a guest password, and plonked it down in front of him. Then she and Anton went up to bed, leaving the lights on, the dishes unwashed, and her fingers firmly crossed.

In the morning, she found Tuan sound asleep at the table. On the screen was a Microsoft Word document that ran to eighty pages.

That left her with one affidavit still to complete: that of Duc, a man she had only met once on the roadside near Dien Bien Phu, a Montagnard from a primitive hill tribe, to whom Anton claimed he would entrust his life. He was the witness to her claim that the village wells had been deliberately infected, and that Paladin had recruited tribesmen to go into China in order to spread the virus there as well. She desperately needed his testimony, but where was he, and how could they reach him? He had a cell phone that she'd observed Anton trying to call on a number of occasions, with limited success, when they were on the run in Vietnam. Of course, he lived in the mountains, where coverage was mostly non-existent, and internet was not an option. Could she trust Sinclair Baines to track him down, or was this the part of the story that would prove to be her Achilles heel?

Now that she was using the secure encrypted link provided by TAILS and the TOR network, she felt more confident about messaging Sinclair directly. That confidence was boosted by his overnight admission that he had real doubts about the validity of the numbers being provided by the Vietnam government, and about the reliability of the WHO.

```
Accepting your theory about what has gone on here,
we'd have to say it is in everyone's interest to
boost the figures and pull China into the mix. In
the wonderful world of international slush funds,
pandemics are big money, and the WHO's man here is
already hinting that that's about to be announced.
My next port of call is the CEO of Nui BioLab, so
the sooner you can send me the statement from your
microbiologist witness, the better. Don't worry,
I'm as keen as you are to ensure that no one
suspects the story we want to break, but the more
time we spend sitting on this, the more chance
there is that it will leak.
```

She thought about this for some time before answering.

She hoped to God that her trust in him was not misplaced, because
between them, she and Anton had concluded that they had no other way
of getting a signed statement from Duc, unless Caroline sent his details to
Baines, together with a version of Duc's story as he'd told it to Anton, in
deliberately imperfect English.

* * * *

Later that morning, the three of them got into the Peugeot and set off for
Cambridge, seventy miles away. Tuan was in a better mood, having taken
ownership of his part in the story as a result of writing it himself, and his
relationship with Anton had noticeably thawed on the back of the previous
night's brandy.

In Bury St. Edmunds, they found a digital print shop, where they were
able to print out copies of two bank statement files they had downloaded
to Caroline's laptop, giving the residential addresses of Tuan in Hanoi and
Anton Faraday in Kensington. Arriving in Cambridge at 1:30, they found
King's Notary & Apostille Service closed for lunch.

'Only Mr King can certify documents,' the receptionist explained, 'and
he won't be back until two thirty. Do you have an appointment?'

Caroline shook her head. 'Your website says no appointment is
necessary.'

'You'll need an appointment. Besides, we don't certify same day.'

'We'll wait,' Caroline replied.

And so, they sat in silence. At 2:45, Mr King returned from lunch. He
was ruddy and affable and smelled of beer. Of course he could witness their

documents. He'd be delighted. Passports and bank statements? Excellent. He'd notarize them under his seal for eighty pounds each, on the spot. And would they like these documents to be accepted outside the UK? Attaching an apostille certificate would authenticate their use in all countries that were members of the Hague Convention. Yes? Well worthwhile, and only one hundred pounds extra.

'Would it be possible to get digital copies of the certified documents?' Caroline asked. 'We need to send them straight away.'

'Ah!' Mr King enthused, 'an excellent option. My receptionist will scan them and put them on a memory stick for you. That will be just one hundred pounds extra. Each.'

Anton peeled off the notes, while Mr King looked away, as if cash were somehow in poor taste. Then he left, and the receptionist sighed and went off to find a memory stick.

'When you delete those files,' Caroline said on her return, 'they aren't actually deleted at all. Is that right?'

'They go into the file marked "bin,"' the receptionist answered, as if that were obvious.

'So, delete doesn't really mean delete.'

'Oh, if you want them deleted permanently, you have to completely empty the bin,' she explained, looking at her watch pointedly.

Caroline smiled and laid on her New Jersey accent. 'Thank you. That would be real helpful.'

As they drove back to their hideaway on the marshes, each was buried in thought. For Caroline, this was what she had aspired to for so long: the life of the investigative journalist. However this turned out, she sensed that her life was already irreversibly changed. It was frightening but true that her built-in sense of moral outrage at the world had lain dormant within her for years, waiting for this moment to explode into life. She could never have turned away from it, the way Anton was prepared to do. Danger was the price to pay for accepting the challenge. Self-loathing was the price for ignoring it. Once those statements landed on EANA's desk, there would be no opportunity for second thoughts.

As soon as they were safely home, Caroline posted copies on her dropbox—the one that she'd given her parents access to in case anything happened to her on her travels.

'That's everything you two know,' she said. 'There's nothing more we can add.'

'I say send it,' Anton replied. 'The sooner it's out there, the sooner we can stop hiding.'

'Tuan?'

'I'm ready.'

'And what about Duc?' she asked. 'We need his evidence that the virus was deliberately spread through the village drinking wells.'

Anton was adamant. 'Send his statement unsigned in the meantime. I trust him to stand by it. If EANA doesn't run with this, send it to everyone. This is what you want, Caroline. Just do it.'

SEVENTEEN

Ngo Nam Koi left Hanoi before dawn, picking up the DCT05 highway north for Lao Cai before the morning chaos began. His Yamaha 125cc bike had a high-revolution whine that reached a sweet spot at somewhere around 110 kilometers per hour, and at that speed, he estimated he'd reach Lao Cai in three hours. From there, his timing was less certain. The route from Lao Cai to Lai Chau was winding and mountainous for a hundred kilometers, and it could be treacherous unless he cut his speed back dramatically. He might not reach the turnoff for Sinho until midday.

Sinho was the only address he had to go by. The man he was to find was known only as Duc. He was a Dao mountain guide, and he needed to sign the papers that Sinclair Baines had given Koi, with instructions to try to be back before nightfall. There was a cell phone number, but it was either turned off or out of range.

Koi was wearing his green fatigues without insignia, as he wore every day, and the zips on his jacket and trousers held his Smith & Wesson Bodyguard .38 Special, his cell phone, and his KleerVu plastic ID holder and money clip, safe from pickpockets' hands. Beneath his crash helmet, he wore a black cotton balaclava, and beneath that, he wore the cotton face mask that everyone in the north of the country was now shamed into wearing. It was already hot at 6:00am, and he sweated profusely beneath the black balaclava, but the wind dried it out instantly.

He'd read the papers that Duc was required to sign, and he felt it was not something that someone should put their name to if they wanted to avoid trouble. But this man was a Moi, and that was what the Moi did: make trouble. So, let his ancestors look after him.

At Lao Cai, he stopped and refueled his bike, ate two deep-fried spring rolls and a fried banana, drank lemon grass tea, and went to the toilet. He made a quick call to a contact at MobiFone and asked for the name of the registered owner of the SIM card number he'd been given for Duc. It was a prepay in the name of Dao Kim Duc. No address.

Then he began the slow, tortuous ride heading west on QL4D through Sapa, the road potholed and blocked with construction barriers. The harder he pressed, the more mud was thrown up in his face. At the top of Tram Ton Pass, he stopped and wiped his visor clean. The air was thin and clear, and a thousand meters below him, the pass snaked around the mountain down to fast-flowing indigo rivers and terraced rice fields, while above loomed Mount Fansipan, casting its shadow all the way to the Chinese border.

The Tram Ton Pass wound down to Lai Chau, and he upped his speed, gripping the handlebars as if he were a dirt bike rider, grinning to himself beneath his face mask like a daredevil teenager, daring the juddering front wheel to twist and unseat him, blind to the tourist brochure scenery to the side of him. Along the Nam Na River valley's new roads, he reached eighty kilometers per hour before turning east at Nam Cay/Chan Nua onto the single-lane steep climb to Sinho, zigzagging for forty kilometers. After a series of switchbacks, the scruffy mountain village lay before him, shrouded in mist and drizzling rain, ringed by limestone pinnacles and scatterings of small Kim Mein villages on stilts, puffing wisps of blue smoke into the cool mountain air.

He parked his bike in the town square and found the busiest *com pho* joint to get some hot soup. The people were a mixture of Red Dao and Kinh. The Kinh were the occupiers, noisy and confident. Koi was Kinh. At a table filled with Dao, he asked for Dao Kim Duc. They looked at him with cold eyes and shook their heads. He ate his soup quickly and left.

Next to the street market, he found the police station, occupied by one man asleep at his desk. He woke slowly, exposing bad teeth in a corruptible face, peering at Koi's press identity card in search of money. No, there was no register of the town's inhabitants. The Dao were secretive. They sacrificed animals, and they received money from America. At the herbal baths on the outskirts of town, they swapped spouses on 'Free-Loving Night.' If he wanted to find someone, he should go there and take off his clothes. No one felt threatened by a naked man, not even a Kim Mien Dao.

The town was quiet. The street market had closed, and the petite dark-skinned women, with shaved heads under brightly colored turbans, had begun wandering back to their stilt homes, laden with baskets of vegetables. Koi walked, leaving his bike in front of the police station. For a man with his experience with danger, it was not difficult to tell that his presence had disturbed the balance of trust in the rice and noodles shop, or that the sight of him caused a shadow to cross the faces of the women returning home.

Koi liked danger. It was his familiar. He wrote Duc's name down on a scrap of paper, adding the words *Nguoi ban* ('friend'), and gave it to the woman minding the herbal bath house. Then he went behind a brushwood screen, took off his clothes, and lowered himself alone into a concrete pool of opaque steaming water, lying back with his eyes half closed, listening.

He wasn't entirely surprised when ten minutes later, three Dao men appeared in the doorway. He got out of the bath and dressed while still wet. The men didn't attempt to relieve him of his gun, or check his identity. They spoke with their hands. They had six hands—the hands of carpenters and blacksmiths. He had two hands—the hands of a killer.

They walked out of town and took a steep path down to a small hamlet that he could see through the trees, perched precariously above the craterous valley below. When first he heard the slow, sonorous sound of a beating drum, he stopped, questioning his escorts with his eyes. He knew what it was. They knew what it was. They nodded and kept walking.

Duc lay on a table in the dark. The room was full of dark people. The body was dressed in short embroidered vest and baggy indigo trousers. There was a bullet wound in his temple. The bullet must have been soft-nosed—no powder burns. No one spoke. The drumbeat vibrated through the floorboards of the stilt house. Below them was a thousand-meter fall to the rocks at the base of the mysterious and brooding mountain.

Koi took out the papers that Sinclair Baines had directed him to get signed. He started reading them aloud, awkwardly translating from English. In the dark, he stumbled over words. When he came to the end, he remembered why he had come. He needed a signature. Who would give him one?

No one moved. No one spoke.

'Who did this?' he asked.

There was no answer.

What he'd read described the deliberate poisoning of wells in order to infect the people of the mountains. It had been organized by Westerners, protected by the *Kinh* government. Koi knew as he read it that the people in the room knew it already. Any one of them could sign it.

He took up Duc's stiffened hand and separated out the thumb, then knelt down and took a piece of Duc's baggy trousers in his mouth. He sucked upon the indigo fabric with as much saliva as his mouth would produce, until it was soaking wet and his mouth had turned black. He rubbed Duc's thumb in the fabric, then pressed it onto the last page of the document, leaving a blue-black imprint.

Straightening up, he took out his cell phone and held it up for the room to see. What he said loosely translated as, 'I am his brother, and his brother is me.'

He took two photographs: one of the body, and one of the bullet entry point in Duc's temple. Then he left the room and walked back to the town square. There were two sides to the plastic identity card holder he kept in his pocket. One side was his EANA journalist's registration, and the other side was his *Tong Cuc 2* insignia of the General Department of Military

Intelligence. It was the TC2 side that he showed to the occupant of the police station who had sent him to the bath house. This time, the man was a lot less sleepy. The body with the bullet in its head was Moi. He shrugged. Clearly, the man had committed suicide. Dao could bury people any way they liked. There was no register of their names.

Koi unlocked his motorbike and headed back down the hill on the TL128 to Lai Chau. The farther he descended, the quicker the mist cleared, and soon the vast sunlit landscape opened up beneath him, the implacable mountains, home to the spirits of ancestors, the *Ban Ho*, stretching far into the distance—a repository for the secrets of eons, the dreams, longings, tragedies, and fears of all the peoples who had sought refuge there.

By nightfall, if all went well, he should be safely back in Hanoi.

EIGHTEEN

As far as Sinclair Baines was concerned, they now had their story. The email he'd received from Caroline attaching Faraday's and Tuan's statements sealed it. Together with the document he'd given to Koi to get signed by the mountain guide, there was enough damning evidence to justify them running with it, and as he'd hoped from the beginning, it had the potential to release a torrent of follow-up stories, provided they planned it right.

Anglo Swiss, Nui BioLab, the Vietnam Health Ministry, the British and the Americans, the WHO—Christ, they were going to need his whole team briefed and ready to go, and then some. The London Bureau would have to be primed and ready as well. It needed a war room, and he already had the opening line for the first briefing.

'This is murder—mass murder on a grand scale.'

Caroline had now chosen to move away from the simultaneous communication with Liddell, Kate Manning, and himself. She'd elected to use the encryption service, trusting his judgment about redistributing. What that meant was that he was sitting at the top of the triangle, the place where he'd always wanted to be—and where, in this case, he deserved to be.

There were those who believed that the best way to discover news was to create it, and the responsibility for running with it lay with those at the top. If you wanted to be at the top, however, that was not an attitude that would help you get there. As the East Asia bureau chief, he now had four contributing writers on staff, three regular freelancers, and a string of irregulars. Caroline Brinkley fitted the last category. Irregulars didn't research and write to instruction; their fingers danced across their keyboards to the beat of their own drummer—which carried risks. In the news business, one often had to make a snap decision as to whether to run with the story being pitched, or give it a miss and hope someone else fell flat on their face if they picked it up. With this story, Baines had made a snap decision to run with it. He'd accepted the risks.

London might consider itself the center of the world, but in his judgment, nowhere could safely claim that position anymore. He might subtly remind Bryan Liddell of that when he called him. Locating the EANA office in Hanoi, rather than in Hong Kong, Tokyo, or Singapore, had been his recommendation. They already had a dedicated China office in Beijing, and with so much space being given to the economy and politics of that nation, his argument had been that the emerging countries of South East Asia would be overlooked without a presence in one of them. Besides, all a correspondent needed was an internet connection, an airline ticket, and a sensitive nose, he'd argued. It didn't matter where he or she was based.

Events since early June had proved him right. The avian flu epidemic had spread into South China and was teetering on the edge of becoming a pandemic, with the anxious gaze of the world now fixed firmly on Hanoi. It was Sinclair Baines and his reporting team who had first delivered that story to the news wires, while the lead-footed bureaucrats of the World Health Organization and the United Nations labored to get their spokesmen on the ground. By mid-July, EANA had been filing three stories a day and had the ear of every official who was allowed to open their mouth, but by mid-August, the WHO had wrestled control of information away from the hospitals and government departments, drowning it in bureau-crap.

Then Caroline Brinkley had called. He'd never met her. She was just a voice: young, American, direct, and focused. She'd filed a story about the scene on the ground in Sapa, which was good for local color, and he'd been happy to pay for it. Then she claimed to have an angle that had a whiff of conspiracy about it, but if true, it sounded too good to pass up. It was his skill in handling her that had brought that story to life.

He'd sat on these witness statements all day, waiting for the London office to open so he could call Bryan Liddell. Now he was starving, and Mrs Qui was taking an age to make his order.

The air conditioning system in the food court was famously efficient, reducing the temperature indoors to ten degrees lower than the steam bath out on the street, despite all the cooking taking place inside. But it wasn't the temperature that caused a brief chill to pass over Baines as he pondered the implications of Caroline Brinkley's claims. It was the momentary chill of fear at the thought of the power and cold-eyed ruthlessness of the corporate and government agencies on whom they were about to declare war.

The moment passed, and excitement returned as he called Liddell. It was nine o'clock in London.

'I have the statements,' he announced, 'signed, sealed, notarized, and damning as hell. This is murder, Bryan—mass murder on a grand scale.'

'How come I don't have them?'

'She's chosen to use my private encryption service. After reading this stuff, I don't blame her. You and I should do the same. It's too damn explosive to risk being leaked.'

'We agreed that Kate Manning would be in the loop as well. I'm not going out without our libel arses covered, so get that firmly fixed in your head.'

'Well, I suggest you deliver it to her in person. But when you see it, you'll maybe need to rethink the idea of taking it to Anglo Swiss for comment. All I can see is an avalanche of threats and injunctions, and probably D-Notices from your government as well. We're going to have to grow balls on this one.'

They agreed to switch to encryption, and Baines would send through the three statements, with the mountain guide's unsigned, pending Koi's return. From there, they'd draw up a plan and communicate one-on-one by phone only; no more emails.

If only he could persuade Caroline to do the same.

Finally, his asparagus and crab meat soup arrived.

'*Mang tay nau cua,*' Miss Anh announced softly. 'Sorry it take long time.' She hesitated. 'Mr Sinclair…'

'Yes?'

'Mrs Qui say, if you phone your order, I can bring to your apartment.'

NINETEEN

Kate Manning read in silence, turning each page over on her desktop as she finished it. Several passages were retrieved and read again. She didn't make notes or use a highlighter.

While she read, Bryan Liddell paced her office, inspecting the bookshelves filled with unread leather-bound volumes of the Bodleian Law Library, casting quick glances in her direction to try to gauge where she was, and whether or not her facial expression matched what she was reading.

As she reached the last page, he stopped his foot-tapping and stood over her, hands buried deep in his jacket pockets like an impatient football manager stuck on the sidelines.

'Well,' she said, turning the last page face down and laying her hand on it as if it might fly away, 'I can see now why they believe their lives are in danger.'

'What we are alleging here,' Liddell stressed, recalling the words Baines had used half an hour earlier, 'is nothing short of mass murder. We need to urgently rethink our whole strategy.'

Kate stood up as well. She didn't want to react until she'd properly absorbed it—and there was a lot to absorb.

'Who else has seen this?' she asked. 'Everyone that you *know* has seen it, and anyone who *might* have seen it, no matter how small the possibility. I want to be sure.'

'You, me, Baines, Brinkley, Faraday, the microbiologist … and the notary.'

'The mountain guide…?'

'They're still trying to find him.'

'But no one else at EANA?'

'Not to my knowledge. Baines is being particularly cautious about the possibility of leaks, but I'll ask him.'

'And Karim Farzan?'

'No. We've reverted to using a P2P encryption service, so there's nothing on our office server. I'd prefer that he stays out of the loop.'

Realizing her door was open, Kate moved quickly to close it. Her concern was obvious. She returned to her desk and sat down again.

'Bryan, I think I'm going to have to withdraw my initial advice. Having these witness statements notarized and certified is very useful, but it won't alter the reality, which is that the allegations are extremely dangerous. This is no longer about mitigating exposure to libel claims, or providing the accused with a fair right of reply. If we took this to Anglo Swiss, we'd never make it to print. We'd be swamped with injunctions and suppression orders that would sink us without trace. Not to mention the financial pressure they'd put on Wilton McGwyer.'

Liddell shrugged. He was a big boy. He wasn't hearing anything he hadn't expected.

'So, what's Heathcote Manning's advice now?' he asked. 'Publish, and be damned—or hope that our witnesses get killed first, saving ourselves from trouble?'

She didn't have a reply to that. Whether Liddell ran with the story or declined it was his decision to make. They both knew the consequences, and she had absolved herself of professional liability. But if her mind was clear on that issue, her heart was deeply troubled.

* * * *

Liddell returned to his office and busied himself with the rash of daily stories that were requiring his sign-off. The decision about the Anglo Swiss story was momentarily parked. He'd wait until Baines called him to confirm that the mountain guide's statement was safely locked down, then the two of them could talk strategy. Someone would have to lead the charge on this story, and that someone was Sinclair Baines.

He'd been back at his desk for an hour when Karim Farzan appeared again for the second time in two days. He watched him disappear into Megan Hastel's office, and he wondered what was so important about her financial reporting that it called for the high-flying attentions of a director of Wilton McGwyer on a daily basis. Whatever it was, he closed Megan's door behind him, and he didn't emerge again until fifteen minutes later. This time, instead of heading for the elevator, he headed for Liddell's office, gliding through the open-plan desks like a poised ice-skater, smiling his acknowledgment to the writers and subbies, who would have no idea who he was.

'Bryan, am I catching you at a bad time?'

Liddell got to his feet. 'If we're talking financials, it's always a bad time. Come in.'

Farzan chuckled and took a seat. 'I was asking Megan to present her monthly reports in a slightly different format,' he explained. 'I hope you don't mind. It helps with our investment newsletters to have our unlisted equities presented in a comparable style to the listed ones.'

Liddell shrugged. 'Sure. As long as ours aren't printed in red, you can have them formatted in any way that suits.'

Farzan's face turned serious. 'The line between red and black is very thin in the media business, as you well know, Bryan,' he replied. 'And one of the things I think we need to discuss is risk.'

'Risk?'

'Kate Manning called me the other day about our attitude toward establishing a contingency fund for libel claims. It made me realize we don't have one.'

'You don't have an attitude, or you don't have a fund?'

Farzan crossed and uncrossed his legs. *Women do that*, Liddell thought. Men who did it shouldn't be trusted.

'The point she made,' Farzan answered, 'was that opponents in libel cases are very good at assessing the financial breaking point of the media outlet being sued. She wanted to know, in the case of EANA, whether it was Wilton McGwyer's breaking point that was applicable, or whether it was EANA's alone.'

'And what was your response?'

'I replied that it was EANA's alone, and that I rely on Heathcote Manning to identify anything that might attract a libel claim, and on Bryan Liddell's good judgment to ensure that it doesn't get released if that were the case.'

Liddell sat up straight and frowned. He was a Yorkshireman, and he could have sworn that he was, in a roundabout way, being threatened.

'We're a news organization, Karim,' he replied firmly, 'not a public relations outfit. If we dropped a story every time somebody decided they didn't like it, there'd be no news worth printing.'

Karim crossed his legs again. The cost of his bloody suit would be enough to drain EANA's cash resources, if Megan's reportage was anything to go by, so he knew damn well that Liddell weighed the odds every time he published something. What the fuck had brought this on?

'Well,' Karim cautioned, 'I thought Kate Manning was right to make the point, and I just want to be sure we're all on the same page.'

* * * *

Koi parked his Yamaha at the entrance to the Royal City apartments, chaining it to a bollard before descending to the food court. He was hungry and hot, shedding his helmet and balaclava as he walked. The pretty girl, Anh, told him that Baines had been in earlier and taken his meal upstairs to his apartment. She said he'd ordered two deep-fried rolls as well and forgotten to take them, but she didn't know his apartment number. Koi told her it was apartment 2709, but he'd take the rolls up to him personally, and he wanted two for himself as well.

As he waited, he took out his cell phone for the first time since he'd left Sinho and looked at the two photographs he'd taken. He wanted to be sure that there were no burn marks on Duc's temple. There weren't. Suicide victims put their gun right up to their head, so they could feel it with certainty. Professional killers wanting to fake a suicide did the same thing. If he'd stayed in Sinho longer, he might have tried to learn what other strangers had visited the town before him. But he knew the Dao wouldn't tell him, because he was a Kinh, and he knew the police wouldn't tell him, because Duc was a Moi, and one more dead Moi was not a crime.

He wouldn't send the images to Baines, but would transfer them by Bluetooth when he saw him upstairs. Then he'd delete them. He didn't want the evidence on either his computer or his phone.

* * * *

It was lunchtime in London when Sinclair Baines called to report Koi's news of the shooting. The sonorous beat of the funeral drum down the line was almost palpable. What had previously been a decision with scary implications based on the facts revealed had now become a decision that risked being powered by moral imperatives. Moral journalism was something to be avoided.

'More than ever,' Liddell cautioned, 'this means that we have to question every word of these people's testimonies.'

'I agree,' Baines acknowledged. 'The stakes are too high.'

Though he hated saying it—hated even thinking it—Liddell felt obliged to state the obvious. 'You know, this has the potential to destroy us as a company, Sinclair. While we may be outraged by what we've been told, is it necessary for us to take on opponents who will have no hesitation in trying to bankrupt us? Yes, they undoubtedly deserve to be exposed, but what good does it do if we go down as a consequence?'

Baines was not unduly surprised. 'I guess Caroline Brinkley doesn't need us in order to get the story out there,' he conceded reluctantly. 'There are plenty of internet news sites that would be only too happy to run with it. But these accusations will feel like nothing more than a pinprick to the bastards responsible for all this. It's making the accusations stick that will be the challenge, and that's one hell of a task.'

There was no mistaking the despondency in his voice.

'You sound doubtful that we can do that.'

'It will require all our resources, and I'd have to be sure of your backing.'

'Kate Manning is convinced we'd be locked down with D-Notices and injunctions the minute they got a whiff of it,' Liddell warned. 'How would you suggest we get around that?'

They both went silent. Having to think like a public prosecutor was not new to either of them, but the consequences of failing to make the charges stick seemed particularly dire in this instance. The question Liddell had thrown at Kate Manning earlier that morning, before he'd learned of Duc's murder, had been left unanswered for good reason. 'So, what's Heathcote Manning's advice now?' he'd asked. 'Publish, and be damned—or hope that our witnesses get killed first, saving ourselves from trouble?'

Put crudely, it was one down and three to go.

As if reading his thoughts, Baines reminded them of how they'd got where they were. 'Remember, Caroline Brinkley came to us because she has good reason to fear for their lives,' he stressed. 'On that score, she's now been proven right beyond doubt. But it's the glare from the spotlight of public accusations that she believes will protect them from being further attacked. What's not proven is the identity of the attackers, but it's my guess that no one named in those statements would want to see their accusers deliberately harmed once the statements are out in the public arena.'

'I'm not forgetting that,' Liddell made clear. 'It's top of my mind. What I'm questioning is whether that strategy relies on us.'

'It relies on credibility, Bryan. That's what we can provide.'

The death of Duc should have made the decision to proceed easier for Liddell, but unfortunately, a serpent had entered his room earlier in the form of Karim Farzan, and it had flicked its tongue at him, reminding him of the harm its venom could cause.

'Give me an action plan that I can sleep on overnight,' he instructed. 'What can we actually prove beyond doubt, and how would we go about doing it? Then I'll decide tomorrow.'

TWENTY

Liddell came into work slightly later on a Saturday morning. News never stopped, of course, but he was past the age when he needed to work seven days a week in order to be indispensable. Saturday, however, was the day when Sunday papers were substantially put to bed, and he liked to ensure that a healthy quantity of EANA's output was featured.

The early Saturday edition of *The Times* went to bed around midnight and was delivered in the dark, while most Londoners were still asleep. Most Londoners, it had to be said, tended to read the digital versions of papers over breakfast, if they had time. Assuming they could afford to pay for it, that is, because unlike the more popular *BBC News* online and the tabloids, the quality and prestige of *The Times* were sheltered behind a paywall.

On a normal weekday, Bryan Liddell liked to scan the online editions on his laptop as he rode to work on the Central Line from West Ruislip between 7:00 and 8:00am. He checked the front pages of all the dailies each morning, for obvious reasons, but it was very seldom that he took a deep dive into the middle sections, or did much more than quickly scan headlines and skylines to see what was trending, or what might pre-empt stories EANA's own staff and contributors were planning to file that day. With the Saturday edition of *The Times*, however, he allowed himself the luxury of scanning the printed version, saving the arts and sports supplements to be read on the way home.

The story that appeared on page 37 was outside his train journey reading range, and it wasn't until he was sitting at his desk, and Kate Manning was shouting at him urgently down the phone at 10:15, that he was forced to find it. The headline would not normally have grabbed his attention, but the standfirst stopped him dead.

Secret Agreement Helps Beat China to the Punch
Anglo Swiss BioLab reveals how years
of co-operation helped in development
of new Asian bird flu drug and vaccine

'Have you read this?' Kate demanded. 'It's a direct contradiction of what your reporter is saying. Anglo Swiss is claiming that the governments of Vietnam, the United States, and Britain have been working together on drug development and trials for over ten years. They say that, quote, "the Paladin Foundation was engaged to advise on the protection of a special environmental area to prevent degradation of the habitat by local tribes, and this has allowed them to ensure the survival of the rare plant from which CD8Magna has been synthesized." But that's not all—'

'Okay, okay, I'm reading as fast as I can, but let me take this in.'

'Go down to the second-to-last paragraph.'

'Shit.'

'Deep shit, Bryan. The way this reads sounds to me as though someone saw your story coming.'

Nui BioLab, the wholly owned subsidiary of pharmaceutical giant Anglo Swiss BioLab, announced that the release date for a new vaccine to protect against the bird flu strain is due to be announced in the coming weeks. Although Stage 3 development is almost complete, the release has been delayed following receipt of an extortion threat, which has resulted in an arrest warrant being issued, and an Interpol alert being raised, for an ex-employee microbiologist at their Hanoi facility.

'I'll call you back, Kate.'

'Alright, but I can't help thinking that we might have just avoided shooting ourselves in the foot.'

The updated 9:00am edition of *The Times Online* had moved the story to the front page of the business section. There was no byline or dateline, and the reason for that quickly became apparent, at least to Liddell. At 9:00am, EANA's own *news@eana.co* domain for incoming media releases had received the exact same story, word for word, from a London strategic communications company on behalf of its client, Anglo Swiss BioLab UK Limited.

The only other newspaper carrying the story was *The Sun*, the second national daily in the News UK stable. So, the pre-release had been given to News Corp the afternoon prior. *The Sun's* treatment was, of course, more sensational.

Life-Saving Vaccine Coming
Security breach delays release

From the moment Caroline Brinkley's story had first landed on his screen, Liddell had known that it was trouble. Was Kate right that they had just dodged a bullet, or was the trouble now only going to ramp up?

* * * *

When Bryan Liddell alerted him by phone about the breaking news, Sinclair Baines felt like he had been rear-ended, hit from behind by a Mack truck. He hadn't seen it coming, he hadn't prepared for the whiplash that momentarily turned his brain to custard, and inevitably, it was taking him time to recover from the shock and assess the damage.

The person he was most pissed off with was himself. He'd known that Caroline's story was true, and he'd probably known that Liddell and the lawyers would lose their nerve about publishing it. So, why hadn't he gone ahead and sent it out without involving them? Well, the answer was simple: he hadn't had the balls.

He knew damn well where he'd learned this caution, but it disgusted him that he hadn't managed to outgrow it. He walked and talked like a grown man, but he was no more a man now than he was when he'd first entered this news-gathering racket. As a twenty-eight-year-old kid on the *Boston Herald*, he'd started out thinking that he understood the world he was licensed to write about. No one had warned him during media studies at Central Connecticut State University about how big business and government were run. They taught him instead that he had an obligation to tell the truth. That was the line all wannabe journalists were fed.

Well, that all changed pretty damn fast in Boston when he started filing stories about City Hall corruption. He was very quickly made aware that he was no match for the cold-eyed men standing in the corner of his editor's office while he was being instructed to look elsewhere. And he'd been a naive kid when he'd leaped from his dinky Volkswagen after being rear-ended on a late-night street some days later, only to suffer an attack that left him in the hospital, having lost sight in one eye and with a burst spleen, but with no evidence of his attackers.

But all that had been eleven years ago. He'd had an excuse back then. After three months in rehab, he'd applied for a job with the Associated Press in Singapore, resolving that if he were ever rear-ended again, he'd stay seated behind the wheel and keep the engine running. Was that going to be his position now?

Or was he going to get out of the car and find out who the fuck had rammed him?

* * * *

The flow of news releases involving Anglo Swiss came quickly. At midday, there was an announcement from the headquarters of the World Health Organization in Geneva that the World Bank had approved a one-billion-dollar Pandemic Financing Facility for the Vietnamese government to aid in their fight against the spread of the avian influenza virus and to help design a nationwide vaccination program in anticipation of the forthcoming release of a broad-spectrum vaccine developed by the Anglo Swiss subsidiary, Nui BioLab.

In time for the BBC News at six came a feel-good announcement that Anglo Swiss was donating a half million doses of CD8Magna to the health authorities in the Guangxi and Yunnan regions of South China to aid in the treatment of patients infected with the virus there. And two hours later, the government of Ecuador revealed that it had declared a twenty-thousand-hectare area of mountain forests in the El Oriente region to be a protected area under a management plan drawn up by the Paladin Foundation for the Environment. What, exactly, was being 'protected'? 'Pharmacologically active substances in nature.'

These last two unfolded on Bryan Liddell's iPhone as he rode the Central Line to East Ruislip, then caught the repeating BBC news in the Snug Bar at his usual stop-over opposite the Ruislip golf course on his way home (tomato juice and Tabasco sauce with a generous helping of Worcestershire sauce to give it body: a Virgin Mary, English-style). He presumed that Sinclair Baines was realizing at the same moment what was crystal clear to him: that the people accused in the story they had considered running were so well equipped with money, resources, and moral disengagement that they couldn't be shamed or corrected by public exposure of the truth; they were above it, immune to it. The truth would only hurt the teller.

He lingered over his Virgin Mary while digesting this bitter thought until, by his calculation, bath-time would be over at home, and he would be able to read his granddaughter a bedtime story while his daughter, Tracey, prepared their supper. Tracey, an expensively schooled graduate in gender affairs and social policy, was, of course, a solo mum, which meant she had come back into his life at a time when he'd been anticipating a need to either find a domestic partner again, or resign himself to crusty bachelorhood. Not having to make that choice had come as a great relief. Domestic chaos and toys on the floor had proven to be a small price to pay.

So, he strolled home past the golf course, smelling the summer air and wondering why this contentment that he only felt the closer he came to his cottage door was not felt when it had been his wife and baby daughter whom he'd been returning home to thirty years ago. What had caused it to skip a generation like that? Was it something he'd learned in the interim, or was it something he'd let go?

Cock Roche had joked with him one night, during his drinking days, that the most effective anti-ageing agent for a man was the love of a young woman. Liddell had tried that, but without success. Now he'd have to reply that it took a three-year-old to prove the maxim true.

'Dad,' Tracey greeted him, 'I told her that you wouldn't read her *Winnie the Pooh* unless she was already in bed when you got home.'

'And is she in bed?' he asked loudly.

A small voice answered. 'Almost.'

Well, almost was good enough. He'd willingly enter the world of *Winnie the Pooh* with her, because it was the stuffed bear, Pooh, the world's greatest romantic, who'd said, "I hope you live to a hundred, and I hope I live to one day less, because I never want to spend a day without you."

As he climbed the stairs to lead his granddaughter into that world, he tried to block out the thought that another girl, of a similar age to his daughter, had found herself in a world of evil and corruption that day, where death was a commercial commodity.

TWENTY-ONE

After returning from Cambridge on Friday night, unaware of the stories that had yet to break, Anton and Caroline had taken a walk in the woodland behind the cottage in order to have some time alone, and to voice their thoughts about how they were going to reveal themselves in public once their story was released.

Anton was adamant that they should go to his house in Kensington and openly make it their base.

'If there are going to be press conferences, let them be held there. If there are going to be photographers, let them camp outside. The more visible and accessible we are, the better.'

'What about Tuan?' she'd asked. 'He's the one most at risk, because he's the one who knows everything.'

'We can find somewhere nearby where we can keep an eye on him. It's not difficult to hide in London, if you've got people helping you.'

The rain had stopped, and the wind had dropped, but the ground underfoot was damp, and the foliage of the trees, as they brushed past, was laden with water. A milky moon was struggling to break through the clouds, too weak to light their way. They'd stopped and held each other, Caroline remembering the first time he had held her in his arms in the garden of the hotel in Sapa. She'd kissed him then, impetuously, believing they were on the verge of becoming lovers, though he'd never said anything to make her believe that; it had just been a feeling. Now they were on the verge of something else, and she was fighting hard to suppress a feeling of dread.

'I feel like I've talked you into this against your will,' she'd whispered. 'I want justice, and you want peace. Perhaps it's not possible to have one with the other.'

'Maybe we'll discover that it isn't possible to have either.'

She'd pulled away from him. A moorhen screeched. An owl hooted, startling her. She wanted to be back indoors with the locks bolted and the lights on. She turned and ran.

But Anton hadn't followed, savoring the sounds and smells of the night, knowing that he'd be catching her up only in order to offer her comforting words in which he could not vest either honesty or belief.

When he did finally get back to the cottage half an hour later, he'd found Caroline sitting in silence in front of her computer, and Tuan sitting at the kitchen table, holding his head in his hands. Neither of them had spoken as he entered. On the screen of Caroline's laptop was a photo of his friend Duc, with an ugly bullet wound in his temple and parts of his skull fractured, a sign that pathologists and other professionals would recognize as indicating that a soft-nosed bullet had been used.

* * * *

On Saturday morning, Caroline woke at the same time as the marsh warblers, just as the light changed in the eastern sky, anticipating the arrival of the sun. The sun was still half an hour away, but the warblers liked to be up early. These were things that Anton had taught her in the days they'd been there. She was surprised to find that she had slept at all, because her memory was of tossing and turning, driving her head into the pillows in search of a palliative thought—any thought—that would encourage her to rise up in the morning and re-enter the fight.

Anton, on whose shoulder her head had lain, conscious of avoiding his damaged chest, breathed softly in tune with the slow rhythm of his heart.

She unwound herself from his body, realizing that she didn't want him to be awake. They hadn't made love properly since their last night on Cat Bar Island—before the horrific events that had forced them to flee Vietnam. They'd been driven then by adrenalin, and relief at finally revealing the truth about the conspiracy they'd uncovered. Orgasm was a cry of hope and longing. Neither of those were emotions that she felt now as she swung her legs out of bed and went to the bathroom to splash water on her face, wondering at the pull of tension and grief that had sucked the vitality from her face. Then she went outside and breathed the salt marsh air.

Were they partly responsible for Duc's death? If she'd never embarked upon this story, would his knowledge of what was going on in the highlands have remained unknown?

By the time she returned indoors, the two men were up, and the smell of toast was wafting through the kitchen. She opened her laptop and checked her email. There was a message from Bryan Liddell with no subject. It contained a link to a page in *The Times*, but she didn't have a subscription to *The Times* and couldn't open it. While she was trying to find a way around that, Anton brought her a cup of coffee and a piece of toast.

She snatched at his hand and smiled. It was a loving smile. She was relieved that she felt love and wasn't faking it. They needed to be close. That was her wish for the day.

'Can I have some peanut butter?' she asked.

He found it for her.

'And jelly…?'

He shook his head in disbelief.

'Jam!' she explained.

He found that for her also.

They laughed, and he sat down and watched her as she spread this offensive (to him) mixture of ingredients onto the perfectly buttered piece of plain English toast, then continued watching her as she consumed it, mouthful by self-conscious mouthful, until it was finished.

'There,' she said. 'That's how I'd like my toast in future.'

'Yes, madam. Duly noted.'

The day had started as well as could be hoped, she thought.

* * * *

By mid-morning, the day had turned to custard, as the English say. Liddell had scanned and forwarded two stories from *The Times* and one from *The Sun*. They were copied to Sinclair Baines and Kate Manning, with no attempt at encryption.

Anton had tried to warn Caroline, but she'd been determined to see her name in lights, convinced that being right would protect them from being wronged. What Anton knew (and how did he know it?) was that Good had fewer armaments at its disposal than Evil. Was that just another definition of cynicism? Her father, a longshoreman from New Jersey who had risen to be the secretary and treasurer of the local chapter of one of America's most important trade unions, had told her before she was old enough to understand that it took only a single word to tell a well-formed lie; no elaborate sentence was needed. She'd poured so many words into her attempts to expose the truth that she'd overlooked the possibility that a single word could undo her.

In Tuan's case, that word had proved to be 'extortion.' Who would listen to him now that that word had been let loose (by Interpol, no less)? All his knowledge of the falsified drug trials and the illegal creation of hybrid strains would be dismissed as the desperate attempts of a low-level, deluded extortionist to divert attention away from his ill-planned crime. It wasn't necessary to kill him, the way they'd needed to kill Duc. They only needed to discredit him.

Caroline knew Tuan, and she knew he'd fester over it until he felt compelled to seek revenge.

So, what could she do? Should she broadcast her stories to the world's media, like Anton had suggested from the beginning, or had the rug been so successfully pulled out from beneath them by the stories that had now been published that no one would believe them? And what was her story in the absence of Duc and Tuan? It was exactly as Anton had described it the night they'd arrived on the Suffolk coast, and he'd asked if she was sure she wanted to do this.

'The spin they'll put on it will see your claims disappear into the ether, instantly dismissed and forgotten,' he'd warned. 'By the time they've finished, even you will be doubting your own story. Are you prepared for that?'

TWENTY-TWO

Monday morning. Copies of yesterday's Sunday papers lay on Kate Manning's desk. Beside them lay the three statements of Caroline's witnesses, which Bryan Liddell had brought her, and which she'd now taken from her office safe.

Portions of the statements had been highlighted with an orange felt marker, as had sections in the newspapers that she'd flagged with adhesive tags. The stories that had first appeared on Saturday had been picked up by the Sunday papers and amplified. A quick internet search revealed that the same stories had crossed the Atlantic and been picked up by *The Washington Post* and *The New York Times*.

The purpose of Kate's highlighting was to draw attention to the similarity of passages in the microbiologist's disclosures and the press releases put out by the public relations company for Anglo Swiss.

While the evidence of Tran Minh Tuan was dense in its rendition of technical detail, it was blindingly clear in its intent. This man was making the claim that his company, Nui BioLab, had deliberately violated recognized scientific codes surrounding the safety and testing of medicines by falsifying test results and creating hybrid viruses, specifically for the purpose of being in a position to control the supply of the vaccines needed to protect against them.

Kate Manning had no background in microbiology or pharmaceuticals, but she did have the type of mind that could dissect complex sequences of information, and reorder them in ascending order of relevance. That was not just a product of training in law, but a genetically inherited trait. Tuan, she concluded, was the sort of person she would like to have in the witness box. His concerns were in relation to the consequences of mammalian transmissibility resulting from reassortment with human influenza viruses, and the enormous risks involved in falsifying the results of human trials. There was nothing in his statement that indicated a disenchanted employee seeking revenge, or setting himself up for compensation for his silence. But for the fact that Nui BioLab had got in first with their extortion claim, Tuan would have been seen simply as a well-informed, conscientious whistle-blower.

The question that hung in her mind was, how had Nui BioLab got its timing so right, its language so precise?

That was the question that she put to Bryan Liddell and Sinclair Baines when they met for a telephone conference late Monday morning. Liddell came to her office, and Baines came down the line from Hanoi. The truth was that Kate was carrying a degree of guilt into this meeting, and she had to get it off her chest first.

'Let me start by admitting that I went outside the strict confidentiality sought by Caroline Brinkley and advised Karim Farzan—in general terms only—that we had a question regarding our ability to withstand a libel claim. But no one except me has seen the draft story, or had access to the contents of the witness statements you gave me. The printed copies provided to me by Bryan have been kept under lock and key in my safe. I'm satisfied that this office is not the source of the leak in regards to the microbiologist's evidence.'

Liddell scratched his head and looked grumpy. 'Well, my copies are encrypted, and my computer is password-protected. That leaves you, Sinclair.'

'Ditto.'

'The thing that puzzles me,' Liddell mused, 'is that if Karim knew we were sitting on a potentially libelous story, why didn't he mention it to me?

Why would that be, do you think, Kate? Had you promised to keep him informed about the story as it developed?'

'No.'

That wasn't a sufficient reply, she realized.

'I went to see him because I wanted to know what Wilton McGwyer's attitude was toward the contingency funding of libel litigation. It goes to the heart of the advice I can give.'

'And what is their attitude?' Liddell asked sarcastically. 'I don't suppose he promised to write you a blank cheque.'

Kate ignored the sarcasm. 'He seemed to be more concerned about any potential impact on Wilton McGwyer's intricate network of investors. I said that the price sensitivity of shareholdings was not what should influence your decision, or my advice.'

Baines laughed skeptically. He was in a hurry. 'There's a quicker way of saying that, Kate.'

'Yes, well…' She smiled.

'This is not about covering our asses,' Baines continued. 'This is about acknowledging two realities. Number one is the fact that the story is damn true. Number two is that someone has sabotaged it. One witness has been murdered, two witnesses came close to being murdered, and another witness has been silenced by false accusations. So, what are we going to do about it?'

'We're not going to take on a fight that we can't win,' Liddell warned. 'We're not justice warriors or vigilantes. What do you say, Kate?'

'In law, I'd have to say that libel is a cheque-book game, and with your balance sheet, you need to stay out of court.'

'Great!' Baines spat down the line. 'That's law. Now tell us about justice.'

* * * *

None of this sat comfortably with Kate later. They'd satisfied one another that the witness statements had only ever been exchanged via encrypted files between Caroline, Baines, and Liddell. Koi, the EANA employee who had discovered the murder of the mountain guide, had only seen the one statement that he was instructed to get signed; he was not a party to the rest of the story. But it was just too coincidental that the media swarm released by Anglo Swiss UK should have so accurately targeted the claims to be made in Tuan's affidavit.

The next move was up to Liddell, and Kate was glad of that, because it was not a decision she'd want to make. She could advise him as to the consequences, but that was all. If there was one consolation, however, it was that she suspected that the timetable had now been altered as a result of the initiatives taken by Anglo Swiss and their publicity team. The pre-emptive strike was no longer an option for EANA. That option had been stolen from them.

As events had unfolded over the seven days since they'd first received Caroline's story, Kate's personal life had been altered in a way that had taken her unawares. For anyone other than Kate, this development in her life would have been regarded as cause for joy and celebration. But for the self-contained, driven careerist that Kate had become in her thirty-six years, it was destabilizing to the point where she was losing trust in herself and her own judgment.

Following her lunch with Karim Farzan on Tuesday, she had returned to her office and fielded a phone call. It was Sophie Cunningham from Wilton's. They had played squash together that morning.

Sophie's voice was tense. 'Karim said you refused to stay and have coffee with me,' she said angrily. 'Is that true?'

Kate was taken aback. 'I didn't refuse to have coffee with you. I told him I needed to get back to the office.'

'No.' Sophie was adamant. 'He said you didn't want to have coffee with me. *Me!*'

'Sophie, that simply isn't true. I don't know why he'd say that.'

'Well, he did.'

Too late, Kate realized that Sophie was pulling her leg, and having trouble stifling her giggles.

'Alright, you got me. I'm sorry I didn't stay and have coffee with you. Okay?'

'So, how are you going to make it up to me?' Sophie teased.

In that moment, something that had its origins in preconfigured pathways, networks of nerve cells in the forebrain and spinal cord, caused her neck and cheeks to flush, and the lobes of her ears turned cold. She cleared her throat. 'Why don't I buy you a glass of wine after work?' she suggested tentatively.

'Done.'

They met at an outdoor bar at St. Katharine's Dock, because Kate had been unable to think quickly, was not a frequenter of bars, and had formed the fleeting impression that this place looked like a pleasant spot to be on a summer's evening, having passed it once or twice on her way home to her apartment nearby.

The disturbance of her sympathetic nervous system, which had earlier caused her skin to flood with blood, had now subsided, and her cognitive processes had regained dominance. She had changed out of her work garb into a tracksuit, the only casual attire that she kept at the office.

Sophie had decided to keep the earlier phone call charade going, which made it easier for Kate, who found herself surprisingly uncertain about how to handle the tone of the conversation.

'Shall we order a glass of wine?' she asked.

'You're not going to palm me off with a glass,' Sophie quipped. 'Let's order a bottle.'

It seemed that both had forgotten that Kate didn't drink. A bottle of cold sauvignon blanc disappeared quickly, while Sophie made merry with Kate's debt to her, which she promised was not going to be paid off easily, hinting that it was going to be an ongoing game for her, a suggestion that— after two glasses of wine—Kate found herself relaxing into rather willingly. Along the way, Karim got a pasting as a pompous Persian prick with no sense of humor (and a lot of other personal things that solidly destroyed any suspicions Kate might have held about Sophie having slept with him).

It was so nice sitting in the late afternoon sun, getting tipsy and enjoying her younger companion's wicked humor and good looks, watching her animated face as she exuberantly pouted and stretched her full, brightly colored lips. The sheer lusciousness of her just across the table was a sufficient intoxicant in itself, without the need for alcohol.

'There's something I need to ask you,' Sophie said at one stage, towards the end of the bottle. She leaned across the table and peered into Kate's eyes with a look so penetrating that Kate felt her neck beginning to flush again, her heart rate increasing.

Then, infuriatingly, Sophie sat back, as if she'd forgotten what she wanted to say.

'Ask away.' Kate smiled. There were elements of getting drunk that she'd forgotten she enjoyed.

'Is it true that you sued the law firm where you interned for sexual harassment, and were awarded squillions?'

'Yes,' Kate replied, her lawyer's demeanor returning with a rush.

Sophie yelped with delight and high-fived her. 'You go, girl!' she shouted aloud. 'How much?'

Kate gulped down the last of her wine. 'It was a confidential settlement. Both parties agreed to keep it that way.'

She could feel herself shutting down.

Sophie leaned forward again, running her tongue around her lips lasciviously. 'What did they do to harass you?'

She wasn't picking up on Kate's body language, or the tone in her voice.

'Some senior male partners thought female interns liked to be groped.'

'What about senior female partners?'

'The men didn't grope them, only junior interns.'

'No, what I meant was, did senior *female* partners try and grope you, too?'

Just as they had done earlier, Kate's neck and cheeks started to flush, and the lobes of her ears turned cold.

'Females don't grope, Sophie,' she replied quietly.

'Would you sue them if they did?'

There was no escaping her eyes, or the pinkness of her tongue.

'That is a very weird question,' she answered, trying to look away.

'I just want to know where I stand,' Sophie said quietly.

The assumptions Kate had made and clung to about her own sexuality were washed away later that night in a lava flow of unrestrained abandon. What she'd longed for, it seemed, was skin, and moisture, and intimate probing. What truly defined her was not control, discipline, or restraint, but the absence of control, and the greed for someone else's pleasure. Just like that.

And now, when she heard Sophie's voice down the phone, she caught herself smiling openly, and she felt the twinge of anxiety that all people who were not fully in control were forced to feel. She had entered new territory.

'Listen, I've got something dangerous I want you to do for me,' she said to Sophie, once Bryan Liddell had left her office.

'That sounds fun. What is it?'

'I want you to steal Karim's phone for half an hour.'

'Steal as in borrow, or steal as in *steal*?'

'Borrow the phone and steal its data.'

'How do I do that?'

It required Sophie to first borrow his cell phone battery charger. Then, while he was in his two-hour partners' meeting (no phones allowed), she would charge his phone for him. While pretending to do that, she would connect the Android charger to her computer using the USB cable, having first downloaded an Android file transfer program off the internet at the address Kate gave her. A notification would then come up on her screen asking if she wanted to use the USB to transfer files. She'd be given a choice of folders: Internal, SD, or Removeable, listing the information stored on the phone. By clicking on the desired file or folder and pressing Command + C, she could then copy it to her desktop.

'What files do I want?'

'Contacts, phone log, messages, and email. Put them on a stick for me, and I'll buy you dinner tonight.'

TWENTY-THREE

Though the cottage was tiny, the distance between its three occupants had become enormous.

Tuan occupied the kitchen, huddled over endless cups of black tea, chain smoking while writing in an exercise book Faraday had found for him in David Goode's desk—page after page, some in English, some in Vietnamese, very precise, very cramped. If he was angry, it didn't show. The one annoyance he expressed was over his failure to have brought his laptop and research files with him while under pressure to escape Vietnam.

Caroline, like Diana the Huntress, ran through the forests of the internet in search of prey, her quiver filled with arrows, the arrows tipped with indignation and revenge. When she spied who had betrayed them, her aim would be straight and deadly.

Faraday had retreated to the attic and commenced a portrait. It wasn't of anyone in particular. He hadn't started with an image in mind, didn't even lay down an outline in charcoal. If there was a plan, it was a simple one. Like an unschooled child, he would follow the paint and see where it went, the metamorphosis of color looking to coalesce into a recognizable image, perhaps, or to create a mood that resonated with an ill-defined emotion.

A tube of carmine red that he'd saved with the thought of a Turneresque sky in mind had found its way into a shape vaguely resembling an eye, and run down into the skin of a cheek, which was falling off the yellow ochre of exposed bone. A twisted line of black pain wound up from one corner until it turned into a mouth opened to reveal the white space of the canvas, and only when he took a two-inch brush and filled the edges with deep, dark forest green did he realize he'd outlined a head. It was Duc's head—and now, Duc was dead. Faraday stared at it for a long time, as he should, for no matter how short the time in which he'd known him while living, the time he would know him dead was going to be long.

That he should have chosen to retreat into the space in front of the easel was hardly surprising, for that space had been his sanctuary for over twenty years. What was surprising was that on this occasion, he had spontaneously eschewed the guidelines and precision necessary for copying from life. The discipline that he'd brought to painting during those twenty years was an indication of the degree of control that he'd managed to exercise over his life as a whole. By burying himself in work, he'd left no room for the wild horses of emotion, opinion, or outrage to ride roughshod over him. Everything had been quietly contained, bound and safely tied up within him.

And what of Caroline? Had he needed to fall in love with her in order to be free of the fraud he'd committed on himself—the fraudulent conviction that he couldn't love fully? If love was the complete surrender of oneself willingly to another person, not necessarily wisely, perhaps that was a further symptom of his constant, nagging need for control. Yet falling for Caroline had happened so quickly that it was foolish to trust it. The pros filled a full column of the ledger, but what would happen when they started to list the cons?

The reason he was upstairs painting while she was downstairs searching for the person who had betrayed them was that his view of mankind was that of the evolutionary biologist: that mankind's traits, whether 'good' or 'bad,' were unalterable. Her view was that the bad could be defeated, leaving only the good to survive. Such a dichotomy of belief and approaches to life would surely leak into their feelings around love.

As he looked at the image of Duc that had emerged from his

unconscious—allowed to emerge because he had been shocked into loosening the bindings of control—he sensed that implicit in his view of the inalterability of mankind must be an acceptance on his part that he should not attempt to alter another person's beliefs. After all, all beliefs had a biological basis and were an intrinsic part of each individual's persona. He had no disagreement with her about the truth of their experiences, or the conclusions that had led to the accusations they'd made. The difference was that he saw the challenge as lying in their ability to retain their convictions while preserving their safety. She saw the challenge as being their ability to bring the perpetrators to justice, and their safety would be assured by … what? The superiority of their moral position?

In which case, why were they hiding in the Suffolk marshes? Maybe it was time to get back to London and face their threats front on.

* * * *

Caroline and Baines exchanged emails throughout Monday afternoon. They had begun as one- or two-liners. The witness statements had gone from her computer to his alone, fully encrypted, on the understanding that he would forward them to London by the same method. The TOR network was the dark web, and he'd assured her it couldn't be hacked, so how the hell had he allowed their contents to go astray? If it wasn't on his end, then it had to be on Liddell's.

Perhaps it was the fact that Baines was her only hope for finding answers in Vietnam that prevented her from cutting the connection, but by mid-afternoon, their exchanges had shifted from mistrust to collaboration again.

He had already made a list of unknowns that he intended to investigate. It was the list that Bryan Liddell had asked him to draw up on Friday as an action plan (when Bryan was still needing to be pushed into deciding to go ahead—a decision that he'd left too late). Top of the list: who killed Duc? Was it the same person who had hired the crew who kidnapped Caroline and Faraday on Halong Bay? How could the US and UK be linked to the conspiracy to boost the spread of the epidemic, and could the WHO be shown to be complicit in falsifying figures and eventually declaring a pandemic?

What if none of these links can be proven? Caroline typed. *It's too late for unsubstantiated accusations.*

I can't help feeling that your man, Tuan, the microbiologist, could blow this thing out of the water, Baines asserted. *He's the one they're scared of.*

Scared enough to stick Interpol on him, she typed back. *We Americans invented rendition, remember? There's no way Tuan's safety can be guaranteed.*

I get that, but there are two distinct stories here. There's the claim that the virus has been deliberately spread, but our chief witness is dead.

You mean murdered.

Yes, murdered. Which looks bad, but doesn't prove the claim. Then there's Tuan's separate claim that the virus is a mutation bred in the lab so that a vaccine could be specifically designed for it, and that vaccine is potentially dangerous. Ask him if there are others at Nui BioLab who could be persuaded to blow the whistle with him.

She thought that was unlikely. Tuan had been moved around rapidly towards the end, as if they already knew he was a security risk to them. If there'd been others in the same position, he would have said so. But she'd ask.

Could there be any other single person we haven't thought of, Caroline wondered, *who could blow this whole thing apart if we had him by the balls?*

Sinclair didn't reply. He had the beginning of an idea, but not one which he was willing to give form yet.

*   *   *   *

Megan Hastel watched Bryan Liddell heading towards her from the bar at the Cheshire Cheese and squirmed uncomfortably in her seat. It wasn't that she regretted being here, or that she was uncomfortable about being seen drinking with a colleague—her putative boss. It was her sense of vulnerability to shame, as if in a dream, she had found herself naked when all around her were fully clothed.

The feeling had started when she looked up from her desk to find him standing over her earlier. He'd smiled, but his eyes seemed to be elsewhere. His body was in the room, but not his energy.

'Join me for a drink,' he said without warning.

She didn't ask when or why, just nodded. 'Alright.'

She closed her laptop, picked up her handbag, and followed him down in the lift and along the lane to the pub. He might have said something about why—it wasn't even lunchtime yet—but she didn't hear it if he did. She might have said something, too, but her subconscious was speaking, rather loudly, about this feeling of nakedness.

He led her to a corner table and went to the bar to order, not asking what she wanted, but returning with a tray with two wine glasses and a bottle. Then he filled the glasses and passed one to her.

'Megan,' he said, 'you told me the night we had dinner together that you had spent your married life living with an alcoholic, and what you'd learned was that you weren't an alcoholic yourself. You told me that this gave you the freedom to enjoy drinking without risk.'

'Did I say that?' she asked.

'Yes.'

'It sounds correct. Is that what you want to talk about?'

He looked around unhappily, searching for words. 'What I know about addiction,' he confessed, 'is that it is only skin deep. Scratch it, and it bleeds.'

It wasn't her that was naked, she suddenly realized; it was him.

'Something happened yesterday that made me want to scratch,' he explained, 'and I know enough to recognize that drinking is a poor disguise for self-loathing, but it's the only one I know at this moment—and you're the only person I know who properly understands that.'

She was about to take a sip, but decided to put her glass down. 'If you know that…' She frowned. '… then you must know that drinking just gives people another reason for self-loathing, without addressing the first.'

He put his glass down, too.

It took her a while to realize what was happening, and why he was doing it like this. He had a deep shame that he wanted to confess, but he lacked a confessional. He was a brusque man, a damaged man—a man like so many who believed that it was a sign of weakness to reveal self-doubt. But as he was harder on himself than others, his self-doubt was a high hurdle for him to jump. The bottle that he had placed on the table between them was a hurdle also, but a lower one to clear, and she, being a veteran observer of this process in a man, would be there to give witness to his fall. Falling was a necessary part of the process of dealing with his guilt.

When he'd finished telling her the bare outline of the story that he had been sitting on, and how his indecision had left brave people in jeopardy and evil people in command, a spark had returned to his eyes, and the glass on the table was still untouched.

'What disgusts me most,' he stressed, 'is that I had allowed myself to be swayed by what I felt was an implied threat from Karim Farzan that Wilton McGwyer wouldn't help if it went wrong. Fuck it, Megan, I'm a forty-year veteran of front-line journalism, not a toady for an effete investment banker. If you knew the details of the story I was sitting on, you'd be horrified and disgusted, too.'

She sat very still and waited. It was something she'd learned to do. Her hands were folded in her lap, and her eyes were somewhere in the impersonal space between them.

'Do you have children, Megan?'

'Yes, I have two daughters.'

'What do they do?'

'One's a teacher, and one's a nurse.'

'Nice. A nurturer and a healer.'

She stirred and sat up straight. 'Bryan, I know about the story,' she said. 'It was passed to Karim when it first came in.'

'By you…?'

'I thought you knew that was part of the reason I was appointed to financial reporting and IT when Wilton's bought the agency. Wilton McGwyer gets a daily extract of emails from the EANA server. Karim employs someone there to highlight news items that they think could be relevant before they become public.'

'You mean, you personally read every email coming in or out of our server?'

'No, there's a software program installed that does it, an algorithm.'

It wasn't clear whether his expression was one of anger or disgust. She tried to keep her own completely neutral. This wasn't about personal privacy; it was about risk mitigation.

He stared at the full glass in front of him, chewing this information over. 'And did you design the algorithm?' he asked.

She shook her head. 'No.' Then she added, 'But I know how it works.'

'Tell me.'

'It scans for commercial sensitivity: company names, products, financial and economic news, geopolitical events. But parsing data is not an exact science. It produces a lot of ephemera, and what I'd call amphigories— nonsense—which is why Wilton's has someone edit it each day.'

'But you… You said you knew about the flu virus story, so presumably, you see the selected transcripts, too.'

She ached to pick up her glass and take a sip, but she feared it would trigger Bryan to do the same. The feeling of nakedness had started to return.

'Karim gave me a copy,' she stated bluntly. 'He brought it to me.'

'The other day, when he came to the office?'

'Yes.'

Bryan sat back and folded his arms. He nodded. A question in his mind had been answered.

'I won't speculate as to why Wilton's put such a system in place,' he mused, 'or why they were motivated to buy a marginally profitable news agency in the first place; that can wait for another day. But what I *am* convinced of is that saving EANA from falling into a dangerous and expensive libel suit is not what they had in mind when getting advance notice of sensitive commercial stories before they break. What would you say to that, Megan?'

Like a cloak falling off his shoulders and slipping to the ground, the self-loathing with which he'd entered the bar was cast aside as he assumed a new mantle: that of indignation. He was, she knew, a cynical, hard-boiled journo. Nothing should surprise him. He could guess at the worst, and probably would.

'I try not to speculate, Bryan,' she answered timidly.

How could she cover her nakedness? If she picked up the glass of wine, it would quiver in her hand, and he would see that she was exposed.

'Well,' he announced with some satisfaction, 'now that you've explained the vulnerability of our server, I'll have to think seriously about an encryption policy for sensitive items. How would your bloody algorithm like that?'

There was only one way now that she could put her clothes back on and they could leave the bottle of wine on the table untouched, and that was to tell him the truth. Which she did.

TWENTY-FOUR

Faraday lifted the kitchen floorboard and returned the shotgun and cartridges to the cavity beneath, where they had lain undisturbed for the five years prior to their arrival. He put the kitchen scraps in a plastic shopping bag, and the unused dry goods in the pantry, then walked through the house one last time, checking the windows before turning off the electricity and locking the front door. The unconscious oil sketch that had assumed the identity of Duc still sat on the easel, where he'd left it the previous night before coming downstairs and announcing that they were leaving in the morning.

Once the decision had been made, the tension between them dissolved. Instead of waiting to be flushed out into the open, never knowing where and how they'd be ambushed, they'd face their adversaries head-on. If, as Sinclair Baines had now admitted, the entirety of their accusations against Anglo Swiss BioLab, Paladin, and the US and UK governments was known to those parties, and had been successfully debunked or defused by them before they could be published, then there was nothing to be gained by remaining in hiding.

It was a two-hour drive from the coast to the outskirts of London. At Leytonstone on the A12, where they stopped to use the lavatories at the Tesco superstore and order takeaway cappuccinos, they decided to reactivate their cell phones to check for messages and buy the day's newspapers. The very ordinary nature of these actions helped to restore a sense of normalcy, cracking the protective shell they'd formed around themselves, and for the first time since leaving Uncle's house in Vietnam, they sensed the possibility that they could return to the mainstream of life.

Faraday had four missed calls on his phone, and three messages in his voicemail. Three of the calls and two of the voice messages were from Robbie at Lutyen's Gallery, urgently asking him to call back. He decided not to return them until they were settled back home in Kensington. The third message was from David Goode, his friend from New York, whose hideaway cottage they had just left. The sound of his voice, announcing that he was in London for the week, lifted his spirits, but he decided that now was not the time to talk to him either.

If Faraday and Caroline felt that a weight had been lifted from them, the same couldn't be said for Tuan. Assuming that Nui BioLab's press statement was telling the truth, an Interpol warrant was out for his arrest, and any branch of the British police, immigration, or security services would be aware of it. The first place they would look for him would be in Caroline and Faraday's company, so taking him back to the house in Kensington was not an option. They'd rejected the idea of leaving him at the cottage on the marshes, as it would make him feel vulnerable, not having a vehicle or any means of escape. Their conclusion was that a boarding house in West Brompton was the safest solution, and he could stay in touch with them using the pre-paid burner phones. Tuan was the one remaining real threat to Anglo Swiss, and Faraday was certain that whatever he had been writing in his notebook over the previous few days, it would not prove to be a letter of contrition seeking forgiveness.

They dropped him off in Avonmore Road and waited while he verified the vacancy sign outside a suitably anonymous rooming house. Having already made the mistake of using his credit card once, Tuan was persuaded to accept cash from Faraday and offer that as pre-payment of a week's rent. It was a part of town where Tuan's Asian face would look less conspicuous than Caroline's or Faraday's, but they were nervous, with good cause, having no idea how all this would end.

Returning to the car, Tuan confirmed that the landlady was happy, and he asked Faraday for his home address.

'A courier will come with a packet addressed to you,' he said, writing it down. 'You will need to sign. Please tell me as soon as it arrives.'

* * * *

It had been almost exactly three months since Anton had opened the door to find Jonathon Appleby from Christie's standing on the steps, clutching the counterfeit painting under his arm that had started him off on his journey to Vietnam—three months in which he'd had occasion to wonder whether he would ever find his way home again, and if he did, whether he would return to the same life he'd been living for the past twenty years, or whether his life had now changed forever.

The hydrangeas in the front garden had been deadheaded. Bridie, his half-day weekly housekeeper, had apparently run out of things to do inside and had turned her attention outdoors. The brass doorknob and knocker had been polished to perfection, the front steps scrubbed like new. If the house was being watched, there was no obvious sign of it, and he was able to park in a resident's permit spot right outside his front door, realizing as he did so that he didn't actually have a resident's permit, never having felt the need to own a car.

Only when they had unloaded and crossed the road to his front gate did he remember that he didn't have a house key. Everything in his travel luggage, barring his cell phone, money belt, and passport, was sitting on the bottom of Halong Bay. Cursing his stupidity, he returned to the car while he called Bridie, who, at best, would take three hours to get there. They had no choice but to wait.

Sensing that Caroline was already anxious about them sitting outside his house, and wanting to relieve the tension, Faraday began to laugh.

'What's so funny, brainbox?' she demanded irritably.

'I've just realized,' he pointed out, 'that the clothes we're wearing were bought in a street market in Haiphong, and we both look like performers from a holiday camp pantomime.'

'Is that really your greatest worry at the moment—that we're not well dressed enough?'

'No, but we have three hours to kill, and when Bridie gets here and opens up, I'll have wardrobes full of clothes I can wear, and you'll have nothing. So, come with me.'

Overriding her objections, he pulled her out of the car and steered her down to Kensington High Street.

'I don't have any money,' she objected.

'You have better than that: you have a boyfriend's cash card.'

'That way leads to indenture.'

'Consider it a gift—without ties.'

'There's no such thing. I'd rather steal.'

'Steal from me, then.'

'What's the punishment?'

He stopped. 'Home detention.'

She shook her head.

'Three weeks?' he added hopefully.

She kissed him forcefully, but she was frowning. 'We can't make promises we can't keep,' she insisted.

After walking High Street on both sides to Phillimore Gardens and back, he followed her into Kathmandu and found a seat, while she went off to rifle through the clothing racks and the travel packs, giving him a chance to return Robbie's calls, which, judging by their frequency and tone, involved matters of some urgency.

Their conversation was almost entirely one-sided and lasted barely a minute, before Faraday cut it off and turned off his cell phone. He was using one of the cheap burners he'd bought, but the nature of Robbie's outburst, and the thought that he was using the Lutyen Gallery landline, which might be monitored, suddenly alarmed him.

'I'll contact you later,' he promised before hanging up.

When Caroline appeared in front of him, looking as though she were ready to go hiking through Yellowstone National Park, he was lost in troubled thought.

*　*　*　*

The thought that troubled Bryan Liddell at that moment was that his natural habitat had been destroyed, leaving him no place to live. His entire adult life had been spent at a keyboard of one kind or another, transcribing his thoughts or editing those of others in order to produce a product generically known as the news. News did not leap from the keyboard to the computer screen fully formed. It followed a gestation path that had many twists and turns, some caused by the alteration of facts, and some by the interference of judgment. News was a human product, delivered by a human mind—his mind—and now that he knew a peeping Tom had been planted in his mind, he could not trust it to willingly do his work.

Megan, her cheeks flushed and her hand trembling, had looked into his eyes with the shame and intensity of a reluctant executioner.

'Your VDU is connected to mine,' she'd whispered.

'My VDU?" He was confused.

'What appears on your screen can be captured by a screensaver on mine once you decrypt it.'

Her eyes hadn't wavered. Her pupils were dark, her irises pale, her eyeballs white. He had the impression that she was focused on a point behind his own eyes, somewhere deep within his hippocampus, where the thought might be forming that would cause him to erupt in fury.

He didn't. 'How?'

'I fitted a DGI to a VGA adaptor, which runs to a second monitor in my office. Encrypted material passing through our server triggers an alert.'

'Why?'

'Because Wilton McGwyer wants encrypted material collected in addition to normal traffic.'

The realization that he should have felt an overwhelming sadness, rather than anger, intrigued him. It was a feeling he'd wanted to hold onto, sure that it contained a clue to his psychopathology. Megan's face swam in and out like a fish in an aquarium, silent and staring, waiting to be startled.

It never occurred to him to pick up his wine glass and down its contents.

As she'd sat so immutable, locked onto his face, he wondered why she made no move to apologize or excuse herself. There was a strange willfulness in her manner, as if she were savoring the danger, expecting him to lash out, sure of deserving it, like someone who saw punishment as the inevitable and necessary end for fear.

'So, Karim Farzan had copies of the three witness statements,' he'd confirmed, more to himself. 'And he's had them since before the stories run by Anglo Swiss that pre-empted them.'

She didn't answer, and he had stood up slowly and walked back to his office alone.

Sure enough, there was a cable running from the back of his screen into the skirting board cable tray that ran out of his office and into Megan Hastel's. He pulled the adaptor out of its port, threw it on the floor, and ground it with his heel until it snapped.

Yet like a wife caught *in flagrante delicto*, an employee caught stealing, or a hero caught cheating, his keyboard and computer could no longer be trusted. Nothing he had written there was free of taint. Anything he would write there in the future would have the stench of censorship attached to it. It would no longer be news; it would be eavesdroppings.

Half an hour after he'd returned to his office, Megan poked her head around the door.

'Would you like me to resign?' she asked.

He didn't answer, but instead, started typing.

FROM: Bryan Liddell
TO: Caroline Brinkley, Sinclair Baines, Kate
Manning
COPY TO:Karim Farzan, Megan Hastel
SUBJECT:ACCUSATIONS REGARDING ANGLO SWISS BIOLAB
AND OTHERS

<u>CONFIDENTIAL - BE ADVISED AS FOLLOWS:</u>

Regarding Anglo Swiss BioLab and others concerning
the bird flu epidemic in Vietnam, be advised that
EANA declines to publish the story filed by
Caroline Brinkley or the witness statements
provided in support of it. This decision has been
taken following publication of stories released on
behalf of Anglo Swiss BioLab UK Limited that
directly contradict information contained within
Ms Brinkley's story.

EANA has received legal advice that this would
likely trigger action for damages to be taken
against EANA,and EANA's shareholders have advised
that they will not provide the financial backing
to defend such action.

Without judging the merits or otherwise of the
material submitted by Ms Brinkley, I must instruct
all those who are privy to its contents to maintain
the strict confidentiality under which it was
circulated.

Further, I wish it to be known that EANA will
not hesitate to revisit this decision should any
threats or physical harm be levied against any of

After clicking send, he phoned his old friend, Cock Roche. News didn't need a sober drunk to mind it. News was a drunken agglomeration of fantasy and lies, a fairground mirror ball that reflected humanity's grotesque and leering face back at it for its own amusement. Round and round it went on a carousel held together by the gravity of spin, never daring to stop.

TWENTY-FIVE

The story that had been anticipated by *The Sun* in its piece the previous weekend, relating to the upcoming release of a broad-spectrum vaccine developed by Nui BioLab, had a twist to it. The twist lay in Anglo Swiss BioLab's announcement the following Wednesday that it would share its patent, once granted, with two other top ten pharmaceutical giants, in order to help scale up production and distribution. The names of the two other companies were not released, fueling speculation, not least of which was reflected in the financial markets, where stock prices of certain big pharma companies were taking off. The biggest gains were in Anglo Swiss BioLab, up forty-five percent that week and still climbing.

This was not the sort of announcement that would normally be expected to interrupt sexual foreplay, but Kate Manning was relatively new to foreplay, while still being finely attuned to the nuances of subtexts that might impact one of her clients. Hearing the announcement being read on the television news in another room, she lifted her head from Sophie Cunningham's breast and neatly rolled off their bed to go capture the tail end of the news item before it finished.

Too late to catch whatever graphics they'd chosen to show, she returned to bed, placing her hand between Sophie's legs while slipping her tongue into her mouth, amazed at the ease with which she separated her pleasure sensorium from her thoughts. It had been her doubts about her ability in this regard that kept her from giving in to her impulses in the past, "reason trumping emotion" lying at the heart of the lawyer's paradigm.

Sophie had an ease with the quick achievement and release of orgasmic spasms that allowed Kate to disengage ten minutes later with a clear conscience, put on a gown, and go to the kitchen and make tea while she waited for her laptop to warm up. The memory stick that Sophie had used to extract files from Karim's cell phone had been uploaded earlier that afternoon while Karim was in a partners' meeting. The log recorded all incoming and outgoing calls for the previous six months, but it was only the last ten days that interested Kate. Wherever a number, whether incoming or outgoing, was already in Karim's contacts, it was identified by the name or initials he'd entered. Only if the number was not reflected in the contacts list was it shown numerically.

Since the day when Kate had received the first of Caroline Brinkley's emails outlining the story behind the avian flu pandemic, Karim had made or received over two hundred phone calls. Identifying the contacts from the nicknames or initials by which Karim stored them was going to require Sophie's help. Her willingness to betray her boss did not derive solely from her desire to help her new-found lover; it had its origins in a long-standing desire for revenge against a male whose deep-seated misogyny had allowed him to presume that a young female employee was a fruit that he was entitled to pluck. A nasty and frightening encounter with Karim in his office while working late one night had primed her for this moment.

Despite the overwhelming euphoria that had gripped both of these women during the last few days, when they had coincidentally thrown themselves into a love affair, its physical expression had only been a part of it. It was the thrill of outwitting a man like Karim that excited Sophie now, and it was the indignation she felt about the treatment of Caroline Brinkley that inspired Kate. The intimacy of a shared conspiracy helped to make it even more thrilling.

If it took them all night, Kate determined, they would decipher Karim

Farzan's role in the sabotage of a story that needed to be told, and then they could decide what to do with the power that knowledge would give them. She was sure that Karim would not have been motivated by a need to protect himself from losing money if EANA were sued. No, he would have been motivated by the money he could make on those escalating stock prices.

* * * *

For Sinclair Baines, the email issued by Bryan Liddell had not come as a surprise. He didn't blame Bryan, and he couldn't fault Kate Manning's advice. Perhaps if they had been less circumspect, more willing to accept the evidence once they had seen the signed witness statements, they could have been justified in publishing on the grounds of 'public good,' but he accepted that their hesitation had allowed them to be gazumped. To go ahead and publish in the face of the stories that Anglo Swiss had pushed out would be economic suicide.

Yet now more than ever, Baines was convinced of the truth underpinning Caroline's story. The precision with which the main claims made by her witnesses had been targeted, and subsequently defused by the releases put out by the pharmaceutical giant, was beyond coincidence. There had been a leak, and he was sure Liddell knew its source. But while this was a setback, it was far from being the end of the matter. The truth could be unraveled by finding other strands to pull.

His Hanoi office still had a requirement to feed updates on the epidemic to the world's media, but he sensed already that the mainstream media was putting its own people on it. EANA needed stories they couldn't find for themselves. Besides, the inevitable effect of twenty-four-hour news coverage, resulting from the explosion of internet-fueled distribution channels, was that stories quickly expired due to exhaustion. North Korea, ISIS, Trump— no matter how keen the interest and speculation surrounding these stories at their height, public attention needed to take a break. The same was true of bird flu, unless it suddenly spread worldwide—or if they could find an angle that no one could ignore.

But if Liddell's cancellation memo had come as no surprise to Baines, the phone call he'd received from Anton Faraday had. It came at 8:00am while he was finishing his breakfast in the food court, and it was so unexpected that it had taken Baines a moment to realize the identity of the caller.

'You mean, Anton Faraday, the painter?'

'I'm calling from London to let you know that we have decided to ignore the threats and reveal our whereabouts.'

'You and Caroline?'

'Both.'

Then there was a brief silence, which Baines wasn't sure how to fill.

'Your panda painting is sitting on a chair in my office,' he remembered. 'What would you like done with it?'

Faraday seemed genuinely surprised. 'How come?'

'Didn't Caroline tell you? You left it at the hotel when you went off on that thing on Halong Bay. They gave it to me because … I don't know, I kind of gave them the impression that I was official. What do you want done with it?'

'If you like it, hang it on your wall.'

'Are you kidding? I've seen what your paintings fetch. I don't have that sort of insurance.'

'It's worthless. It's a copy.'

Ah, Baines thought, so this was the counterfeit painting he'd mentioned in his affidavit. He'd forgotten that detail. It might pay for him to go back and read everything again.

'Well, they did a good job,' he observed. 'I'll do like you say and put it up on the wall. It'll remind me of where this whole thing started.'

Why was Faraday ringing? Why wasn't it Caroline?

'So, what made you guys come out of hiding?'

'We're no longer a threat.'

'But your story…'

'It isn't going to be believed now—unless something happens to one of us, causing someone like you to pull it out of your drawer and say, "Look at this, this is why they got killed." That's why I'm phoning. The story has no further purpose other than to protect us.'

'You want me to keep it in my drawer?'

'*You* tell *me*.'

'I hope you're right, because these people don't seem to give a fuck about anything.'

'I'm glad you've noticed.'

Baines left the remains of his congee and walked outside. He didn't bother to put his face mask back on, and he noticed that he wasn't alone in this. Crisis fatigue was starting to creep in. People were getting on with life.

'Listen,' he said, 'stories like this are more common than you think. You only notice them when they become personal. I think you're smart to walk away from it, and there's a good chance that they'll let you, if they're certain you've got nothing else to reveal. That's what I'm assuming here—you've got nothing more that can harm them, right?'

'You got it. There's nothing more to tell.'

That was his message.

'Then I wish you well—and Caroline, too. Tell her I'd like to talk to her in a day or so, because she's a good journalist, and I want to get a payment to her for the work she's done, and try and find a way for her to keep filing copy in the future. I mean that.'

'I'll tell her. I'm sure she'll be happy to hear that.'

Then Faraday gave him his number, emphasizing that he was back on air again, using his own cell phone, before abruptly taking his leave before any further discussion could develop.

Baines walked out onto the Royal City forecourt and flagged down a xe om taxi to take him to the office. Assuming that *was* Anton Faraday on the other end, and regardless of whether the call had been listened to or not, he was pleased with the way he'd handled it. There'd been no mention of the microbiologist, Tuan; no mention of the mountain guide's murder; no mention of the roles of the US and Britain. Faraday hadn't been calling to wrap up loose ends and bring an end to the matter; he'd been calling to give the appearance that he was shutting it down. That was smart. Maybe he knew, or hoped, that his phone was being monitored.

But it sure as hell wasn't over.

* * * *

Faraday called Robbie's cell phone later that evening. He'd been unable to find a public telephone that wasn't broken, and he had finally decided to use his burner, feeling certain that his own phone was hacked, and hoping to hell that Robbie's wasn't. He also hoped that the period in between had allowed Robbie to reflect on the facts and get his reportage right.

'Start again, Robbie,' Faraday demanded. 'What precisely did they say?'

'They said they're from the Criminal Taxes Unit.'

'They had identity?'

'Inland Revenue Criminal Taxes Unit. They marched into my office unannounced and read this letter of authority to me—like reading me my rights or something—about them having powers of arrest and entry without warrants, and how they could search and detain me on any reasonable grounds: emails, phone records, accounts...'

'Why? Did they say why?'

'They said fraud and money laundering. I had no idea what they were talking about. And then they said, very specifically, that they wanted *everything* relating to transactions involving the sale of your paintings, going back to when we first started representing you.'

'When was this?'

'Three days ago.'

'Just me?'

'Just you. Well, of course, I said that was impossible, because I'd have to go back twenty years, and nobody keeps records for that long. But then I thought about that package that Ralph had in the safe at his parents' apartment, which he wanted you to have, and… I don't know, Anton, but I was alarmed. First Ralph's horrible death, and now this. I thought you'd come to the funeral, but I haven't heard from you for weeks, so I was afraid something had happened. God knows, I'm not really coping, Anton. I wanted to warn you, and I kept trying, but you weren't answering, And I realize you're right: if they're really serious, then they've probably tapped the gallery phone, but…'

'But…?'

'What do I do?'

Faraday did a quick check of his body's responses and found that his heart rate was slow, his breathing was even, and his senses were unusually alert. He wondered if it was possible that he had unconsciously learned to adjust to stress over the last few weeks, to the point where his nervous system was making judgments as to relativity. His response was revealing.

'Nobody dies here, Robbie,' he replied. 'Tax audits are a pain in the butt, designed to be unpleasant, I guess. But if you've got nothing to hide, you'll be fine.'

Faraday couldn't say so to Robbie, but what he was hearing was actually reassuring.

'You're right, of course,' Robbie acknowledged, 'but things like this remind me of Ralph—everything reminds me of Ralph. And I can't help wondering… You know what he was like, and…'

'The papers he left for me are probably the names of people who received copies of my Harbinger Collection works, Robbie. He wanted me to know who bought my lithographs. That's all, nothing more. It was all very innocent.'

The relief in Robbie's voice was palpable. 'I can just tell the truth, then?'

'Don't mention the envelope addressed to me, because it's personal, and it's none of their business. I'll come and get it from you tomorrow. Meet me in Berkeley Square at eleven o'clock. By the fountain. After that, just tell the truth. Open your records to them, and everything will be fine.'

As he ended the call, Faraday turned to Caroline and reassured her as well.

'If they were planning on killing us, they wouldn't bother with organizing a tax audit of Lutyen's. It's just a warning that they can make things awkward. But we can sleep easier tonight.'

They spent the evening continuing to settle in to his house, identifying their spaces, filling neglected rooms with the spirit of their presence, checking cupboards, playing music, news-hopping on the television. With each day that passed, it had become clearer to both of them that they were two self-contained individuals. They were comfortable in each other's company, but not dependent on it. They enjoyed loving each other, but their separate identities were unwilling to be subsumed by coupledom.

Climbing into bed alongside his sleeping companion, he thought about Sinclair Baines's matter-of-fact advice that 'stories like this are more common than you think.' If that was true (and he had immediately recognized it as being so), then what was the proper response?

In the morning, they attempted to make love. It was a nice idea, if thwarted by the wound in his groin and the pain in his rib cage. But the uniquely restorative combination of warm skin, soft touch, and entwined limbs brought them closer together.

Over breakfast, undertaken in silence, it became apparent that they were locked in their own thoughts, and not yet ready to fully air them. This was Faraday's house, and that's how it felt to Caroline. And while the dangers of the last few weeks had been shared equally, the story was hers to tell, not his—and that's how it felt to Faraday.

While dwelling on this conundrum, they were startled by a loud banging of the front door knocker, the first interruption since they'd arrived, and the first test of their nerves. After surveying the front steps through the spy-hole, Faraday opened the door for the driver of a DHL courier van that was parked on the footpath outside the house.

'Package for Mr Anthony,' the driver announced. 'It needs a signature.'

Faraday's first instinct was to tell him he had the wrong house, but checking the address, he realized it was correct, and his name had been inverted. The sender was from Hanoi, with a Vietnamese title, and a return address that looked like a post box number. He signed for it, checked the street for signs of anything unusual, then closed and bolted the front door again. The bolts were not a symptom of his nervousness, because he always bolted the front door, but he had to admit to feeling unsettled. Coming back to his own house had given both of them a sense of security, but he'd been certain that at some point, contact would be made by someone who had a message for them. Whatever form that contact took, it was unrealistic to expect the message to be welcome. Their best hope was that it would be survivable.

He felt the DHL packet cautiously, getting an impression of the shape of its contents. It was hard and metallic. He thought he could detect a cord or cable attached to it. The padded envelope was sealed with an additional strip of broad adhesive tape, which he sliced through carefully with a pair of kitchen scissors before attempting to peel back the self-adhesive flap. It wouldn't budge, forcing him to take up the scissors again and cut into the envelope itself, keeping the opening pointed away from him and holding his breath against the possibility of inhaling anything toxic.

Caroline watched anxiously as he worked slowly to expose the contents, cutting down two sides until he was able to open it fully. Only when he'd identified the metallic object as an external computer hard drive in a red drawstring bag with Tuan's name on it did he remember Tuan's warning that something would be delivered. It also sharply reminded him that Tuan was the one remaining person who could be considered a serious threat to their adversaries, yet they had not formulated anything resembling a strategy for ensuring his safety.

Caroline looked to him for an explanation.

'It's for Tuan,' he assured her, removing the hard drive from its bag.

'He should have told us,' she complained.

'He did. He said a packet was going to arrive.'

'But he didn't say it was a hard drive. What's on it? What if it had been intercepted?'

She was right. They'd entered a different world now; nothing was as simple as he was trying to pretend.

'We could ask Tuan… Or we could look at what's on it, and *then* ask Tuan,' he suggested, handing it to her so she could make her own decision.

An hour later, he called her brother on one of the pre-paid phones and made arrangements for one of them to drop the package off, admitting that they had opened it in order to verify it was intended for him. He didn't admit that they'd looked at the files on the hard drive, or that their contents were such that he needed to know who Tuan had trusted to send it to him, thus widening the circle in the process.

'Who did you call to arrange this?' he asked. 'Getting it sent to my home doesn't make it safe. What if it had been intercepted?'

'I'm not foolish, Anton. I trust my friend. No one will know that he sent it, because he's intelligent, and he'll have made another copy, just in case. Besides, you don't care that people know where you are. Where else would I have it sent?'

This was the tone of the arrogant bloody prick he'd first met in Hanoi, letting him know that everyone else was a fool. It seemed that he'd got his confidence back. Whether that was a result of having the contents of the hard drive would no doubt become apparent, but he hoped for all their sakes that it didn't mean he would now abandon all caution.

'Okay, Tuan, but remember, there's an arrest warrant out for you, and the best way of finding you is going to be through me. So, the next time you have a bright idea that involves me or Caroline, fucking well discuss it with us first.'

He cut the call short to emphasize his displeasure, but not before telling him that either he or Caroline would let him know when they'd get the hard drive to him.

'And I need a laptop,' Tuan stated. No 'please,' and no 'thank you.'

Caroline, meanwhile, had printed out the list of folders in the hard drive's documents file. It ran to ten pages. The number of individual files contained within all those folders must have run to tens of thousands, which explained why the hard drive's storage capacity of two terabytes was almost full. This was a significant chunk of Nui BioLab's research data, and Faraday had no doubt that the person or people possessing that data would be in great danger.

TWENTY-SIX

Virginia Allsop's history with Kate Manning's father, Gerald, now Judge Manning, went back forty years, which meant that she had known Kate since the day she was born, watching a bright but overly serious young girl (an only child) grow into an overachieving female clone of her father, with a reputation for fighting her clients' corners. She was not only delighted by Kate's surprise visit, but intrigued by it, for Kate had made it clear that she wanted Virginia's advice.

For Kate's part, the decision to call Virginia on short notice was motivated by the acceleration of events relating to Anglo Swiss, and the recognition that the woman who had bestrode the financial reporting press in the United Kingdom for decades, first at *The Economist* and now at *The Financial Times*, was better equipped than any other to guide her towards the correct meaning and value of the information she'd discovered.

'I had lunch with your father only last month,' Virginia revealed. 'Did he tell you?'

'No.'

'He was in great form. We've been friends for so many years, you know. All he could talk about was you, and what a great reputation you're carving out in libel. The point he was making, I think, is that you should be the FT's first port of call in the event of our needing defense. He's so proud of you. Oh, and I will definitely take his advice on board … just so you know.'

Kate laughed modestly. She liked this woman—a woman who had made it in a man's world, as if it were such a natural thing to do.

'He's got his uses, the old man,' she replied, 'but I need to warn him about nepotism. If he keeps it up, I may have to change my name.'

'Oh, don't do that. You'll never stand in his shadow. Now, tell me what you've been up to.'

Kate thought about the calls that Karim had made once he'd learned about the story EANA was sitting on, and more importantly, the calls he had made in the two days prior to the weekend announcements from Anglo Swiss, and she decided she shouldn't be impetuous. Caution would serve her better.

'I wanted to get your advice on the subject of insider trading,' she said. 'It's something that I've been alerted to, but I have to confess, I know little about it. Of course, I know its definition and the rules around it, but as soon as I start to research precedent and case law, I get the feeling that there's something I'm missing.'

'Well, now you've really got me intrigued.'

Virginia sat up and tried to summon a waiter. They were in a coffee shop in Kingsway, surrounded by the London School of Economics, where "the doyenne of financial reporting" occasionally lectured. The shop was filled with students, and noisy enough to make talking quietly somewhat of a challenge.

'Okay, here's the seeming paradox,' Kate explained. 'The line between informed investment decisions and insider trading is so narrow that I get the impression it is proving impossible to police. Is that why so few insider trading charges are laid, or are there other reasons? Like, where is the Financial Conduct Authority in this, and where is the financial press?'

'Goodness!' the other woman exclaimed. 'If I gave you my honest opinion, I'd be a traitor to the city of London, and all my preciously cultivated confidants, from decades of promoting the noble cause of capitalism, would ostracize me on the spot. You can't go making observations like that in public, Kate. Everything we do in the city—every analyst, researcher, and dare I say it, financial journalist's aim is to get as close as humanly possible to the facts that only the insiders know. People make fortunes from those facts. The game relies on them. Do you think a company would make a billion-pound takeover offer for another company if it didn't have full and reliable inside information about that company? They'd be pilloried. There's the source of your problem.'

Kate shifted forward in her chair. She knew this, but there was a different question she wanted to ask.

'If you had overwhelming evidence of deliberate insider trading on a large scale, would you as a journalist make it public, or would you take it to the Financial Conduct Authority?'

'Hmm…' Virginia suspected that her answer was going to disappoint. 'I would advise anyone with such information to take it to the FCA. They're the people with the resources to investigate and prosecute.'

'Yes, but they don't, do they? Hardly anyone gets prosecuted.'

'Well, it's an area where proof is not always easy to establish.'

Virginia ordered a second coffee. Kate declined, diving into her briefcase to extract a note she'd printed out for reference.

'I want to read you something,' she said. 'This is a comment from a merchant banker about a story you ran covering a prosecution brought by the FCA. Quote: "The time and money spent by the FCA in chasing these small-time players committing small-scale offences is ludicrous. Has the FCA got its priorities completely wrong, or is it deliberate? I know of senior city bankers who have reported major offences, providing extensive documentary evidence, against the highest levels of banking and private equity firms, where jaw-dropping levels of fraud and corruption have taken place involving billions. The FCA responded with not so much as a single phone call of investigation, and in one case didn't even acknowledge the whistle-blower's report. And the press? They look the other way, too. From the FT's reporting of this multimillion-pound prosecution for no result, you'd think they were covering a suburban shoplifting case." Unquote.'

Virginia pursed her lips and shrugged in reluctant acknowledgement. 'Yes, well… What can I say?'

'You could say he's wrong. You could say that if someone came to you with information like that, you'd take it to the FCA and sit on them day and night until they took action.'

'And if they didn't take action?'

'Then you'd force them to by running your own story.'

'Oh, Kate, I wouldn't want to have you as my opposing counsel. I doubt you take prisoners.'

* * * *

The story coming down the wires on Wednesday got maximum attention from the major media—a fact that pissed Bryan Liddell off more than he liked to admit. It wasn't that the attention was unwarranted. If you'd spent three months cranking up fear of an emerging pandemic spilling out of Asia, as the press had, you couldn't very well play down an announcement like the one coming out of the WHO or Anglo Swiss BioLab.

On the left was the frightening thought of the pathogen let loose in Vietnam spreading around the globe. Was this the horror pandemic that would turn into the greatest threat facing mankind? (What a fucking beat-up!) On the right was the World Health Organization, looking as ever for science to deliver salvation. Enter Anglo Swiss BioLab. In truth, it was an announcement of an announcement. A vaccine was on its way. *Watch this space.* The end of the end of the world was nigh.

The core of the announcement was a pledge to share manufacturing and distribution with two other giant pharmaceutical corporations, in order to 'reduce cost and speed delivery to vulnerable countries.' No one, it seemed, had the wit to ask questions about the vaccine itself, and how it could be developed in such a short time. This was a story about good guys, and the world desperately needed good guys. At this stage, the two partners with whom they would share licenses and royalties weren't even named. Those in the business speculated that it might hinge on shared experience in the vital area of vaccine expertise, such as familiarity with the chosen adjuvant. Was it Merck? Glaxo? Share traders were already taking bets, and the stock in those two entities had risen in anticipation by 27.5 and 29 percent, respectively. Anglo Swiss was up 45 percent on the week following its earlier announcement, and nearly 65 percent on the year.

What Liddell realized was that this had now moved on from the need to counter the allegations levelled by Caroline Brinkley; it had developed into a well-planned campaign, to spread a contagion of fear, and to offer a cure to banish it. The documentary footage shot in Vietnam was chillingly effective, and the maths was convincing. To hell with the ethics.

In life, triumph and defeat were binary. Those who never risked trying never experienced either. Falling off the wagon with the assistance of Steve 'Cock' Roche, as he'd done the previous night, had been a defeat. Now Liddell would have to start again. Every dry day would be a little triumph. But the defeat he felt over the Vietnam story also ran deep, and he couldn't start each day again by choosing to ignore it, because that made every new day another small defeat. As Steve had been quick to point out, EANA had sabotaged its own story through indecision. It was a story that relied on the safety and credibility of its sources, and they had been comprehensively undermined.

'Shrug and live for another day, mate,' was the best advice he had to offer.

'People fucking well died, Steve—hole-in-the-head type stuff, not accidental. Just so corporations can fleece governments of billions, with the assistance of those same fucking governments.'

'Yeah, so? People died in Iraq, too—half a million of them—so that corporations could make billions with the assistance of governments. Has it affected demand for Blair at speaking engagements? Have Bush or Cheney been charged with war crimes? Shit, Bryan, what's got into you? Stop taking it personally.'

One good thing had come out of it. After four drinks, standing at the top of the cliff, he'd stopped drinking. The decision that he'd had enough had been his to make. He could allow alcohol to win and push him off the cliff, or he could stare it down. For the moment, alcohol had lost.

When Kate Manning called and asked if they could meet after work, he took it as a sign that she wanted to talk in private. His feelings about her were ambivalent. It had been her advice on the threat of court action that had stalled his decision-making, and it had been her questioning of Karim Farzan's financial resolve that led to Wilton McGwyer making it clear that they had no appetite for libel suits. While he accepted that she was doing her job, he despised himself for not having done his.

They met at six thirty at an outdoor café bar in St. Katharine's Dock that she seemed to know. To his surprise, she was not wearing her usual straitlaced work attire, but was looking fashionable and younger. It suited her.

Her manner, however, was little changed.

'This is off the record,' she greeted him, rising to give him a peck on the cheek.

She ordered sparkling water for both of them, not asking for his agreement.

'Is it off the record for Karim Farzan, as well?' he asked. 'I wouldn't want to be blindsided again.'

She smiled, but didn't think it necessary to apologize. 'It's a personal matter, and I'm asking your advice as a friend. What can you tell me about the Freedom of Information Coalition?' she asked.

'You mean BlowSafe? It's a dumping ground for whistle-blowers, a place to upload data that they've stolen.'

'Is that what you call it—BlowSafe? It sounds like a porn site,' she teased.

'If whistle-blowers want to get their information into public hands safely, they put it up on BlowSafe and remain anonymous. As opposed to, say, Wikileaks, which takes ownership of the hosting site, and by inference, of the information posted there, deciding what will and what won't be made available at any time. If you're a member of the Freedom of Information Coalition, you can use that data as you see fit.'

'Is EANA a member?'

'No. People don't pay us for stories they can write themselves, or get for nothing. They pay for items that are new, or where they don't have their own sources on the ground. The journos who participate in the BlowSafe site specialize in investigative journalism, usually for political or idealistic reasons, and they cooperate together to uncover corruption. Then they distribute their findings worldwide. Why the interest?'

'Would the Caroline Brinkley story have been the sort of thing to post on that site?'

'No. That story was not based on incontrovertible facts so much as allegations. The allegations would have had no worth so long as they were anonymous. Is that what you're thinking—that she should post it on a whistle-blower site?'

'No. I think it's altogether too late to run it now that the drug company has won the high ground,' she admitted. 'I agree with the decision you made, though I hate that you had to make it, because it upsets my ideals about what makes a just world.'

He sighed. 'Yes, well, there are lots of things we have to live with in this business. Just as you have to in law.'

It was late in the day, and he hadn't eaten lunch. Torn between making this conversation short and heading home, or ordering something to eat and finding out what direction Kate was heading, he realized that the opportunity to talk about ideals with someone younger made him uncomfortable. It was something he'd avoided with his own daughter, for fear that it would expose an unbridgeable gap between them in their world-views. Kate and Tracey were both products of an education system that emphasized progressive liberalism, gender politics, and anti-patriarchal social levelling. If he were to have any hope of a cordial conversation with them, there would be a multitude of subjects he needed to avoid.

Now Kate was raising the specter of 'ideals.' He didn't do ideals.

'Look, I need a bite to eat. Would you like something?'

She declined, having a dinner date in an hour's time. He ordered a basket of fried calamari with an aioli dip, knowing the ingredients came pre-crumbed from a frozen catering pack and would only need five minutes in a deep fryer.

'You've got another reason for asking me about BlowSafe,' he prompted her. 'What's on your mind?'

'A client has information that points to financial malpractice. Actually, it points to fraud. The information on its own needs context and interpretation around it, but for anyone familiar with how the system works, it will be blindingly clear and worthy of exposure. I've looked at the submission guidelines for the coalition's site, the level of anonymity possible—provided the rules are carefully followed—but my client is concerned about two things. Firstly, her data is meaningless on its own—'

'"She"? Your whistle-blower is a woman?'

'Is that somehow relevant?'

'Not in itself, no,' Bryan acknowledged, though it was not the sort of information he would choose to discard.

'She's a whistle-blower, and the data has been stolen,' Kate emphasized. 'Isn't that how these things work?'

'Bang on.'

'But the minute she puts context around it, she risks being identified.'

'And the second concern?'

'There's a history of the media taking a hands-off approach to this particular subject, until a regulatory body is persuaded to act—and even then, they tend towards under-reporting its significance. That's the harsh reality.'

'What subject are we talking about here, Kate?'

She looked long and hard into her iced sparkling water, stirring it around before finding an answer.

'Insider trading.'

'That's the biggest game in town,' he conceded, 'but a hard one to pin on people.'

'It wouldn't take much for an investigative journalist, under her guidance, to connect the dots joining the data, and make a compelling story exposing major players—and that's probably what should be posted on the site at the outset. That way, it's in the public domain, and the media and authorities who ignore it become open to being judged themselves.'

Bryan's fried calamari arrived, and he fed two rings into his mouth very quickly, while they were hot.

'Media outlets don't get blamed for their omissions,' he cautioned. 'You're probably right that a certain type of outlet would pick up the story if they trusted the data. It's a reasonable assumption. Then there might be others who would keep it at arm's length by reporting on it only as a story being run by someone else. "*The Guardian* today is reporting information that, if true, would implicate such-and-such, a well-known blah-de-blah, in insider trading"—that sort of thing.'

'That's all it needs.'

Kate was encouraged. She reached over and stole a calamari ring.

'But my client isn't an investigative journalist, nor can she run the risk of being exposed. So, what should she do? Who do you know that could help?'

TWENTY-SEVEN

Faraday could feel himself falling into bad habits. After the DHL packet had been delivered, he returned to his studio to kill time until his planned meeting with Robbie. For days prior to him leaving for Vietnam, he'd stood in front of his easel, fiddling around with a painting of a weaver bird caught in a dizzying blur of frenzied activity, as it used all its energy to build a nest good enough to tempt a female mate. An hour of dabbing at it here and there had done nothing to improve it, and he put his brushes down and lifted the canvas off the easel.

It was just another painting of a bloody animal, and the doggerel written in the margin did nothing to elevate it. He must have known that this conclusion wouldn't change with time, for he'd now reached a stage of self-discovery from which there was no turning back. That was why he'd put his brush down and left for Vietnam so abruptly, as if sensing that that was where he'd find the evidence of his years of corruptibility. And now that that matter was settled, where did it leave him?

The defining moment of one's life is when dreams collide with reality. But had the painting of wildlife, and being paid outrageously well for it, been his dream? Or had that been Ralph Lutyen's dream? Had he just been a convenient medium through which others could satisfy their greed? And without painting, what was he, and how should he lead his life? As a justice warrior, like Caroline, an avenging fury bent on redeeming himself through revenge? Revenge was not an ideology. There had to be another way to live.

Jonathon Appleby came to the phone immediately.

'I found the person who produced the counterfeit painting of the panda,' Faraday told him. 'I traced him to Vietnam, just like you said.'

Appleby was delighted—relieved and delighted.

'But there was one thing you never explained,' Faraday added. 'What made you suspicious that something was wrong?'

'I'd like to be able to say it was my impeccable eye for copies,' Appleby confessed, 'but it was simpler than that. You see, we were instructed not to publish the painting in our catalogue, either printed or online, but to offer it up as a last-minute entry. Now, that's a red flag, because if you want the best price, you give it maximum exposure. You'd only give an instruction like that if you were wary of it being challenged. Are you mindful of laying any charges?'

'No.'

'That's a relief. And did you trace the vendor at the American Embassy in Hanoi?'

'How did you know he was from the American Embassy?'

'Did I not tell you that was where we were asked to send it?'

'No, you didn't.'

Perhaps he had, and Faraday hadn't been listening. Would it have made the difference, or was there a pre-written script to which fate adhered, and *not* knowing was included in that script? Destiny had meant him to search Ho Chi Minh City, the Mekong Delta, and Hoi An. How else would he have met Caroline, Duc, and McAvoy? Where but in the War Crimes Museum in Saigon, and during a fevered night watching *Apocalypse Now* in the Rex Hotel, could he have inhaled the breath of Vietnam's suffering, feeling it deep within his lungs? And how, without traipsing through the rain and mud of a Can Tho canal, could he have learned of the lurking presence of the snakehead fish?

His camera was at the bottom of Halong Bay, but its images were imprinted within him.

At 10:40, he caught the tube to Green Park and walked slowly up to Berkeley Square. The wound in his thigh was healing, but he worried that the hospital in Haiphong might not have removed all the bullet fragments. With that, and his ribs still giving him discomfort, he felt he was walking like an old man.

Robbie, who was early, watched him approach, thinking the same thing.

'Anton! What's happened to you?'

'I'm fine. I cracked a rib. It's taking time to heal.' He was relieved to sit down. 'More to the point, how are you?' he asked. 'Are the tax people still giving you a hard time?'

'No. I did what you suggested and showed them every business record we held. Suddenly, they lost interest and left.'

'But you didn't tell them about the safe in Ralph's parents' apartment?'

'Of course not.'

'And the package…?'

'I'm sitting on it.'

'What do you mean? I thought you were going to bring it.'

Robbie looked around furtively, then lifted a buttock from the bench seat. Faraday looked down and saw the edge of a yellow envelope. Robbie giggled nervously.

'Well, I'm not used to this sort of thing, Anton. I didn't want anyone to see me passing an envelope to you like a spy.'

'Good thinking. And how do I get it from underneath your bum?'

'When I go, I'll just get up and leave it there.'

'Brilliant! You'd make a great spy.'

'Anton, I was upset that you couldn't make it to Ralph's funeral. He would have been so happy to see you there.'

'You think he was watching, do you?'

'But of course. Can you imagine Ralph missing his own party?' Robbie gave the forced laugh of a man who was bearing up.

'And what are the police saying about the break-in?' Faraday asked.

The forced laugh quickly died. 'They have no clues. "Professional burglars" is all they'll say—violent eastern European gangs who got misled by Ralph's outward appearance of wealth. Since we opened our doors to immigration, West End galleries and retailers have become sitting ducks for them.'

He paused and gathered himself. 'Ralph left the gallery to me, Anton, and he always said he wanted me to carry it on. My fervent wish is that you'll agree to us continuing to represent you. We've always put you at the top of our list, and I'd hate to not have A. J. Faradays hanging on our walls. Will you consider staying with us?'

'I'm flattered, Robbie, but I have very little new work to offer. Just an African weaver bird, in fact. And I'm half thinking of going in a new direction.'

'Anything,' Robbie said gratefully. 'Anything that's a Faraday.'

Suddenly feeling better about the day, Faraday decided he'd stop into The Ritz, order a glass of wine, and have a look at the contents of Ralph's envelope undisturbed. He might even order a light lunch, and call David Goode while he was at it.

* * * *

Caroline returned to the house at lunchtime. They had now determined that there was no need for caution in their coming and going. No one was watching them from the street, and their use of cell phones and the internet had become so circumspect that anyone eavesdropping would be tearing their hair out. The whole thing had turned into a game—a game they were becoming good at.

The one area where extra care was needed, if they were to avoid exposing him, was in their contact with Tuan, but that had become like a game as well. After getting his message that he urgently needed a laptop, Caroline had gone down to Kensington High Street with Anton's credit card and bought him one, then walked all the way to Olympia before diving into the back streets and taking a deliberately circuitous route to Tuan's bed-sit on Avonmore Road, making sure that she wasn't followed.

Despite the letdown she'd experienced over her story having been gazumped, she hadn't lost her enthusiasm for continuing to pursue it. If she hadn't been sure before that investigative journalism was the path she wanted to follow, she was damn sure of it now that the world she'd always suspected existed (the world that her Irish-American parents had warned her needed to be fought with all the energy decent people could muster)— *that* world, *this* world, which had brazenly exposed itself to her in all its callous, unpitying criminality—had carelessly lifted the veil on itself and allowed her to look in.

Seeing the ravenous hunger with which Tuan set up the laptop she'd bought for him, and the hard drive with its enormous cache of files, made her realize how frustrated he must have been waiting for them. She'd read enough to know what the files contained, though she didn't admit that to him, and she knew that their contents were at best sensitive, and at worst highly damaging to his ex-employers. So, who had he trusted to send it to him?

'My friend,' he snapped.

'What friend? Does he know the danger you're in?'

'My danger is nothing compared to what will happen if the vaccine is released.'

'What will happen? They've already announced its release.'

Tuan picked up the red notebook in which he'd been writing so furiously back at the cottage on the moors. 'This explains it.' He waved the book in her face. 'When people read what I have to say, and we get the files from the development program on my hard drive reviewed by independent experts in drug development, the vaccine will have to be withdrawn.'

'And how will we do that?' she demanded. 'Who do we get to review your files that world governments would listen to, in deference to the World

Health Organization and the biggest international pharmaceutical companies? You're wanted by Interpol, Tuan. You can't even appear in public to argue your case.'

It wasn't what he wanted to hear. 'Listen to me,' he said. 'I know what I'm saying. When I'm ready, I'll tell you where you can access my notes. Even you will understand. You can't stop now. You have a duty.'

So, this was far from over, but she'd need to quell her impatience until Tuan was ready. In the meantime, she'd choose to gloss over what she'd discussed, telling Anton only that Tuan was grateful for the laptop and would pay him back as soon as he was able. With every passing day, she realized, she was telling him less of her thoughts, sensing that he didn't share her burning anger, and she didn't want to hear his counter-arguments, no matter how reasonably he expressed them.

On the way back from seeing Tuan, she'd been to Waitrose and done some shopping. If there was one thing she'd learned about Anton, it was that his equilibrium depended on a well-stocked fridge, with lunch and dinner dictating a rhythm to the conduct of the day. When the rhythm was upset, so was Anton.

Though it was foreign to her nature and lifestyle, she'd decided that she'd lay out the quiche Lorraine and salad she'd bought and heat a French baguette in the oven, the smell of which would surely bring Anton down from his studio in anticipation. Whether this "little woman" peacekeeping gesture on her part would be to his liking, she couldn't be sure, but it was worth a try.

* * * *

Caroline's route to her man's heart would have to be tested on another day, however, for after finding his way to a quiet corner table in the Rivoli Bar at The Ritz, ordering a glass of Nuit St. George, and opening the envelope from Ralph Lutyen, Faraday's thoughts were seized by the events of a different age. Aiming for The Ritz had been, in itself, an attempt to escape the reality of the present, to quell the dull intestinal ache that anxiety had induced while they were on the run, to dispel the one-dimensional view of the world that left no room for perspective or levity.

Ah, levity! That was the lure that had guided his leaden footsteps here, where a single glass of wine, while he was sitting in a lushly brocaded chair in a polished jewel-box interior, cost him as much as a room cost for a week in the Flowerpot Hotel in Hanoi. Sadly, such an impetuous moment of self-indulgence had seldom occurred to him in the time since he'd first met Caroline. Indulging in expensive treats was not in her nature—which made this moment alone all the more appealing.

As he'd suspected, the envelope contained a distribution list. There were thirty pages in all, formatted to fit an Avery labelling system, forty labels per page. He knew what he was holding. It was the list of 1,200 recipients for the Harbinger Collection of hand-signed lithographs, featuring rare and threatened wildlife species, that the Paladin Foundation had commissioned him to paint, turning it into a fundraising exercise targeted at the rich and fiercely anonymous benefactors who had seed-funded the foundation. *Fiercely* anonymous.

But anonymous no more.

For a West End gallery owner as addicted to celebrity and money as was Ralph Lutyen had been, having that stolen list hidden in his parents' apartment safe, knowing that he would face reputational ruin if he was ever discovered using it, must have gnawed at him night and day.

Had he ever been tempted to mine its riches, Faraday wondered? Just a little bit? Just a select name here and there? 'Mon cher President, excuse my unsolicited intrusion, but I wanted to let you know (in the strictest confidence) that a Pierre Bonnard of the very highest quality has come into my hands for private sale, and knowing of your good fortune in owning his exquisite *Table avec des Fleurs Bleues*, it occurred to me that…'

How could he have possibly resisted? Faraday had openly challenged him to prove that he hadn't surreptitiously skimmed money out of Paladin's scheme, but he'd been on the wrong track. Now that he saw the distribution list, he realized why Paladin had guarded it so jealously. These were the names, physical addresses (for courier delivery), and private phone numbers of large donors to a shy—to the point of being secretive—foundation. It would be a serious breach of trust if the list had fallen into the wrong hands, for Faraday was sure there were other things apart from wildlife that brought them all together.

There were a few names that he recognized, but he couldn't confidently say why, except they were not to be found in the world of celebrity, and the world of high finance was not one that he'd ever followed. Perhaps Ralph had left it to him for purely sentimental reasons. This was, after all, a list of people with one unique thing in common: they all owned an expensive, exclusive, and personally signed portfolio of lithographs featuring the paintings of A. J. Faraday.

Thank you, Ralph. He raised his glass, emptied it, and then returned the list to the yellow envelope.

It was the thought of people in high finance that reminded him that he'd failed to make the call to his best friend, David Goode.

'Where the hell are you?'

'I'm in the bar at The Ritz Hotel on Piccadilly.'

'Stay there. I'll see you in twenty minutes.'

If he was after levity, this was exactly what he needed.

TWENTY-EIGHT

Louis Rey of Nui BioLab didn't need media training. He was a practiced technocrat, overlaid with equal measures of confidence and charm, knowing when to slide from an infectious enthusiasm for the wonders of scientific discovery to the safe haven of commercial sensitivity.

The infectious enthusiasm side of his public face had been in full swing for twenty-four hours by the time Sinclair Baines reached him. The CD8Magna story had been run out of the Anglo Swiss head office in Geneva, keeping the focus well away from Nui BioLab in Hanoi, but the forecast release of VAXX-Avia was altogether too big a story for the Vietnam operation to be left out of it. As the world's media descended on it, Louis Rey and his team had been ready for them with slick video clips, reader-friendly clinical texts, and heartwarming human stories of hope.

Louis had the perfect face for it: a warm mouth coupled with a furrowed brow. Baines got to meet him in private at the end of a day that the people of Nui must have regarded as a triumph for well-organized public relations. The meeting had been set up by a nervous but eager-to-please Richard Dibble, who'd stressed that the WHO was keen that the East Asia News Agency be given special treatment. The expectation was that this would be an interview focused on the implications of the global research cooperation that had led to the vaccine's release, rather than any details of the science behind it (for that was beyond the expertise of EANA).

Once the pleasantries were over, this was where Baines started. He opened his notebook, retrieved a pen from his inside jacket pocket, and looked up with a smile of anticipation, ready to commence.

'So, let's begin,' he said. 'I didn't realize just how interconnected the world of health research is—particularly when it comes to vaccine development—until Richard Dibble at the WHO explained it to me. You're really all in the same room, aren't you?'

'But of course,' Louis acknowledged. 'The scientific community is one of continuous collaboration and peer review, which is how we make progress, and now, with blockchain technology, there are decentralized platforms for information exchange that help to dramatically speed up new development.'

'That's what really interests me, Louis,' Baines explained, 'because I don't think the general public understands how the scientific community works.' He laughed. 'Well, by that, I mean that *I* damn well don't know how it works. So, if you can help me get my head around it, maybe I can help our readers do the same.'

Louis looked a little skeptical about that possibility, but his expression suggested that he was willing to give it a try. 'Where can I start?' he asked helpfully.

'Well, I guess the surprising thing about the news of this vaccine's imminent release is the speed with which you've got it through the maze of clinical trials in order to meet regulatory standards. I mean, this bird flu epidemic only really took hold in the highlands in June, and here we are in September, with a vaccine almost ready to come out of phase three trials. That's how it looks to outsiders. How did you do it?'

Louis did not look pleased by the question. 'My understanding is that this interview is not for the purposes of discussing virology in detail,' he said, 'but I need to correct you. The "bird flu," as you call it, has been endemic in domestic poultry and wildlife, throughout Asia in particular, for decades in one form or another. Viruses mutate. The ability to achieve mammalian transmissibility has always been a possibility for which we plan.

In that sense, this epidemic, which is now being declared a pandemic, is entirely coincidental to our work, which has been going on quietly for a number of years.'

Baines wrote quickly. 'And fortunately,' he said, 'you somehow knew that it was going to emerge—not as H5N1 or H7N4 or whatever, but as a mutation not seen before. You haven't allocated a number to the neuraminidase, but you've obviously identified it. Was that possible because you had been experimenting with new strains, and already knew the potential for mammalian transmissibility—perhaps as a result of reassortment with the human influenza viruses, as some people are claiming? Isn't it the case that, when flu viruses come together by infecting the same cell, they swap genetic material and produce hybrids? What do they call it— 'gain of function'? I see that the *Wall Street Journal* reported that the US Center for Disease Control and Prevention had begun a series of experiments to see how the bird flu virus could result in a human pandemic some time ago. Were you involved in that?'

'Mr Baines, I am afraid you would require a far greater knowledge of epidemiology to discuss such matters with me in detail. There is now a large network of research laboratories around the world working in this area, and we all exchange information. Fortunately, we are an important member of that network, and now that puts us in the position of being able to respond to what could be a global emergency. Once the vaccine has completed phase three, there will be any number of peer-reviewed papers dealing with the science. With all due respect, I believe the media should wait until then.'

'I get all that,' Baines conceded, 'but I really want to show people just how remarkably complex the layers of this operation can be. Putting aside the fortunate fact that you somehow managed to predict the structure of the mutated virus, I am astounded that so many international agencies are confident that they will be in a position to give approval to a vaccine so quickly. As a for instance, I read in your press statement that you have already agreed to bring the vaccine to Gavi countries at the lowest possible price.'

'Yes. Gavi, the vaccine alliance, is a very important agency that brings together developing countries and donor governments to ensure that the widest possible protection is available everywhere.'

'And I read that the World Health Organization, UNICEF, the World Bank—or at least, the IMF—and countries like the USA and United Kingdom will all be involved in subsidizing that initiative.'

'That's right, and many private foundation donors as well.'

'Wow!' Baines exclaimed. 'That makes the story even more remarkable.'

'In what way?'

'Well, you've not only managed to run stringent clinical trials—human trials with control groups and auditing and all that stuff—over many years, presumably, including with people infected with the exact same virus, and people at risk of being infected, but then you had to get all this evidence through a pile of health agencies and peer groups. And as if that weren't enough, you then had to get a sign-off from these huge international bureaucracies at the WHO, the IMF, and the World Bank—and didn't I see that those three all happen to be based in Geneva? Well, hell, I have to say that it makes the story of Genesis seem like a walk in the park, Louis.'

Louis Rey's frown had started to deepen. The *'aww, shucks'* style Baines had adopted clearly threw him.

'It goes without saying,' Louis said, 'that it is not a simple process, nor a cheap one.'

Baines was quick to agree. 'So, when the WHO announced this week that the World Bank had approved a one-billion-dollar Pandemic Financing Facility for the Vietnam government, does any of that come back to you— the money, I mean?'

'No. We will rely on vaccine sales and the sales of our neuraminidase inhibitor, CD8Magna.'

'Ah, yes. I noticed that your parent company has donated five hundred thousand doses of CD8Magna to the Guangxi and Yunnan regions of China. That was very generous. But I think you've said that antivirals have to be taken within forty-eight hours of infection and are impractical as a preventative drug. Yet many countries have already begun stockpiling that product in anticipation of a pandemic, so presumably, they are confident that they're going to need it. I see also that Ecuador has set aside twenty thousand hectares of mountain forest in the El Oriente region as a protected area for the plant species you use for synthesizing your neuraminidase inhibitor. Am I right in thinking that's to be managed by the Paladin Foundation for the Environment?'

'I believe so, yes.'

'And they were involved in managing and protecting your seed plants here in the Northern Highlands. So, I'm curious to know what the connection is. Well, to be blunt, what's in it for them?'

Louis could not help readjusting himself in his chair. Body language, pure and simple. 'They're a non-profit foundation that oversees a number of ecological initiatives, including, in this case, pharmacologically active substances in nature.'

Baines looked up from his notebook. 'And their president, Charles Van Heeren, is also the chairman of Anglo Swiss BioLab—that's a statement, not a question—which explains what's in it for them, I guess. Sales of CD8Magna must be quite substantial. What sort of figure are we talking? In the billions…?'

Louis suddenly looked vague. 'I don't have up-to-date figures on that,' he mumbled. 'It's a question for Geneva, but development has not been cheap, as I've explained.'

'That's exactly the story I want to tell, if you'll let me,' Baines explained. 'People think pharmaceutical companies make fortunes off of ill health, but they have no comprehension of the costs of research and development, or the gambles the drug companies take in trying to get approvals and patent protections. Do you see where I'm coming from?'

'Yes, I'm sure it would be helpful to make that point.'

Baines dived into his pocket and took out a typed sheet that he'd prepared in advance for the meeting. 'I made a list of all the organizations I could identify that must have been involved along the way in your remarkable work, starting here in Vietnam with the Ministry of Health, then all the national agencies, like the FDA, the CDC, the NIH, and the MHRA in Britain, right through to the international funding agencies that we've already discussed, like the World Bank's Pandemic Fund, and…'

He handed it to Louis and waved his arms expansively in the air.

'… and the idea that I had, which Richard Dibble suggested I put to you, was that I get a brief comment from each one of them that I can collate into a story that properly explains the monumental achievement represented by this vaccine's development. And what Richard is really saying is that this might be possible if you could give me your main point of contact for each of these organizations, which would not only save us time—it's a long list— but it would be an extremely useful endorsement of what I want to say.'

Louis Rey laid the piece of paper down on the desk in front of him without looking at it. 'But what you don't understand, Mr Baines, is that our industry can only operate if information exchanges and commercial agreements are conducted under the strictest possible security arrangements. Even to give you contact names would be a breach of those arrangements. I'm sorry, but in this age of misinformation and disinformation, it's not possible. You should speak to the WHO. Since a pandemic is being declared, they are now the one official source of information, in line with international health regulations.'

Baines took the paper back, slowly folded it up, and put it back in his pocket. 'Okay, well, I guess I'm going to have to do it the hard way.' He closed his notebook and made an awkward show of fitting his pen into his jacket pocket while Louis watched him with equal measures of confidence and charm.

'One last question,' Baines said brightly. 'Two questions, actually. Your announcement of the forthcoming release of the vaccine said that it has been delayed as the result of an extortion threat made by one of your microbiologist employees. What was the nature of the threat, and can you reveal the employee's name and status?'

The confidence remained, but the charm was gone. 'Those matters are sub judice, Mr Baines. Now, if you don't mind, our time is up.'

* * * *

It was a matter of some concern that Mrs Qui had taken down the poster of the chicken and duck with the red X slashed across it, quietly reintroducing her chicken broth pho and spicy orange duck with lime leaves. The poultry came from Laos, she explained, and vendors were allowed to sell it. But Baines felt uneasy about that, knowing how basic it was to the local diet, and how corruptible Vietnamese officials could be under the pressure of financial inducement. He passed on the recommended pho and plumped for the pork. Swine flu over bird flu.

Koi ordered his usual *mam kho* from an adjoining food stall.

'Is there anything that would stack up as evidence?' Baines asked.

Koi shook his head. 'You ask me to find out, and I find out. You want evidence, then I have to say I not find out.'

'Okay,' Baines accepted.

He didn't know what uniform Koi was wearing now, or what uniform he'd been wearing when he went to talk behind his hand to the shadowy figures in the Haiphong gangs, or the TC2 branch of intelligence. Did both of those groups think he was a member of the other, or did they know he was like the wire that connected two tin cans in the primitive days before telephones were invented?

'But you somehow got them to say American, right?'

'Black American.'

'Oh, so it was that specific?'

Koi slurped his salted fish stew, eyes down. 'That's what you ask,' he muttered.

'But what if I'd asked if he was a bald white Englishman?'

'You didn't.'

Baines was too exasperated to eat. 'Fuck, Koi, what value is this to me? They might agree to anything, and we'd never know.'

Koi looked up as if insulted. '*I* know,' he said bluntly. 'Black American.'

That might have been enough for Koi—hell, it might even have been enough for Baines—but knowing was only a starting point in the journey to establishing the truth. And Koi knowing that the order for the pirating of the Halong Bay junk had come from a black American—which could only mean Sam McAvoy from the American Embassy—was unlikely to ever be proven.

'Is this from the mafia, or from intelligence?' Baines persisted.

Koi's shrug suggested that it could have been either, or perhaps that there was no difference. Should he pass this on to Caroline Brinkley as fact, then? It might be helpful to her, as it was to him, to know that at least the story wasn't sliding backwards, but it had no other value. McAvoy, no doubt, was CIA or Office of Intelligence analysis, or some other likewise dangerous spook who had free license to operate anywhere and anyhow with impunity. That bit was a given. Okay, he wouldn't waste further time on it.

'Koi, I want you to call on Richard Dibble of the WHO late tonight when you think he'll be asleep. He's in room 5209 at the Lotte Hotel.'

'How I know he asleep?'

'Good point. I want you to knock loudly on his hotel door at a time when he *should* be asleep.' When was he going to learn that with Koi, his translation of English was literal?

'He should be asleep when I should be asleep,' Koi replied, smiling and cracking the bones in his neck.

'Make it one o'clock. Knock on his door at one o'clock. Very loud, so he wakes up.'

'Why?'

'Tell him you want his passport. Study it. Write down his passport number, date issued, and place of issue. Let him think you're from TC2 Intelligence.'

Koi finished his stew and pushed the bowl away from himself. 'Then?'

'Then hand it back and leave.'

'Why?'

'To make him worry.'

Miss Anh brought a pot of jasmine tea and two cups to the table. On her tray were two chilled hand towels, which she handed to them using bamboo tongs. They both knew that this level of service was not reflective of the usual practice in a public food hall, and Baines read more into it than he probably should have. Was she honoring Koi, perhaps seeing him as a person of authority? Or was it a gesture of appreciation for the regular business that Baines gave her and her mother?

Either way, he smiled appreciatively and avoided Koi's gaze.

TWENTY-NINE

Riding on the tube to West Ruislip each day after work was not how Bryan Liddell had imagined as a young man that his life would turn out, yet that very ordinary routine in the company of very ordinary people, heading home unglamorously to a modest domestic landscape was the thing that now defined him. He thought of this often.

Oh, look—he'd got all that stuff about #MeToo, misogyny, inequality, and the time for righting wrongs; there was no resistance left in him about all those things. But what he felt in his bones was that he'd been born to take on fights, and he'd taken them on for forty years. That was a man's role. That was man's destiny.

But now that role was belittled, and it was the source of the problem between men and women. As he searched for a new role, he wasn't confident that he'd find one that could take him into retirement with enthusiasm. The past was no example to follow—destroying a marriage through alcoholism and absenteeism. But what did the future hold? Tracey had accepted him, after years of anger and rejection, only when he'd finally displayed abject shame and acceptance of blame, and not because he now showed any qualities of which he could be proud. Admitting fault might have been admirable, but those faults now defined him. There was nothing else. He rode the train home each night to his daughter and granddaughter feeling like a man who had failed.

The bird flu scare was starting to be built up by AP, Reuters, and others.

EANA—who'd had the biggest story of all to tell, if he hadn't chickened out—was being left behind in the pack. His abject surrender to Karim Farzan's unsubtle threat had neutered him. Even if he told Sinclair Baines to get back into the story again and recover their position as the best agency source on the ground in Vietnam, how confident could he be now that he wouldn't have the rug pulled out from under him again?

Face it, Bryan. You've been exposed as a weak man.

The meeting he'd just had with Kate Manning had only magnified that feeling. She and Tracey were not dissimilar. They were both millennials, educated and assertive, spawned by baby boomers (the despised generation that carried targets on their backs). Where was Kate headed with her questions about how whistle-blowers could get their stories out without being identified? The glint in her eye, the set of her jaw, and the confidence in her own judgment were in such sharp contrast to his own recent behavior that he had felt chastened.

She'd been at great pains to extract his promise of confidentiality. Was that a compliment, a sign of her trust in him, or a sign that she saw him as a patsy? She wasn't actually taking him into her confidence; she was merely asking him for a referral. And he'd given her the name of the BlowSafe site, and Steve Roche as the person who could tell her how it worked.

After she'd written down the details, and he'd finished describing Steve to her, he'd got up from the table and started to leave, but she stopped him.

'Bryan, I feel I owe you an apology. I now know for certain that Karim Farzan warned Anglo Swiss about the story you had. He was the one responsible.'

'I know. You don't have to apologize. It wasn't your fault.'

He turned to make his way to the tube station. Should he have explained what sort of man Steve was? He'd started to go back, then stopped, seeing that Kate was being joined by a glamorous young woman who'd been sitting at a nearby table. They embraced warmly and sat down, holding hands. Seeing that, reading its message, Liddell had been swamped by a feeling of regret, a wave of nostalgia for something he missed.

Before boarding the train, he had called Roche and given him a heads-up, only to discover that he'd already heard from Kate and was heading over to St Katharine's Dock to meet her. For some reason that he couldn't explain to himself, Liddell felt a twinge of resentment that his friend might be about to learn information that Kate had decided to deny to him.

But when he opened the door to his house, stepping over the toys in the hallway and following the trail of cooking smells towards the kitchen, all that was forgotten as his granddaughter called out that she was waiting for her night-time story, the most important story of the day.

* * * *

Liddell's failure to properly explain Steve Roche's personality caused a brief moment of hesitation in Kate Manning's inexorable march forward that evening. Even with the benefit of prior warning, it was probable that she would have checked herself before entrusting her information to him.

Roche was a short man in his early sixties who carried a lot of history in his face. His movements were measured and sure. It was unlikely that he would ever be hurried. By contrast, he spoke without pause in an even flow that displayed no hesitation in thought. His Australian accent was softened by an unusual modulation of tone, as if he had coached himself to acquire a radio voice. It was his voice that fascinated Kate the most, and his eyes. His eyes seemed to miss nothing.

He walked into the apartment, shook hands with Kate, looked around, shook hands with Sophie, accepted her offer of a glass of red wine, and then sat down in the armchair while the two women took the sofa. He saw and understood it all without asking.

'The Freedom of Information Coalition,' he began, launching right into it. 'Cheers. Not a bad drop of red. Am I the only one drinking? Oh, well, it hasn't killed me yet. You know, there's a lot of criticism about the press these days, and of media in general—no depth of reporting, hyped-up trivia, opinion masquerading as news… And then, when something is reported—bloody kids lost in underground caves, tsunamis wiping out Japan—the bloody news is just journalists repeating other journalists. I'll tell you why—in a word: advertising. Newsrooms have been decimated because newspapers don't make advertising revenue anymore. Bloody Google and Facebook have gobbled up the advertising dollars, because marketing pricks think that social media is the only place they'll find an audience. And they're right. So, who's going to keep the bastards honest?'

He took a healthy swig from his glass and flicked his eyes from Kate to Sophie, more to check that they were listening closely than to solicit a reply.

'In the forty years I've been pounding the pavements, I've never pretended that journalists are shining examples of moral rectitude. Jesus, most of us are sluts for a headline, and then on to the next one. But all predators have a purpose in nature, and hunting down the sick, diseased elements of humanity falls to us. If we aren't there to do it, who's going to stop the diseases from spreading? Even now, with the press corps decimated in every country around the world, politicians and corporate thieves are doing their utmost to control the media. Fucking hell, they've got us on our knees financially, and they're still not satisfied. And do you know why? Because there's a behavioral trait in some journos that just can't be eradicated. It drives the bastards mad, because that trait—the need to find and broadcast the ugly truth—just won't go away.

'Shit, this wine doesn't keep; my glass is empty already.'

Sophie got up and moved a side table alongside Roche's chair, then set the wine bottle on it.

'Which brings us to BlowSafe,' he said.

'Bryan said you had some sort of connection to it,' Kate suggested, 'and that you would be able to explain how it works.'

'Okay. Let me pour another glass of wine.' He did so. 'Forget everything I just said, and imagine that journalists really are driven by ideals of truth and justice, that the world is filled with media proprietors who are equally filled with those ideals, and that the great unwashed are hungry to read their revelations, trusting them to be free of bias and corrupting influences.' He laid back his head and chortled. 'Christ, can you imagine such a thing?'

'No,' Kate said bluntly. 'On the evidence I've seen, I can't imagine such a thing.'

'No,' he replied thoughtfully, 'but here's a thing I bet you've never considered. What if there were circumstances where appearing to pursue truth and justice made good financial sense for media proprietors, especially if other people had done the work at their own expense. Could you imagine them doing it under those circumstances?'

'Do you mean,' Sophie asked, 'when doing so improves readership?'

Roche seemed pleased that he could turn and look at Sophie for a good reason. 'A bit of that, sure,' he muttered over the top of his wine glass, 'but…'

He put the wine glass down and took out a packet of cigarettes. Kate and Sophie looked at each other in disbelief, but Roche had lit up before they could even register an objection.

'… headlines don't do much to increase readership, because you're lucky to own a headline for longer than the time it takes to read it. But if there's enough evidence of corruption in the investigative journalism, so that most media are confident in running it, then you're encouraged to follow suit— particularly if it's cost you nothing and you can't be held liable. That's the BlowSafe model. For freelancers like me, it's the ownership of the source that provides the value. If most news is just journalists repeating other journalists, and most of it is rewrites of stories pushed in the media by people with vested interests—politicians, lobbyists, and PR hacks—that leaves just a pitiful percentage of stories that are originals, hunted down by hard-working journos, and they're the ones that can be sold by freelancers like me. Got it? BlowSafe, on the other hand, gives it away, because they're truth warriors.'

He waved his cigarette in the air to summon an ashtray, which Sophie rushed to provide in the form of a saucer from the kitchen bench.

'Thanks, love,' he acknowledged, pressing on. 'For people like me, it's the unpublished gem that's never seen the light of day that's valuable. Sometimes I'll get lucky with a whistle-blower, but I can't guarantee they'll stay anonymous. BlowSafe—which is what you want to discuss, apparently—is set up specifically so that whistle-blowers can bring stories to them confident that at least one or two of their members will take it on. The Freedom of Information Coalition has a couple hundred investigative journalists from all around the globe who're dedicated to exposing corruption and graft. They're funded by donations from all sorts of different bodies. They don't do it for the money.'

Kate, trying not to let her irrational response to smoking (let alone indoors, let alone in her apartment) derail her intentions, got up and opened a window. 'Are you saying that they're inspired by a desire for truth and justice, rather than money?' she said in disbelief.

Roche laughed loudly. 'Too right! Truth and justice are essential parts of the story, particularly if they're couched in terms of indignation and punishment, but what those journos want is to know that the whistle-blower is kosher.'

Kate came back to the center of the room and remained standing. 'I get that. But what's the guarantee that journalists reading the information put up on BlowSafe will carry it further?'

'If the story pretty much writes itself,' Roche acknowledged, 'then the whistle-blower might as well send it out as a press release to everyone and be done with it. The information you leave on BlowSafe needs to be the bait for further research. The trick is to make the bait tasty enough that someone wants to take it. These journos are different creatures.'

Kate seemed disappointed. 'So, there's no guarantee that something sent to BlowSafe will be investigated and published?'

'Nope.' Roche shrugged. 'But usually, a whistle-blower, by definition, has access to information that is otherwise hidden from view, and knows the relevance of that information—and that's a fucking good head start, wouldn't you say? You need to think tactically.'

'But isn't the whistle-blower running the risk of being identified the more research they do?' Sophie asked.

'Yes, but not through any of the processes involved in communicating or depositing information on the site; that's all safe. They've got good encryption systems. The risk is that the whistle-blower is identified because only that person could have access to the information being supplied. That's where you have to box clever.'

Kate picked up the wine bottle and topped up his glass again. 'Bryan Liddell said that you're one of the investigative journalists who has access to BlowSafe, and you're also a freelancer for EANA. Does that mean you investigate BlowSafe stories on EANA's behalf?'

Roche's eyes flicked from one to the other. Kate decided this was a man who couldn't help but sit on the outside edge of truth, so how was she going to trust what he had to say?

'You want the God's honest truth?' he asked, as if reading her mind. 'The God's honest truth is that I sell to whoever I think will pay the most, and that usually means whoever will give the story the biggest and best coverage. I keep an eye on what's happening at the Freedom of Information Coalition, just in case I'm missing something. But I like to be paid. I'm not looking for sainthood.'

'Do you write under your own name?' Sophie wanted to know.

'For EANA, I write as Stephen Roche. For BlowSafe, I'm registered as Steve Murdoch. That's an inside joke,' he added dryly.

'Oh.' They didn't get it.

'Can you show us how to disguise the identity of the whistle-blower?' Kate asked.

'That depends on what you've got. Most whistle-blowers are identified by a process of elimination. If you're the only person who could possibly know what's being revealed, then you're likely to be found out. And if you're the person with the most obvious incentive for blowing the whistle, that can be a giveaway, too. Ask why you're doing it, and whether it's worth it. Like I said, you have to box clever. The other way of being found out is if you let a journo get close to you, and they blow your cover for some reason.'

'How would we ensure that wouldn't happen?' Sophie looked anxious, scowling at her painted fingernails as if wanting to bite them.

Roche shrugged. He'd been here before. 'A journalist will always tell you that they're not obliged to reveal their sources, so you'll be safe. That's your protection, they'll assure you. But revealing their sources might have considerable value to them. That's the risk you take once you start dealing with one. The best advice is to stay anonymous. If you can't do that, forget the idea.'

Sophie jumped to her feet. *God, she has a body,* Roche thought. He lit another cigarette quickly. Kate examined him calmly, mulling over the implications of what he'd said.

'But the whole idea, Mr Roche,' she said calmly, 'is that we would put enough information up on this site to enable journalists to follow through and write their own stories. We'd have no dealings with them. Your job, if you're willing, would be to show us how to do that safely and effectively.'

'But then I'd know, and I should warn you—*Ms Manning*—before you get out your lawyer's hat, that I don't do confidentiality agreements. If you don't trust me, don't tell me. But the bigger question is: do you trust your whistle-blower?'

'Why, I trust her implicitly—*Mr Roche.*' She smiled. '*I'm* the whistle-blower.'

* * * *

Anoushka's was not at all like Annabel's, other than also being in Berkeley Square. That was its point. It wasn't a bit like the Rivoli Bar either, and that was a point that David Goode made as soon as he arrived. So, Faraday had to walk back up Berkeley Street again, and that exposed his limp, which left him with a quandary. How much should he reveal about what had happened to him in Vietnam?

These were two friends from boarding school days, and then through the period of their lives when they'd progressed from uncouth to couth, on to so-called maturity. Their conversational style bore elements of all those periods that they'd shared. It was blokey, sexist, cynical, irreverent, and rife with the piss-taking that males use to disguise their affection for each other. They ordered tapas and a bottle of Krug.

If Faraday couldn't find levity here, he wouldn't find it anywhere.

'I tried to chase a young bird upstairs to her bedroom,' he said, deadpan, 'and tripped and fell down the stairs.'

'Christ, haven't you learned?' David asked in mock horror. 'We're old bulls now. Old bulls never run after heifers.'

By mid-afternoon, the weight on Faraday's chest had lifted, leaving only the cracks in his ribs. They talked about the past, when they'd behaved badly and had fun. And David talked about his life in New York.

'You either love it or hate it,' he said. 'I love it. It's the energy. No other place is so in your face. In business, they don't do niceties. You save that for the mistress or the wife. "Give it to me straight"—that's what they want. "Fuckin' give it to me straight, Dave, and give it to me fast." Christ, it took me the best part of five years to work it out. When it comes to money, we Brits are used to walking around the subject like it's a dog turd on the pavement. We don't want to look at it, or talk about it, or even admit it's there. But in New York, they want to know how it smells and tastes. I'm Jewish; I belong there.'

'And you're in that money game. What is it, exactly? Hedge fund, investment fund…?'

'Yeah, I run a couple of funds now, under an umbrella. We have around twenty-five bill under management. Old money, new money, lazy money, nervous money… The big thing for me is that it's other people's money,

Anton. That's the number one rule: other people's money. Oh, sometimes I hitch a ride, but only when I can see the finish line clearly.'

Faraday shook his head. 'Don't you get nervous?'

'Of course. The thing that makes me nervous is not knowing something. So, I try to avoid that. We have search engines that can track where the smart money is going, and software to help plot its likely course. That tells us when something's going on behind the scenes to move the market. Find out what that thing is, and you can join the game. Call it informed trading, or insider trading—they're much the same thing. Except you mustn't get caught doing the latter. A lot of investing is chart analysis and algorithmic trading, but to beat the market sometimes—beat it big—you need to know what the wider market doesn't know, and act before it finds out. That can fray the old nerves a bit.'

He laughed and ordered another bottle of Krug. Somehow, Faraday suspected that 'fraying the old nerves a bit' was something that David enjoyed.

'So now, my little Jewish schoolmate is rich, and he's conquered New York.' Faraday sighed theatrically. 'While I'm just a dull-as-dishwater painter of wildlife.'

The champagne cork exploded, and they laughed as if everything were totally absurd, and always would be. When David suggested that Faraday come to New York and spice up his life for a week or so, it was time to open up about events in Vietnam.

'I could introduce you to some women in New York,' David boasted, 'who would fall for your arty-farty pose and throw themselves at your feet. One in particular, who—'

Faraday stopped him. 'Maybe I should tell you how I really got my broken ribs. And a bullet hole in the groin.'

He started at the series he'd painted for the Paladin Foundation, and how a counterfeit copy of his panda painting had turned up, originating in Vietnam.

'On a whim, I decided to take a trip and see if I could locate the gallery that sold it. I was feeling bored and flat, and I needed to get out of the house. But it turned into something of an odyssey. I mean, nothing prepared me for Vietnam. It made me realize that I'd been living in a soundproof box with no windows, no idea of what was going on outside. Such a frigging Westerner... It was embarrassing. Anyway, I was down at this place on the Mekong River called Can Tho, and I ran into an American girl there who was teaching English, though she was really a journalist. Her family had adopted a Vietnamese boy back when the boat people were all escaping after the fall of Saigon and the communists were dishing out retribution... But that's another story. Anyway, Caroline and I—that's her name—made a connection of sorts...'

'You mean, you fucked her.'

'No, funnily enough, we only met briefly—like, for an hour or so—and then stayed in touch a couple of times while I was travelling, before we coincidentally both ended up in Hanoi and agreed to meet up in a town called Sapa, in the Northern Highlands, where she was going for a job interview, and I was going to check out the art galleries, such as they were. Well, it was in Sapa where things started to go off the rails in a very strange way. Remember, this trip of mine started because of a forged copy of a painting I'd done for the Paladin Foundation.'

'Yeah, you've said. A panda. I didn't know they had them in Vietnam.'

'The forged painting came from Vietnam, not the panda.'

'Gotcha.'

'Did you ever meet a guy called Kenneth Johnston? He was the Paladin frontman who commissioned my paintings.'

'No. Oh, wait a minute... Maybe... Yes. Is that the asshole who Helene ran off with?'

'Thanks for reminding me.'

'She was one hot chick.'

'Too hot. Anyway, where should he be but in goddamn Sapa? This is proving too much of a coincidence, and I'm thinking this is the prick who's commissioned the forgery, because he had access to the original, but what the hell is Paladin doing here? Though one thing I noticed on my travels was that Vietnam is overrun with NGOs of every stripe, and that, it appears to me, is the perfect cover if you want to run around with virtual impunity in anybody's country—particularly complicated, fucked-over countries like Vietnam. Or Cambodia. Or Laos. And while I'm trying to absorb all this, the area has a major outbreak of bird flu, and people are going down like flies—including me, as it happens. And—'

'Hold on, hold on… Are you saying you caught bird flu?'

'Correct. Nearly died. Three weeks in a coma. If Caroline hadn't done a Florence Nightingale on me, I might not have pulled through. She was busy filing stories on the growing epidemic, and I'm riding out a high fever while trying to process the things I've seen and heard, which are leading me to the conclusion that Paladin is up to no good somehow. And then Caroline's adoptive brother enters the scene, and he works for an outfit called Nui BioLab in Hanoi, and he has some alarming tales to tell. Turns out, Nui BioLab is owned by Anglo Swiss BioLab—which you know well—and they're donkey-deep into drug and vaccine development, including for the SARS bird flu virus. And guess what? The head of Anglo Swiss is the founder of Paladin.'

'Ah, the plot thickens.'

'It's so thick that you could stand a spoon up in it.'

Faraday held his glass of champagne up to the light and watched the bubbles creaming up the side—little pockets of yeasty CO_2, intent on enlivening his palate to make him want more. But he didn't want more. He'd had enough. The sense of fun had come and gone. He wanted to be with Caroline.

'Long story short, we ended up in the middle of a rather complicated situation where people saw us as a threat to their activities, and it got out of hand, and we needed to escape the country and go into hiding at your lovely cottage on the marshes—many thanks once again. And we left it clean and tidy. So, here we are. Cheers.'

'Holy shit! Cheers.'

Understandably, David was not going to let it finish like that. 'Questions, questions... You said something about a bullet hole in the groin. That's heavy stuff. How? Why?'

'A misunderstanding. It was an accident.'

'Oh, sure! And this stuff about Paladin being up to no good—what does that mean?'

'I knew they were funded by a list of heavy hitters, because I knew something about how they raised money—my paintings were a fundraising exercise—but they were very, very private. Any news of their activities was so discreet, you almost got the impression that they didn't want publicity of any sort. Why? Environmental activism, doing good for the world's threatened animals and habitats? These are things that signal virtue in the corporate world. Why wouldn't a Big Pharma company like Anglo Swiss want to send that signal at every opportunity? Especially given Big Pharma's reputation.'

'Right, I agree. Greenwashing is an industry in itself now, particularly in multinationals. So, what's your theory?'

'I think it's a club of some sort. Maybe they're people who are in a position to wield influence in environmental decisions, but who wouldn't be free to exercise their influence if their membership were out in the open.'

'Makes sense. It would be fascinating to know who they are.'

Faraday decided he needed to go to the men's room. He wasn't feeling that bright. Champagne on top of red wine, and only a few mouthfuls of tapas. Time to go home.

He called Caroline and explained where he was, catching up and gossiping with his old friend, and checked in to make sure she was okay. She was fine—busy on a new story angle. She had a quiche Lorraine waiting for when he returned.

Back at their table, he found David deep in thought.

'There must be a way of finding out,' he said. 'Don't you want to know?'

Faraday had left Ralph's envelope on the table, and he tapped it with his fingers. 'I have all their names here. It's a mailing list. I thought I recognized one or two, but I haven't had time yet to take a proper look.'

David was up and alert, edging forward. 'How did you get it? Can I have a look?'

'They all received signed lithographs of my paintings, delivered to their private addresses.'

'Can I look?'

'Sure.'

Faraday drained his glass and finished the last of the tapas as he watched his friend remove the papers and start scanning them. There were thirty pages in all, and he began to turn them over increasingly quickly while compressing his lips and rubbing the side of his forehead in concentration. A third of the way through the pile, he stopped and looked up.

'Shit almighty, Anton, do you know what you've got here?'

Anton shook his head. 'No.'

'This is gold.'

'How so?'

'When you look in the back of a public company's prospectus or financial report, you'll see a list of the main stockholders. The names mean nothing to you, probably. They're all trusts, foundations, investment funds, and banks, and all the big corporations have all these same entities invested in them. Sometimes the holdings are held by nominees. But if you know how to look behind those entities, like we do, and you tot them all up, the individual total investments of the beneficial owners would be in the billions, if not the trillions. And nearly every one of those entities is owned or controlled by one person or family. Not the guy out front—the investment manager or CEO—but the one who fucking *owns* the money discreetly, out of sight. Unless I'm wrong, that's the list you've got here. And I, for one, would kill for a list like this.'

THIRTY

If Anton was enjoying his chance that afternoon to escape the claustrophobic intensity of the all-absorbing drama that had been dominating their lives since meeting up in Hanoi all those weeks ago, Caroline found herself in a troubled state of mind as a result of being left alone for the day.

She had to acknowledge that she had become edgy with Anton—bitchy, even—over his passivity in respect to their threats. The news of his friend Duc's murder hadn't outraged him as much as it should have. The cynicism with which Anglo Swiss BioLab had pre-empted her stories, killing any chance of EANA running with them, barely surprised him, it seemed, as if to say, 'What did you expect?' It shocked her that he didn't share her outrage.

Looking back, she might have had a warning back in Sapa, based on the way he'd responded to learning that it was his friend, Kenneth Johnston, who had arranged for the counterfeit copy of his painting. He hadn't seemed the slightest bit surprised. This was the same Kenneth Johnston who had seduced Anton's long-standing girlfriend, to which his response had been, 'Well, I didn't own her.' Was this a British thing? Was it part of their schtick to keep a stiff upper lip and be passionless? What did James Bond do when his latest squeeze was assassinated in front of him? He asked for his martini to be shaken, not stirred.

But something else was going on with her, and she became aware of it as she was returning home from delivering the data file and laptop to Tuan.

Anton had given her his credit card and suggested in passing that she pick up some food on the way back. In a purely practical sense, there was no other option. Her bank account was in New Jersey, and she was well aware that it had nothing in it. When she billed someone, she got them to pay her via PayPal, and PayPal paid it to her account at Wells Fargo, sending her a notice by email. EANA hadn't paid her since her stories from Sapa, so she'd been living on Anton's credit ever since. This wasn't a problem for him, so why was it a problem for her?

It was a stupid thing. Anton had told her that Sinclair Baines was trying to get a payment to her for the stories that had been killed. He'd also said that he wanted to give her more assignments. This should have pleased her, but instead it annoyed her. It made her feel like somehow Anton was patronizing her—like, 'Here you go, little girl, we'll look after you. But in the meantime, borrow my card.'

Of course, he didn't mean anything like that, but when she took the card out in the grocery store, and then went into the department store on Kensington High Street and looked at clothes (because really, she had nothing to wear) and took the card out again, her resentment had hardened. Should she hate herself for it, or be proud? Ever since leaving college, she'd always paid her own way. It wasn't always easy; sometimes it was really tight. But she sailed her own ship, hoisted her own sails, and chose her own destinations. And significantly, she now realized, she'd never spent more than four days continuously in one man's company, always paying her share of the tab. Now she'd been in one man's company every minute for over eight weeks. And they'd never discussed it!

Sometimes it felt so good that she was certain it was love. But she had to consider the probability that danger and fear had heightened their feelings. Other times, it was bafflingly perplexing, as she realized how different their experiences and approaches to life were. Was that normal? Was she just going through an adjustment period? Probably he was going through the same thing. He was a confirmed bachelor, once badly burned, and he had a financially comfortable life pursuing a solitary occupation that didn't require him to consider anyone else. It would help to talk to him about it. What did her mother say…? 'When women talk, they tell you about their feelings. When men talk, they try to deny your feelings.'

When Sinclair Baines came online to report on his meeting with the boss of Nui BioLab, she was caught between two minds. He opened by asking whether Anton's call to him had been real—that they wanted nothing more to do with exposing Paladin and Anglo Swiss—or was it intended to be heard by anyone who was eavesdropping?

'The latter,' she replied, though even she was unsure. Part of her wanted to stay on the story, in the hope of finding a way back to revealing the truth to the world, but she didn't want to start getting her hopes up again only to have them dashed. Bryan Liddell had made it clear that EANA couldn't risk a court action, so how close to the real truth could they go with any further revelations?

Baines was confident that she could do a piece about Paladin's link to Anglo Swiss BioLab through its boss, Van Heeren, but that was a pretty tame filler piece in her mind, and the information was already in the public domain.

'What's the point of that?' she asked. But what she really wanted to ask was, 'Are you asking me to write this because you're embarrassed that I didn't get paid for my exposure stories?' So, she did.

He laughed. 'No, you're going to get paid for those stories regardless, but it'll take a few days to come through. No, what I want is to keep this thing ticking along until we have a picture too big to be outrun by those Big Pharma spin doctors, or to be ignored by the mainstream media that rely on their advertising and bribes. And I want you to work on it with me. You've got the scientific proof coming from your brother, we've got the affidavits about Paladin's activities spreading infection in the highlands, and I might have a chance of uncovering the complicity of the WHO and the agencies involved in giving approval for Nui's vaccine, if I push hard enough. Put it all together, and it'll be a slam dunk, believe me.'

'I believe you. But EANA won't run with it. Liddell has made that clear. He's a pussy, and someone has him by the tail.'

'Bryan is no pussy, Caroline. He made a sensible call, but if I know him, he'll just be thinking we've lived to fight another day. In the meantime, we do what good journalists always do, which is pursue our stories to the end. I've been frightened off in the past, and I swore I'd never let it happen again. My reading of you is that you won't be frightened off either, so let's do this together.'

He was saying the right things, though she wasn't convinced that anything would be different as a result of Tuan having access to all the research files again. They had a warrant out for his arrest. Would the world's vaccine and virology experts rally to support him, and would the leading science journals commission peer reviews to back him up, when they relied so heavily on the pharmaceutical industry's money? And the WHO? Water off a duck's back.

Perhaps Sinclair was reading her thoughts. 'If I put you on contract,' he suggested, 'would you agree to work with me on this? There's no one else I can trust to do it, and it'll take a lot of legwork. How about five thousand dollars a month to your PayPal account, starting today?'

* * * *

If Bryan Liddell had done the right thing and warned Kate Manning about what sort of man Steve Roche was, she wouldn't have been surprised to learn that he was in Bryan's office the following morning, telling Bryan what Kate was planning. It wasn't that 'Cock' Roche was lacking in morality. He had a very strong moral code, in fact, and that code was one of loyalty to an old friend. On hearing Kate's story, he had decided that it would have harmful implications for Bryan, for EANA, for Kate, for Kate's girlfriend, and indirectly, for himself. He had immediately explained this to Kate, thus leaving him with a clear conscience.

'She wanted to prove that her client had tipped off this Anglo Swiss crowd by hacking into your emails, Bryan. So, she got her girlfriend—a tidy bit of stuff who works for the boss man, Farzan—to steal his cell phone so they could download his calls and contacts. Or shall we say, she borrowed it for a while. You gotta wonder why they took the risk, Kate in particular. I mean, he's her client, for fuck's sake. In any case, if she'd asked you, you could have told her for nothing. So, I don't know what's going on there.

'Anyway, turns out old Farzan makes a bunch of calls in the next few days, and the babe with the boobs identifies them all as his company's sharebrokers. What happens next? The big-dick pharma outfit puts out a rash of press releases announcing their new vaccine, *ra-de-ra*, and pumping up the pressure on the fear barometer, for which they have, *ra-de-ra*, the cure that will save the world. Surprise, surprise, share prices take off, and Farzan's in the boardroom being slapped on the back by all and sundry, while Kate and her girlfriend are thinking naughty thoughts, like insider trading.

'Now, the mystery to me is why a smart young lawyer would want to risk her career by putting herself in the middle of this. She seems to think that she can drop hints on BlowSafe, and somebody will do the work to prove that Farzan's outfit, Wilton something—'

'Wilton McGwyer.'

'… Wilton McGwyer will go down, without any blowback in her direction, or that of the girlfriend. I told her she was fucking dreaming. I also pointed out that if Wilton McGwyer was exposed to charges of insider trading that relied on stories produced by EANA, then EANA would go down as well, because it's owned by those buggers. On top of which, she might like to consider the fact that she advised the accused parties not to publish the stories harmful to Anglo Swiss, and she could find it hard to argue that she was entirely innocent of involvement herself. All for what?'

Liddell nodded his head vigorously in agreement. 'All for what, indeed! Kate has a reputation for being willing to die for her principles, but this doesn't look to me like one worth dying for. How did you leave it?'

'I think I convinced her that whistle-blowers are kidding themselves if they think they can stay anonymous, and as she obtained her information by theft—and breach of trust—she'd be better off looking the other way. She reluctantly agreed. Her girlfriend was more pissed off, but she has less to lose. Now, I gotta get to the pub and meet someone.'

Roche got to his feet and paused at the door, nodding his head towards Megan Hastel's office. 'What you gonna do about the Sheila who bugged your computer for them? Have you fired her yet?'

'It might not be grounds for dismissal. After all, she was hired to do that job.' He was smiling mischievously. 'Besides, I quite like having a contrite woman around. Makes a change.'

* * * *

On BBC's Channel 4 that evening, a woman named Muriel Robinson headed up a program called *The Next Great Pandemic*.

'Ooh, I don't like that Muriel Robinson woman,' Tracey Liddell said to her dad. 'She's so bloody officious, and certain that she's right. If she tried interviewing me, I'd smack her in the chops.'

'Yeah? What's she on about now?' Bryan Liddell was slouched back in his La-Z-Boy recliner with his nose buried in *The Times* crossword from a month ago, not really listening.

'Another pandemic scare, by the looks of it. Just another,' she replied.

Tracey got up and went to make a cup of tea and turn off her daughter's side light, while her dad pondered the clue that read, *Cross-channel swimmer gets cramp under foot while fishing (4 letters)*. He knew the answer must be *sole*, because he already had two of the letters, and he knew the *swimmer* bit was a deliberate red herring (ha ha, nice one, Bryan). But he wondered what sort of person wrote crossword clues, and what else they did with their life. The same sort of question could be asked of himself, he realized.

'Tonight, we're going to ask the questions that health scientists are reluctant to answer,' Muriel Robinson declared. She had the sort of voice that listeners knew would never be used to deliver good news. 'Are we on the verge of the world's deadliest pandemic, or can we survive the threat that bird flu seems to represent?'

Liddell dropped *The Times* on the floor and sat up straight.

'Tonight, we go to Suffolk to investigate the unexplained deaths of birds in the wild, with an expert from the Wildfowl Trust; then to Norfolk to get a comment from a mega poultry farm operator with over one million caged birds about the threat to his business, and to talk to the Unite Union, which believes that thousands of their workers are at imminent risk; then down to Devon for the alarming story of a dairy farmer believed to have caught the bird flu virus from a cow—yes, you heard me right: from a cow—then on to Vietnam, to trace the origins of the virus, and its possible cure, developed by a subsidiary of one of the world's largest pharmaceutical corporations. Throughout the program, we will be talking to scientists and public health specialists from Oxford University, the University of Wisconsin-Madison in the United States, and one of the world's leading microbiologists in the largest hospital in Scandinavia. We will be leaving no stone unturned. So, stay tuned...'

The program lasted for just under an hour, and in that time, Liddell had two cups of tea and ate at least six chocolate digestives. He didn't bother to take notes, because in many ways, he recognized that it was the sort of program that anyone in a production department, with a search engine and sufficient motivation, would be able to put together if they knew the theme required. The theme was standard fare: scare the bejesus out of the audience, point fingers, make accusations, bring in the 'experts,' and then swivel towards the saviors in white coats toiling away in laboratories, while the bosses and bureaucrats conducted late-night sessions in New York, Geneva, Washington, and Malmo in search of that internationally coordinated plan that only required responsible citizens to do as they're told when the moment came.

'Aww, shit,' Liddell said to himself after watching Louis Rey of Nui BioLab smarming his way through an interview. 'When did they put this together? Before they knew about Caroline's story, or after? When Karim Farzan tipped them off, were they already ready to go?'

The Wildfowl Trust ranger, clad in the requisite cargo shorts and boots and carrying a hand-hewn walking stick, raised binoculars to his eyes and peered into the distance of the mudflats that lay before him. His voice was compressed with anger. 'Skuas mate for life,' he barked. 'This is an inhuman tragedy.'

'How can we stop it?' the interviewer pleaded.

'How can we stop it?' the ranger repeated. 'Canada geese are dying, too...' (CUT to dead geese.) 'And they migrate, taking the virus with them.'

'Or bringing it here from Canada?' the interviewer asked.

'Or carrying it around the world from species to species,' Muriel Robinson intoned from the studio.

She had something more compelling for her viewers to watch: acres of plywood sheds on brown muddy paddocks housing over a million turkeys. 'In Britain,' the interviewer intoned, 'we kill over two billion chickens and turkeys a year for human consumption. If the virus comes here, we'll be faced with having to kill two billion birds in a week, and that doesn't even include the egg producers.'

'There goes Christmas dinner,' Tracey said from the doorway. 'I'm going to bed. Good night, Dad.'

'Good night, love.'

The man from Unite Union was more concerned about the possible death of two thousand of its members. 'We want antivirals for all of our workers and their families, and we want them NOW,' he insisted.

An expert from Oxford University said that 150 milligrams of CD8Magna taken daily could be the answer, and the government urgently needed to start stockpiling it.

But the thought that preoccupied Liddell as he switched the television off and lumbered his way off to bed was just how many experts they'd managed to assemble, and how they all had an unerring instinct to turn the discourse towards the acceptance that natural mutation was responsible for the genetic changes that had allowed the virus to cross from birds into mammals; that researchers had been anticipating that possibility; and that the solutions lay in the hands of Big Pharma—Anglo Swiss BioLab in particular.

'Viruses are the psychopaths of the pathogenic world. They ruthlessly exploit their host to replicate and disseminate themselves,' the microbiologist from Scandinavia said.

And the same might be said about spin doctors, Liddell thought.

THIRTY-ONE

'For a cripple, you're more than a half-decent lover,' Caroline murmured, rolling over and poking her feet out from under the bed cover the following morning. She wasn't entirely sure she wanted to quit while both she and Anton still showed signs of wanting more, but she felt motivated to crack on with the day, and who knew? Feeling this way after such a prolonged lay-off, maybe she could lure Anton back to bed again after lunch, by which time she'd be ready for a break from her laptop and the Paladin story she was writing.

'I want to pick your brain about the Paladin Foundation, when you're ready,' she said, pulling on a new sweater and track pants. 'Anything you can tell me about Van Heeren and why you think he set it up. Maybe there's something you'll remember.'

Anton yawned and stretched. 'Uh-huh.'

'Oh, and I want to pay you back for some clothes I bought on your credit card, plus the stuff we bought at Kathmandu the other day, and Tuan's laptop. Give me your bank details. And while we're at it, we need to work out my rent, so long as I'm here. So, give that some thought, will you?'

Then she was gone, racing down the stairs, not having felt like this for weeks. The way ahead was clear. Everything she'd aimed for had now changed from a wish into reality. She was a full-blown investigative journalist with a staff contract and a commission to expose corruption. *Wait until my parents hear about this.*

Better believe it: Caroline Brinkley was back. No more Little Miss Victim, willing to be pushed around, warned off, and intimidated. Money in the bank—and an enemy in her sights.

'Coffee?' she shouted.

'Black … please.'

* * * *

Faraday showered and dressed, hesitating between donning painting clothes or street clothes. Whatever had happened to lift Caroline's mood had the effect of depressing his. He wasn't inspired to return to his easel. He had painter's block, pure and simple. The wildlife trick had been played too often; it diminished him, and the way he felt, he doubted he'd ever return to it. Maybe the act of painting, let alone the genre, was incapable of rehabilitating him now that he'd ripped off his disguise and found there was no one of any substance underneath. But where would that leave him? Ever since he had entered art school at the age of eighteen, painting had been his private and public identity. No alternative had ever occurred to him.

His groin ached, and his chest felt like it was poised to splinter and puncture his lung, despite Caroline's care in avoiding putting her weight on it. So, he'd managed to perform, but it wasn't a performance to make him proud. The same accusation could be laid against him in every area of his life, not just sexual—and from the very beginning of their relationship, when she'd had to nurse him to recovery, right through to his failure to keep them safe during the attack on Halong Bay. Now, while she wanted to pursue these people to the end, no matter the risk—the same people who had corrupted him financially for years—he lacked the stomach for it.

Somewhere inside depression, there was a safe space called indifference. He'd been in it before, and that's where he was headed now. Inside that space, there was an answer to everything, and the answer was always the same: *It doesn't matter*. It didn't matter a damn whether corruption was exposed, because it was like a Mexican axolotl: it would regenerate its arms, legs, tail, brain, and heart, as if nothing had happened. It was a starfish, ready to drop an arm as soon as it was attacked and regrow fifty to replace it. It was a green iguana, able to shed its tail so that it wiggled and squirmed, convincing its attacker that it was dying. And when the attacker went away, the lizard would return, eat its tail, and grow another one. That was corruption.

He bent down to tie the laces on his sneakers and winced in pain. That bastard Kraut and his steel-capped boots had kicked him twice as he lay on the deck of the Halong Bay boat, a useless fish out of water, waiting to be gutted, bereft of fight. Could he have grabbed that boot and heaved its owner off balance until he fell, then leapt upon him, scrabbling furiously for his eyes and throat until the bastard's eyeballs were like squashed grapes in his hands, and he was screaming like Gloucester in *King Lear*? But what anger he would have needed—what righteous outrage and disgust! When in his life had he ever experienced such a towering moral outrage of the kind that was determined to overcome any evil he encountered? If not now, then surely soon Caroline would see that failing in him, for the room of indifference in which he sat was not safe from people looking in.

The mirror reflected a different man than the one who had left the house ten weeks ago for Vietnam. His hair was so long that it would soon need to be tied back, and he'd shed weight from his neck, shoulders, and arms. It wasn't a new look though; it was an old look that had re-emerged, only damaged and aged.

The kitchen was where Caroline chose to work, and he brushed her shoulders and arm as he passed her chair. She hadn't made the coffee, as suggested, but was already deeply embedded in her laptop, lips pursed in concentration, glasses perched on the tip of her nose, a running commentary of murmurs marking her progress to herself. He fired up the espresso machine and washed the dishes from the previous evening's quiche Lorraine. She wasn't domestic; he'd learned that. He was. Living alone for years, he'd taught himself to be. He frothed the milk for her cappuccino and rinsed out the milk canister.

'Why do you want to pay rent?' he asked.

She adjusted her glasses, sat back, and folded her arms. 'To maintain my independence,' she stated firmly. 'I don't like being beholden to anyone.'

'Is this a feminist thing?' He smiled. He knew better than to suggest that it was stupid, but it was … pretty stupid.

'Although I am a feminist, of course, no, it just works better for me. It should work better for you, too.'

'How so?'

'If it doesn't work for you, you can evict me. If it doesn't work for me, I can give notice.'

'How very modern.'

Although he didn't intend on painting, he took his coffee and went upstairs to his studio. The unfinished weaver bird sat on the floor, and he returned it to the easel. His signature doggerel had already been written in the margin.

The sun vaults over shortening shadows, and the veldt bristles with corn.
Flat green strips of cabbage palm are weaved and spittled,
Stripped and torn as the weaver builds his nest.

'That's one of my signature elements, you see,' he'd explained to Caroline in Hanoi. 'Giving it a pseudo-poetic twist to imply that it's more than just another bloody animal painting. I'm stuck with it now; if it doesn't contain some piece of doggerel, people don't believe it's a Faraday painting. Anyway, since writing that, I learned that once mated, the male leaves the nest and goes off to build another. The whole process takes place again and again, on and on, right through spring and summer, until the weaver is worn ragged and his last nest is finally rejected—whereupon he dies. That's what I should have written about.'

'You're kidding! How tragic! Nature really can be cruel,' she'd said with mock seriousness.

'It's simply a metaphor for how women treat men,' he'd replied, with an attempt at a laugh.

'Ah, so you're a chauvinist!' she announced triumphantly.

Was he? Or was that what you'd expect a feminist to say?

Remembering his promise to Robbie, he decided he'd better finish the painting and drop it off with him. Then he noticed a text message on his burner phone from David, asking him to call. He was in high spirits.

'I feel like going out to Marsh Cottage for a couple of nights. Do you want to come? I know you've just been there, but I fancy some country air, and I thought we could just kick back like the old days, chew the fat, walk the fields if you're up to it, and eat at ye olde Suffolk pub down the road. What do you say? I'm back in New York next week, and it could be a while 'til I get back.'

'Um, sure. Why not?'

'Do you have a car?'

'As a matter of fact, I do.'

'Great. Pick me up from the Connaught around two o'clock. And bring that mailing list.'

* * * *

In Hanoi, the temperature was in the high thirties. It was always in the high thirties, and the humidity was always in the nineties. Night or day, it made no difference, which was why the EANA office air conditioning was always running, unless it stopped working. Sinclair Baines, engrossed in signing off on the day's stories from his bureau staff, had failed to notice that his heat pump had silently given up the ghost around 3:00pm, and it was now 5:15. Only when Koi opened his office door and entered unannounced did he realize that his shirt was sticking to him.

'Cai Tho!' he shouted out to his receptionist. 'What's happened to the air conditioning?'

She came stamping in, pushed Koi aside, and punched every button on the control panel.

'It fucked,' she announced. 'I call technician.'

Koi scowled. 'Fucked is *chết tiệt*. Be polite, please.'

'What do you want, Koi?' Baines asked irritably.

'I have bad news.'

'I don't need bad news. I've got enough already.'

'Pho and Congee is closed. I go this morning, and property manager put up signs. He say shop is quarantined. Mrs Qui sick. So, he give me address, and I go there find out. Miss Anh say Mrs Qui get bird flu. Very sick. Go to hospital, but no money now. Miss Anh have to pay rent, but shop is closed. So, I tell her come here.'

'Wait, wait, wait…' Baines got to his feet. 'What are you saying? Why did you tell Miss Anh to come here?'

Koi shrugged. 'She need pay rent.'

'I got that, but why did you tell her to come here?'

'So, she do some work for EANA. She very smart, go to university. And she help you clean house and cook, now that Pho and Congee is closed. Make sense to me, so I bring her here.'

Baines looked up to the ceiling for help. Koi's logic was always difficult to break down, and impossible if confronted head-on. Presumably the girl was waiting in reception.

'Why did they quarantine the food stall?' he asked. 'Why can't Miss Anh keep running it?'

'Mrs Qui break law and cook chicken from Laos. Make her sick, maybe die. You see Miss Anh now?'

Baines smashed his fist down onto his desk. His anger wasn't fueled by Koi's presumptive behavior, but by his knowledge that all of this could be laid at the feet of corrupt powers who cared nothing for human life, and whom he lacked the power to expose. Meanwhile, he was being pressured by Liddell to supply vanilla pieces to help support the story that nature was threatening humanity—bullshit stories, as he well knew.

'Okay, bring her in.'

He took a deep breath and stretched his mouth into delivering a welcoming smile.

'Miss Anh, how is your mother?'

'She is sadly very sick, Mr Baines. But she is strong and will survive.'

'Good. But your shop has been closed, and you need to work, according to Mr Koi. Is that right?'

'That is correct. I finished my university degree last year, but needed to support my mother because she is alone. Now I need work until I can apply for a professional position appropriate to my degree. I told Mr Koi I am willing to be flexible and fill any function that is needed. He brought me to you.'

'Excuse me.' Baines got up from his desk and closed his office door. 'Please sit down. I'm a bit confused. We've never talked before—except for a few words—and now I find that your English is excellent, and you have a university degree that you're not using. What is your degree in?'

She smiled beautifully, as he already knew, but now her gaze was direct, which in Vietnam was not customary. He felt challenged.

'Languages. I studied English, French, and Mandarin in order to be a translator at the Bộ Ngoại giao Ministry of Foreign Affairs. But I cannot apply until October, so I am seeking work until then.'

'How will your mother manage when you're working at foreign affairs, assuming she recovers from the virus?'

'Oh, she won't work again. I'll support her.'

Baines struggled with how to proceed. He was surprised by what he was discovering about her, but also embarrassed, realizing that he had viewed her through the lens of a racial and cultural stereotype, which she had now exposed glaringly. For a moment, he was tongue-tied.

'Do you … do you … not have a father who is able to help?'

'No, my father is dead. I have no brothers or sisters. I told Mr Koi I am happy to clean, cook, run messages. Whatever is needed.'

'But only until October?'

'If I am successful at the ministry, I believe new recruits start at the end of the semester and the beginning of the fiscal year, which is January. So…'

Blowing the agency budget by giving a contract to Caroline Brinkley had been easy for him to justify on the basis of the quality and importance of her reporting, but creating a reason to employ Miss Anh merely because Koi had ambushed him with her hardship story was a step too far. He didn't trust his judgment, but couldn't bring himself to reject her.

'Excuse me. I need to speak to someone,' he said, getting up from his chair. 'Could you wait here a minute?'

He closed the office door behind him and headed for Kim-Ly at the reception desk. 'Cai Tho,' he hissed, 'where the hell is Koi?'

'I not know.'

'Well, you're the Boss Girl. Fucking find him.'

He took his fury to the washroom and tried to relieve it at the urinal. The more he was tempted to find an excuse for taking her on, the more he knew that he would be doing it for the wrong reason. He'd stereotyped her as a little Asian flower in order to infantilize his innocent crush on her. But now that he'd discovered that she was an authentic woman, that harmless little fantasy was destroyed, and he was faced with having to make an adult decision about her.

The washroom door swung open, and Koi rolled in.

'Boss?'

'What do you think you're doing, Koi? We're not a casual employment agency. Did you know she has a translator's degree? What's all this crap about cleaning my apartment and cooking my meals? Are you setting me up?'

'Boss?'

'You know what I'm saying. Don't play so innocent.'

He knew that Koi must have noticed his attraction to the girl, but his personal embarrassment was causing him to overlook something that was too easy to forget. Vietnam played a game in which communism was held firmly in one hand, and capitalism was held equally firmly in the other. Koi was part of that game, and he never knew for certain which hand he was playing. Was he planting a candidate for the Ministry of Foreign Affairs inside EANA's office on government orders?

'I just try to help.' Koi shrugged.

'Help who—her, or me? What are you up to?'

'*Anh* means "clever" in Viet language. I think she has a good name, no?'

THIRTY-TWO

The half-mile track leading to Marsh Cottage was partially overgrown with stinging nettles and blackthorn, which discouraged country ramblers and proselytizing missionaries, but not everyone, if they were determined—and particularly if they didn't mind risking their vehicle's paintwork.

The visitors prior to Faraday and David Goode had not been discouraged to find no one home, nor afraid, it seemed, of being disturbed, because they had smashed the architrave and mortise lock of the front door and left it swinging open.

'Not good,' Faraday said quietly, switching off the engine. They sat and surveyed the scene for a moment before getting out.

'Travelers?' David asked.

'Could be, if they're camped out somewhere nearby and came in on foot. I doubt they'd bring a car in here with no other way to get out. I guess we'd better find out.'

They entered cautiously, pausing to listen, before David rushed straight to the kitchen floorboard where he hid his shotgun, and Faraday checked the other rooms. Cupboards and drawers were open, but nothing that he could see was missing: television, radio, wall clock, espresso machine. Even the booze cupboard was untouched.

'Definitely not travelers,' Faraday confirmed. 'What are we going to do about the front door?'

There was a toolbox of some sort somewhere. They found it in the kitchen pantry. The best it could offer was an old slide bolt, recovered from the derelict woodshed outside. This, they decided, could be used to lock the front door from the inside, while they came and went through the kitchen door that had a Yale deadbolt. There were duplicate keys on an adjacent hook. Faraday offered to bring a locksmith out to make the place secure in the coming days after David had returned to New York.

Before unloading the car, they decided to walk through the woodland to the neighboring farm and check whether anyone was camped there. The wood was long established, with plenty of beech, and the occasional ash tree beginning to suffer from dieback. Here and there were small groups of coppiced chestnut, with signs that someone was still harvesting them for firewood. They didn't speak, absorbing the filtered sunlight from above that seemed to be searching out the airborne insect life.

Walking was easy, the high canopy ensuring that the forest floor was clear of brambles and stinging nettle, but once they neared the edge of the forest, approaching open ground, they had to push their way through blackberry and hawthorn until their way was barred by an electrified wire fence. Beyond the fence was a field of fresh green grass being enthusiastically consumed by a herd of cattle.

'Angus,' Faraday announced.

'Who?'

'Angus cross, but I'm not sure what with. Too big for Hereford.'

'If you say so.'

One or two of the heifers looked up, inspected them curiously, and then shyly moved towards them. The others kept eating.

'Is this a good sign, or a bad one?' David asked.

'It's a good sign. They're ever curious, but wary—they don't like sudden sounds or flapping arms. So, just stay calm and friendly.'

'What happens if they all notice us at once and come charging over? I've heard stories. Will this fence hold them back?'

Faraday laughed. 'They've all noticed us already. Cows have three-hundred-degree vision. They're just waiting to see how the advance guard gets on.'

It didn't take long for the heifers to gain confidence, and soon they had three of them, sniffing and blowing at them in search of a conversation. For Faraday, this was the calmest, most soothing moment he'd had in months. They were beef cattle, and very much in their prime, which meant they would soon be slaughtered, but that thought didn't bother him, because that was the purpose; that was why they were standing in this lush field on a late summer's day. He'd seen old cows and underfed cows back on his father's farm, before Rhodesia became the basket case that was Zimbabwe. These were happy young cows.

'Can we touch them?' David asked tentatively.

'You can try. Hold out your hand and let them smell you. Just don't touch the hot wire.'

No, they weren't ready to be touched. They smelled of freshly fermented grass, and their noses glistened with moisture. The encounter was taking place on their terms, and they invisibly communicated back to the rest of the herd to come and join them as the fund manager from New York wiggled his fingers like a child, willing them to lick him.

'I can't believe the heat they put out,' he said.

'That's because they sweat through their noses. They're the same blood temperature as humans. Nearly all mammals are. The only animals that are hotter are chickens. They're nearly five degrees hotter, would you believe?'

'Fuck, Faraday, you should have been a farmer. I've always said that.'

At that moment, the heifers lifted their heads and scattered, kicking up their heels as a voice called out.

'Hey! You fellas from Marsh Cottage?'

He came lumbering across the field in green boots, shorts, and a Tilley hat, with a black-and-white dog trotting at his heels.

'We sure are,' David called out. 'I'm the owner.'

'Good. Then we're neighbors.'

He was a sturdy yeoman type, weathered and worn by the outdoors, with a hand that was made of hard leather. But his manner was soft, belying his exterior. He whipped off his ludicrous hat to reveal a nearly bald head with thin hair combed over and wet with sweat. As if knowing the abrasiveness of his crusty palm, the handshake he offered was just the barest touch.

'Were youse expecting visitors t'other day, I'd be wondering? Tuesday maybe, or could be Monday of last week?'

David and Faraday looked at each other and shook their heads.

'Two fellas came by, asking if there was a house around here they might have missed, 'cause they knew it was nearby, but they couldn't find the entrance. Said it was a mystery. What did I know? Well, what I knew was that I didn't like the look of them at all, and what I guessed was that it was likely your cottage they were after. So, I said, "No, can't help." Well, bugger me, they got nasty like. "Don't fuck with us," one of them says. So, I go to close the door on them—I was at the old farmhouse at the time—and the other one sticks his boot in it. Shoe, actually—sturdy black shoe. And they're wearing suits with the jackets done up, in summer and all. Who does that? "We don't have time for fuckin' games!" he shouts. "We know there's a place within a half-mile radius," he hisses. Hisses! "Then you know something I don't," I says, and I managed to shut the door on them. But afterwards, I thought that wasn't very nice at all, and I hoped if they did find you eventually, there wouldn't be no one home. Which seems to be the case, right?'

Faraday took it upon himself to reply, for he had no doubt at all that he was the most likely reason for the unwelcome visit. 'That was a very neighborly deed on your part, and it explains the break-in we've had in recent days. But I have no idea who those people were, and what the explanation is for their behavior. Did they say how they knew there was a house hidden somewhere nearby?'

'No, but I remember one of them looking at his phone and saying there was no signal. We're in a bit of a blind spot right here. Maybe he was trying to call one of you, or he was tracking a signal and getting no connection. Who knows?'

'Who knows?' David repeated. He had grown progressively uncomfortable with the whole story, as he should have. 'What's your name again…?'

'Lance.'

'Lance, I'd like to drop by one evening this week and swap contact details with you, because it's great to know your neighbors, and we're not here a lot. Or maybe we can have a beer—say, tomorrow night, if that's okay with you. Do you think we should report this to the police…?'

'Fat luck that would achieve anything!'

'Yeah, yeah, fat luck, like you say, and I can tell you, it's no different in New York…'

At which point, Faraday decided to cut in and change the subject. 'Tell me, Lance, what do you cross your black Angus with? I can tell it's not Hereford, because the frame's too big.'

Lance beamed. 'What's your guess?'

'My guess is Simmental.'

Lance slapped his thigh with delight. 'Well, would you ever? A man who knows his cattle! Not often that a city slicker knows a thing like that. I'd enjoy catching you up over a beer. Why don't we meet up for a drink later before supper at the Wheatsheaf? I'll be there at five o'clock.'

They agreed that would work for them, then took their leave and retreated back into the woods, each with plenty to dwell on.

David was the first to speak. 'Okay, buddy, we've got some serious talking to do.'

* * * *

Everyone has secrets. Like little white lies, they're mostly not worth worrying about. The part of the world that would be affected by the secret being revealed is invariably a lot smaller than the person hiding the secret might believe. That's what journalism had taught Sinclair Baines. He'd learned that there was so much shit in the world that one person's secrets and lies sank beneath the surface of it before anyone had time to notice.

Richard Dibble, however, had a secret that wouldn't sink that easily. His was a dirty little secret of the sort that, if found out, would rise to the surface of the deepest effluent pond that a regional head of the World Health Organization could ever imagine, so strong would be its buoyancy. Sinclair Baines had found out that secret by accident one night in a house near the Bui Vien Walking Street, and he'd tucked it away for a rainy day.

The rain had started falling the moment Koi came to his office reporting that Mrs Qui's business had been shut down, and she was on the brink of dying, because a rat's nest of corrupt officials and corporations had decided that anything was okay when money—big money—was in prospect. Or perhaps it had started falling when he learned that Caroline Brinkley's encrypted emails had been hacked, and that Bryan Liddell had pulled the plug on her story—the moment when Baines was forced to realize that it wasn't just that the details of her allegations were now known, it was that Baines's, Liddell's and Kate Manning's cover had been blown, and they had tamely surrendered to being silent parties to the corruption taking place.

He couldn't seek to penetrate Nui BioLab as he'd planned, or try to win the confidence of Sam McAvoy, the American agent, because they had now been warned. Everything that was said by them would be put through the mangle of double-speak.

What Caroline and Faraday were asking was that their story be preserved as protection against them being harmed—a bottom-drawer insurance policy on which they hoped to never have to collect. Reflecting on that, Baines realized that the insurance cover extended equally to the people they were accusing. It was a standoff, and that's what got him thinking now. What did he have that could tip the balance back in his favor?

Bui Vien Walking Street was a low-rent pedestrian mall for backpackers and bad-boy locals, a neon-lit entertainment strip of bars, clip joints, and fast food vendors, where walking on the wild side was mostly a journey through the fetid imaginations of the people who promenaded there. Backpackers and a certain type of ex-pat were drawn to such places throughout the East, for being ripped off was part of the narrative of the journey through another people's culture, when you lacked the intelligence or will to understand them on another level. Men, in particular, on their own and passing through, thought that streets like this would deliver them an anonymous, out-of-sight experience that they couldn't get at home. Richard Dibble of the WHO was that sort of man.

The clouds had been seeded many months ago, and now they were primed.

He'd asked Baines to have a meal with him, choosing a duck-and-dumpling joint that he favored for its atmosphere and unpretentious décor. He claimed it was the "real" Hanoi at "real" Hanoi prices, by which he meant tables filled with young men in black leather jackets, shouting loudly and drinking too quickly, accompanied by young women in very short skirts whose eyes never settled as they scanned the room for people like Richard Dibble, who, surprise surprise, was quite astounded when one of those young women approached him with an offer that he would never have considered if it wasn't for the fact that, well, her offer had caught him by surprise.

Prostitution is illegal in Vietnam, but so is stealing. Laws are passed for those who choose to abide by them. Baines had been persuaded to accompany Dibble and the girl into the back streets, where a dimly lit house was set up appropriately for the purpose. It turned out that the girl was just bait; the girls in the house were the actual catch. Baines explained to the woman running the house that he was escorting Dibble, and he would be happy to buy a beer, but didn't need a girl sitting on his lap while he was drinking it. Dibble was led away, giving the woman his particular preferences before being guided up the narrow stairs to an out-of-sight bedroom.

Baines had already been drinking beer that night, and he got up to search for a john just as the manager was leading a very young girl by the arm up the narrow stairs to the waiting customer. Perhaps the woman didn't realize that Baines spoke Vietnamese, or perhaps she didn't care, but what he heard her say before he closed the lavatory door was delivered in a very bullying tone.

'You tell him you are twelve. He wants twelve, understand?'

That's what Baines had put away for a rainy day—and now the rain had started falling.

THIRTY-THREE

Debra Manning felt ill at ease. Lawyers were counter punchers; they preferred clients and adversaries to come to them. So, asking Bryan Liddell if she could make an appointment to come see *him* felt like a surrender of power. It didn't help that the atmosphere of a newsroom, with its air of casual cynicism and sartorial indifference, bordering on scruffiness, was anathema to her. But these reasons for discomfort were minor irritants compared to the embarrassment she faced at having to acknowledge the lack of judgment and debasement of professional standards she'd displayed—compounded by the fact that it was a man like Steve Roche, of all people, who had brought her to her senses.

Contrition was the word she was looking for as she waited to be taken into Bryan Liddell's office—contrition with dignity. Not that Liddell was a judgmental man. He'd seen it all, and he probably expected very little from anyone. Which only made it worse, because now he'd be entitled to expect very little from her as well. But what she would plead was that she'd done the wrong thing for the right reason. Karim Farzan had abused Wilton McGwyer's position of privilege as the owners of EANA, breached confidentiality and trust by conspiring with Anglo Swiss BioLab, and profited from those abuses by engaging in insider trading. Of that last one, she was almost certain, and someone should be able to prove it. But as Roche had trenchantly informed her, whistle-blowers hardly ever managed to protect themselves against discovery, and the law offered them no protection if they'd broken it. She should never have asked Sophie to hack into Karim's phone records.

She stood up and went to the water cooler, took a paper cup and filled it, then thought better of drinking it (What was that about? Legionnaire's disease?), and looked around for a place to put it down.

'Debra.' Liddell made an unusual move for him, taking her by the elbow—not in a discomforting way (he wasn't a misogynist), but more in a collegial way that she found quite reassuring. He guided her through the open-plan newsroom and into his office, where he closed the door.

'Nice to see you,' he said. 'Can I offer you anything? A cup of undrinkable coffee, or a tepid brew passing itself off as tea?'

She laughed. 'You make it sound so tempting, but I think I'll pass, thank you.'

How should she start? She hadn't brought a briefcase or any files, which was where she usually started conversations with clients. All she had was a small clutch purse with glasses, a pen, a little notebook, and Kleenex.

She sat up straight. 'I expect Steve Roche has told you about our conversation, and the advice he gave?'

'Sounded like bloody good advice to me.' There was no hint of criticism or judgment in his reply.

'I wanted to thank you for the introduction, Bryan. He was a good recommendation—what you, or he, would call a no-bullshit type of person. That's what I needed in order to make me realize the poor judgment I'd made, and the even worse judgment I was about to make if he hadn't pointed out how things would unfold. He made me realize I was being selectively principled. I'm afraid I'd become emotionally involved.'

Liddell pressed his fingertips together, playing a game of what her father used to call 'pitching tents.' He was waiting for her to reach the point of disclosing why she had come.

'Here's my dilemma, Bryan. I have established that my client passed information on to Anglo Swiss BioLab, which enabled them to pre-empt your reporter's revelations about serious crimes. I've also established—at least circumstantially—that he and/or his select clients used their inside knowledge to profit from share trading. The problem is that I gained the evidence, such as it is, by breaking the law myself, so I can't use it. Until your friend gave me a shocking dose of reality, I had naïvely imagined that I might get someone else to reveal it if I anonymously dropped some clues somewhere like the BlowSafe site. The reason I'm here is that apart from my *mea culpa*, which I feel I owe you, you and I are both in the position of knowing that major crimes have been committed, and for different reasons, we're unable to do anything about it. Forget our client relationship for a moment. Surely there's something we can do as individuals? I mean, at the very least, we need a strategy for protecting your reporter and the people who signed those original affidavits.'

'Hmm…' Liddell stopped playing with his tent formations and spun his chair around to look out into the newsroom. 'What you're finding out is what I found out a long time ago. We assumed that our professions gave us some special powers. In my case, it was the power of disclosure that the press believes it has. In your case, it was the power of judgment that you presume the law has. In reality, we're bound to encounter circumstances where we're both impotent, as this series of events has revealed. What you're expressing is a sense of outrage at that feeling of impotence.'

'No, Bryan.' She wasn't having that. 'It's a sense of outrage at the *injustice*. Surely you share that outrage. Caroline Brinkley clearly does.'

Liddell shrugged philosophically. 'Of course. That goes without saying. And I'm pretty sure that Caroline and her brother haven't given up and are still working on their evidence. When that comes in, we'll have another decision to make. Thanks to Karim Farzan, EANA is faced with a Hobson's choice. We may have to find another avenue for making disclosures, or Anglo Swiss will bankrupt us. I don't have an answer to that yet.'

'But you're not giving up?'

'No, Kate, I'm not giving up. But I run a news agency, and I have to keep pumping out news. I have calls from the legacy media saying they want more material from us about the situation in South East Asia, because that's our stamping ground, and they're being pushed by their proprietors to raise the fear levels. At the same time, would you believe, our own bloody shareholder, Wilton McGwyer, is doing the same thing. How do you think that feels, knowing what we know? No, I'm not giving up. I'm just gritting my teeth and holding my nose as we play their hypocritical game.'

'Then I'd like to make an offer,' Kate suggested. She'd done her contrition; now she needed to offer compensation. 'This is to you personally. If the evidence becomes overwhelming, to the point where you decide a plan needs to be made that doesn't include risking EANA, I would like to help, and I'll remove all conflicts of interest by ceasing to represent Wilton McGwyer. I'll offer my services to you and Caroline on a pro bono basis. Whatever it takes to see justice done.'

* * * *

The Wheatsheaf pub car park had only three cars in it when they arrived just after five o'clock, but the dining room was expecting an influx shortly, as it was humming with waiting staff setting up tables to the soundtrack of Andalusian music. This was a gastro pub—what would have been, in a different setting, a brasserie. What had once been the Public Bar was now expanded, redecorated in pastels and whites (still with a comforting hint of its past history in the seventeenth-century exposed beams), and rebranded the Terrace Bistro. The Lounge Bar was now the Club Bar, and the Snug Bar was still the Snug Bar.

That's where they found Lance, though he no longer looked like a farmer or sounded like one. The Tilley hat, shorts, and green Wellingtons were gone, and in their place was a tweed jacket, corduroy trousers, and brown brogues. Even the accent had changed.

'Gentlemen! Greetings! Welcome to my abode. What can I get you?'

'Is this where you hang out?' David asked with a curious smile. 'Your home away from home?'

'My actual home, actually,' Lance announced proudly with a sweep of his hand. 'I'm the owner, but not the publican. My real job is real estate. I brought the old pub out of receivership three years ago and gave her a new lease on life. What do you think?'

'It looks fantastic,' David enthused. 'I can't wait to try the food. Do we need to make a booking?'

'I'll do that for you. But first, let me get you some drinks, which is the purpose of this establishment.'

Faraday tried not to lose himself in the banter that followed. He felt weighed down by the heaviness of the conversation that he'd been forced to have with David in the hours before this appointment. He'd told him everything, and if there were things he'd tried to hold back, his friend unerringly detected them and tore them loose. These were friends who'd confessed their masturbation secrets to each other at the age of thirteen, who'd called each other Yid and Tyke during schoolboy arguments. Faraday had nowhere to hide. He didn't feel exposed so much as exhausted.

'So, what's with the farming thing, then,' he asked Lance, 'if you're in real estate and property?' It was a Guinness he'd ordered, a pint of the black stuff, and he drank it thirstily. It wasn't Ireland that it reminded him of, but Africa. He'd started to think a lot about Africa recently, about its promise, and the way it then curdled, moldered, and turned to shit, and how few evil people it took to make it that way.

Lance was so much more confident and commanding in this atmosphere than he had been out in the cow paddock that afternoon. He leaned back with an elbow on the bar, never missing a new arrival without a nod of recognition as he drew his new acquaintances to him.

'I had over fifteen hundred acres of the best pasture in East Suffolk ten years ago, and my father and grandfather before me. But there's no money in farming. The councils, the animal rights activists, and the green vegans make sure of that. And don't talk to me about the Whitehall mandarins who spend their days dreaming of badgers' rights and ways to turn the country into a conservation estate. When I finally got sick of it and started selling off pieces of land, I realized that land was the only thing farmers had of any value, and they'd be better off selling it while they can. So, now I'm in real estate.'

'But the cows…?' David said.

'I kept that block in front of your cottage because I needed a quiet place to go and be with animals. If you've never kept animals, you won't know what I mean. But I feel for all the farmers that are getting out, even though it's more money for me as a land agent. It's breaking their hearts, some of them. And what about you—Anton, is it? You must know about animals if you can pick out an Angus/Simmental cross like that?'

Faraday swilled the Guinness in his glass, surprised at how much he'd managed to drink in such a short time. 'I grew up as a kid on a farm in Rhodesia, and I guess I never lost the feeling for being around cattle. You either couldn't care less for them, or you felt an affinity for them. It was a lucky guess today, that's all.' He finished his Guinness in one long go. 'Let me buy the next.'

Lance placed the order with the barman, then turned back and lowered his voice. 'There's going to be a lot of land for sale here in Suffolk, mark my words. The bird flu—this is confidential, mind you—has got into the milking cows out here in East Suffolk, and most of the herds would test positive if the ministry had the nous to test for it. It's in the milk, they say. Probably always has been, but no one tested for it. But the cows aren't sick, and no one milking them is sick, so who's to say? But the farmers aren't waiting; they remember the scandalous way the government treated them during the mad cow fiasco. Why would you wait around to be whacked again if you're already making no money, and your land's the only thing of value? So, if you're looking for land, this is the place to come, and I'm your man.'

After three quick rounds, and more of the same stuff about how there was always a light to come out of doom and gloom, they exchanged phone numbers, then Lance left them with a waitress from Brazil to be seated at a table in the Terrace Bistro. The music had changed from Andalusia to Naples, but the menu was a pastiche of Franglais, and the restaurant was beginning to fill with people in suits, who seemed to presume that their companions were hard of hearing. The car park, which had been near empty when they arrived, was now full of commuting Audis, Land Rovers, and SUVs. East Suffolk had become a suburb of London.

'Did you hear that?' David asked. He'd had three martinis and was spoiling for a high-octane review of what had gone down.

Only a New York Jew could drink three martinis in the Snug Bar of an East Suffolk pub, Faraday thought to himself.

'Your fucking bird flu is in the *milk*,' David went on.

'It's not *my* fucking bird flu,' Faraday protested. 'It's Anglo Swiss BioLab's fucking bird flu. Or maybe not. Maybe it's just the virus birds have always carried, and livestock or all mammals have always carried traces of it. I don't know. How will we ever know? What are you eating?'

David thought he'd have the *fillet steak avec pommes frites.*

'Steak and chips,' Faraday said. 'Feeling adventurous, are we? I'm going to have the *boeuf en croute*, in the hope that it's a good old English beef pie in disguise.'

Why did he feel so angry? What would it take for him to get this damn thing into perspective? Was it the fact that he knew Caroline was starting to despise him for his lack of fight? Dammit, he was more than willing to fight, but fight what? Nature was one thing, but human nature was another. Lance was excited by the money he would make from farmers cashing in their livelihoods. But what about the poor bloody farmers?

'How much are those people in the Paladin Foundation hoping to make out of an engineered pandemic, David? They're your sort of people, so tell me how much you think they hope to gain. I've told you everything I know about Paladin's involvement and its connection to Anglo Swiss. There's no way that the names on that list aren't privy to it in some way. Why else would they have funded the foundation in the first place, and kept it all so secret?'

David shrugged. Maybe he was just so frequently exposed to corruption that he was inured to it. Maybe this was just how business was done at the highest level.

'I gotta say that this is not a new playbook, Anton. Fraud and damages claims are a standard contingency allowance in the financial forecasts of all big drug companies, sometimes running into the billions. Look at Pfizer. Look at Glaxo. Falsifying trials and conniving with health agencies is part of the game. Probably the only thing different about this play they're making with bird flu is that you've seen it up close, and you weren't meant to. A murder or two here or there is probably not unusual, unless you're the one they're trying to murder.'

'Thank you. It's good of you to have noticed. Fuck!'

They laughed. But it wasn't funny, and David knew it.

'You remember I was telling you that most of our trading is research-driven,' he said. 'Well, we have people running software that can tell us who's doing what, where, when, and by how much, within seconds of them doing it. It can pick apart massive and complex data sets using machine learning, which is getting better by the day. We may pretend to be smart, but actually it's artificial intelligence that makes us seem that way. The nerds nicknamed it Hercules. Know why?'

'Something mythological?'

'Hercules had to slay the multi-headed snake, the Hydra. Every time he cut a head off, two would grow in its place. But there's a tiny jellyfish-like organism that biologists have named after that Hydra, which is even more interesting and appropriate than the original. It's an invertebrate, and what biologists have discovered is that its stem cells are in a constant state of renewal. Chop any part of it off, and it'll regenerate. The part chopped off will turn into a new hydra, and if you pulverize it and put it in a blender or a centrifuge, the cells will organize themselves and create a whole new multi-headed hydra again. It's impossible to kill.'

'Okay, I'm familiar with the metaphor. I get the picture,' Faraday acknowledged impatiently. 'So, how does Hercules deal with it?'

'He keeps chopping. His job is to find out what heads grow whenever he chops one head off. Let's start with a two-headed Hydra, like we've got here with this bird flu. People talk about public-private partnerships, like it's something new. Fact is, corporates and governments have been a two-headed Hydra forever.

'Government money comes from the taxpayers—but it seldom returns to them. Private money comes from the shareholders, and it returns to them in spades. The government players who are in on the game deliver taxpayer funds and official enablement, earning their dividends in the form of bureaucratic power, kickbacks, and political sponsorship from the corporations. From what little time I've spent looking at that list of yours, I'd say that's what you've got there: a combination of major corporate shareholders and government enablers. So, now we chop the top corporation's head off—that's Anglo Swiss—and see how many heads are growing underneath.'

'Yeah, alright…' Faraday was getting impatient. 'I get it, I get it. We get the other drug companies involved in the vaccine manufacture, the media, the hospitals and suppliers, the universities dependent on Big Pharma grants, blah de blah de blah… But even if we make all the links, what chance in hell do we have to stop it? You can tell all this to people until you're blue in the face, and they'll continue to follow along like sheep. I keep telling Caroline, no one can stop it.'

Just then, the food arrived. It looked good. Lance waved to them as he paused at the check-out desk. He looked right at home.

'Maybe I haven't explained this clearly enough,' David said. 'We use Hercules to track money, from the top down. Take someone like Bill Gates. His capital came out of IT, and he still invests in IT beyond Microsoft, so we get Hercules to follow that down through the layers. But his personal investment vehicle, Cascade Investment, has a diverse portfolio that branches out into many spheres—including pharmaceuticals, by the way—and Hercules follows them down through multiple layers that include vaccine research and development, healthcare systems, and Christ knows what. But then, he's also got foundations and philanthropies, so Hercules tracks their investments and interests, too. Did you know he's a major funder of the World Health Organization? Oh, yes, layer upon layer, man—that's the miracle of AI-guided research. One day everyone will have access to such tools, but right now, Hoffman, Latrobe, and Goode have got the best version in the industry.'

'So, you don't rely on your superior brains and intuition,' Faraday said teasingly. 'You get old Hercules to follow the money, so you can coat-tail on it. Smart—but where does that leave me?'

'Give me a hundred and twenty names from the list,' David replied, 'and I'll get Hercules to follow the money. When you know how that flows, you'll know everything you need to know. Just the names; I don't need the addresses. It'll only take a week, and if you like the results, we can run the rest of the twelve hundred.'

THIRTY-FOUR

Koi stood in the background and let the two officers in their Tong Cuc 2 uniforms do their work. The underage girl and the whorehouse manager nursed their bruises stoically, allowing the drama to play out in the time and manner that their two interrogators had determined to be necessary. They expected to be hit, and they expected to pay. Madams stuffed their underwear with cash just for that purpose, and that cash was already on the table.

In the adjoining room, bare of furniture, Dibble sat on the floor, back to the wall, and listened to the shouting, the slaps, and the women's theatrical cries through the half-open door, seeing a future so dark that tears of sympathy ran down his cheeks, mingling with his sweat. His sympathy was for himself, for his destroyed career and reputation. His sweat was partly heat and partly fear. His life was over.

One hour after arriving at the military intelligence detention compound, Koi left the room and called Sinclair Baines. He told him the address and said that he would be ready in forty minutes. 'Take a taxi and call once you are outside the gate,' he said. Then he returned and read statements to the two female prisoners, which he'd written in longhand on paper bearing the insignia of the Vietnam People's Public Security. The statements were short, and he spoke them aloud in Vietnamese. The only portion that appeared to be in English was the name Richard Allen Dibble. It was mentioned twice.

When he had finished reading, Koi passed his pen to each of the women and made them sign. As they did so, he photographed them, using the same

Android cell phone that he'd used to photograph Duc's corpse in the Dao funeral house in Sinho. Then he took them both into the room where Dibble sat huddled against the wall. He made them crouch down beside the *người hướng tây* and each place an arm around the man's shoulders, before taking two more photographs, and then ushering the girls out, closing the door behind him. He didn't speak to Dibble—nor, out of fear, did Dibble speak to him.

In a country where the uniforms of police authority were festooned with brilliant scarlet epaulets, buttonholes, and hat bands, the man in the plain, unadorned military fatigues was clearly of a special caliber. The fact that the others followed his instructions, and that he never once looked the Westerner in the eye or addressed a word to him was proof enough that Koi was going to be the arbiter of Dibble's fate.

When Baines called to say he'd arrived at the barracks, Koi came out to meet him. They told the cab to wait, then went inside. The two men in uniform were dismissed and instructed to take the women back to the house where they'd been picked up. The cash on the table was shared out between them. Once they'd gone, Koi opened the door to the other room.

Of course, hope lurks around any human being who has been left bereft by fear and desperation, and it only needs a small opening to rush in. The sight of Sinclair Baines brought Dibble to his feet, fumbling for the words that might dispel the nightmare into which he had innocently stumbled.

Koi put up his hand and barked out loud. *'Câm mi ng!'*

Baines stood in silence. Then Koi started to read the statements aloud in Vietnamese.

'They say you had sex with a twelve-year-old girl,' Baines translated. 'They say you asked her age. They say you were cruel and harmed her. They say you threatened them, and they were afraid of you.'

As in death, the body of a man is an empty vessel once the spirit has gone. The tall Canadian, who could wipe the floor with him in basketball free throws, looked like he would never thread a hoop again.

'Sinclair, please… Sinclair, I didn't know… I wouldn't… I didn't…'

Koi read on, not looking up. When he'd finished, he folded the statements into three and passed them to Baines, then left the room and closed the door behind him. They heard the outer door open and close shortly after.

'You were seen eating earlier at the restaurant on Pham Van Dong,' Baines explained. 'Someone from the CA probably followed you to the house. If they were looking for a show trial, they wouldn't have called me at this stage.'

'A show trial? No, no, no… I didn't know her age; they didn't tell me! You've got to help me explain. This can't get out. Tell me what to do.'

Baines went to the door and looked out. The room was empty. His cab was waiting.

* * * *

In the junior suite on the Club Floor of the five-star Lotte Hotel half an hour later, the air conditioning silently maintained a comfortable twenty-one degrees—a pleasant change from the EANA offices. The king-sized bed had been turned down, the crisp Egyptian cotton sheets folded back into a triangle on either side to allow ease of entry for the legs of tired guests after a day spent dealing with the torrid heat of Hanoi. Two Belgian chocolates in small fluted cartons were set temptingly on the pillows. The lighting had been dimmed, and the room was seductively lit by silk-shaded side lamps.

This was the world occupied by the senior echelons of corporations, government bureaucracies, and NGOs—like the senior representative from the WHO, Mr Richard Dibble. Baines had always known more about the people he interviewed in rooms like this over the years than they would ever have realized. These signs of indulgence were secret witnesses—the floor space, the depth of upholstery, the sheen of soft furnishings. The silence.

'You know,' Baines reflected (because he was the only one talking), 'hotels like to pretend they're watering holes for capitalists, but the crazy thing is that they're run like fucking bureaucracies. They have rules and hierarchies that the staff slip into seamlessly, creating an entropic world within. I remember in the middle of a Lebanese firestorm of Hezbollah mortar bombs and Israeli missiles, the bar at the Commodore Hotel in West Beirut never surrendered its adherence to the structure demanded of us correspondents. Bar stools were not for newbies; they had to be earned. Death was never acknowledged. No one was asked to pay cash. When windows were blown out, room service continued unabated.'

Dibble didn't answer. He was slumped in an armchair, staring into the endless void of his now futureless life.

'But I don't hear any fucking mortars or missiles now, do you? So, why the hell is that hamburger and fries taking so long?'

Baines got up and walked to the window, pushing back the sliding drapes so that he could see the moving lights of the city.

'One of the problems we've got here, Richard, is that there's a meme that's been capturing headlines. Memes are like a genie: once they get out of the bottle, there's no way to put them back in it.'

Dibble turned towards him and brought his eyes into focus. They were red. His face looked like a punching bag. 'What do you mean? What meme?'

'Well, you know about the #MeToo movement, right? Some asshole film producer gets fingered for sexual harassment, and soon everyone who pushes his luck with a reluctant woman has to lose his job. #MeToo: that's a meme. Guilt by accusation. Another meme is pedophilia. White men in Asia: that's a meme. Sexual abuse in aid organizations: that's another. Oxfam, Save the Children, the UN and Red Cross: they've paved the way for you. Wear a charity T-shirt in Thailand or Cambodia right now, man, and they'll point the bone at you, believe me. So, that's what's going on here, and what you need to figure out is whether or not you're going to be the fatted calf that needs to be sacrificed by the World Health Organization.'

Dibble's voice was weak, not that he had been talking. His larynx was constricted with fear. 'I don't understand. Why have they let me go?' he croaked.

Baines turned and looked at him. 'They haven't let you go. They've given you a choice.'

'What choice?'

At that moment, room service arrived with the burger and fries that Baines had ordered, all nicely laid out on porcelain plates, with white laundered napkins and little pots of ketchup and American mustard. And thoughtfully, they'd even included a bottle of Coca-Cola in an ice bucket, which Baines hadn't ordered, but it made him smile, thinking that maybe it would go well later with a bourbon from the mini bar.

'This, I think, is where I come in,' he answered in reply to Dibble's question.

As he told it, it seemed to make sense. Actually, it didn't really matter whether it made sense fully or not; a man who's been thrown a lifeline doesn't stop to question whether it's made of braided flax or nylon. The question Dibble should have been asking was why the Vice Police had called Sinclair Baines once they knew the identity of the person they had in custody.

'Journalism is run like a restaurant kitchen,' he said, dabbing the fries in the ketchup. 'Every story is a dish, and every dish has a condiment and a plate of sides. They arrive hot and appetizing, capturing the guest's full attention. He digs in, his eagerness decreasing as his appetite is quickly satisfied. Then he starts thinking of the ice cream being spooned from the tub downstairs, the chocolate sauce being heated, and the choices to be made for breakfast to be delivered to his room in the morning, unaware of the sous-chefs starting their prep work for tomorrow's dining room buffet. That's before the half-eaten hamburger and the dirty plates have even been collected from the room on the twenty-seventh floor, where the customer is now tired of that meal he was served, his appetite jaded.'

Halfway into the hamburger, Baines pushed it aside. He wasn't really that hungry.

'That's journalism,' he said. 'One story runs into another, on a treadmill of endless production. Just like a hotel kitchen.'

Dibble had the look of a tired dog about to be euthanized. He waited.

'The story of a pedophile from the WHO being arrested for abusing a twelve-year-old girl is not a bad one, from the Vietnamese point of view. I mean, it shows them in a good light, protecting innocent children from being prey to predatory white men, etcetera, etcetera—but it's a snack rather than a meal, as far as that particular meme goes.'

He got up and went to the mini bar. Sure enough, there were two little bottles of Jack Daniels, and a nice whiskey glass with a solid base. He didn't need ice.

'No, the main meal—the reason they called me—is the one that involves the WHO's participation in the falsification of drug trials, and the magnification of epidemic statistics, because from the Vietnamese point of view, that story would be better written in a way that takes the spotlight of complicity away from Vietnamese agencies, and shines it on those corrupt Westerners who assume they run the show in every country they land in … and … and they already *know* that story is going to be written one way or the other, and that's why they phoned me and said, "Give your friend Mr Dibble from the WHO a choice."'

'What choice?'

'Give me enough evidence of the involvement of US and UK agencies in Nui BioLab's falsifying of research data, short-circuiting of safety trials, and complicity at every turn in the approval process, and you won't be put on trial for abusing the innocent children of Vietnam—for the whole world to see. Is that fair?'

The person who needed a stiff drink was Dibble. Did he drink bourbon? Yes, he was sure he did. Baines unscrewed one of the miniature bottles, poured it into a glass, and handed it to him. It went down in a single gulp.

'What if there is no such evidence?' Dibble asked. 'Suppose I give you copies from our files, and they fail to support your suspicions. What then?

The WHO is not the villain you believe it is. We employ thousands of people of all nationalities: scientists, public health experts, people dedicated to saving lives. Do you really believe they're all involved in some sort of grand conspiracy? I understand what drives you, Sinclair: you're a journalist, you want a big story, and you're determined to put corruption at the center of it, because that sells. But the real story is hard to accept because people can't get their heads around it.'

Baines took his glass and refilled it with the second mini bourbon. 'Here, have another. Now, tell me about this real story of yours.'

Dibble took a deep breath and downed the second shot. 'The real story is that viruses are designed for survival, even better than humans are. They mutate and cross species—whatever's necessary to continue living—and that makes them a constant threat to us. The WHO exists in order to deal with that threat, wherever it arises, anywhere in the world. We're just trying to stay ahead of it. That should be your story.'

Baines rummaged through the mini bar again. There was nothing else there that he fancied.

'Richard, I won't argue with you. That's a story that you guys never tire of putting out, and for the most part, I'm sure at some level, you believe it. Except you know—and I know—that this virus didn't just mutate and cross species of its own accord; it was deliberately helped along in a laboratory, remember? So, cut the crap.'

He could feel himself getting angry. How could this man cling to the line that he was fighting a threat to the world, while knowing that he was complicit in creating that threat?

'H5N1 doesn't kill people, you asshole!' he shouted. 'Unless you find the right spike gene to add to it. That's called deliberate genocide for profit.'

Dibble's head dropped.

'And it's the profiteers I'm after, Richard, and you people who aid and abet them—you slime bags who turn a blind eye, take the pay-off, and make the rules that don't apply to the rulers. It's a power and money game with big winners, and ordinary people are just the poor fucking pawns.'

'And what if it's impossible to prove?' The alcohol had given Dibble the courage to resist. 'What happens to me if you don't find what you want?'

'No, you've got that the wrong way around, Richard. It's what happens to you if *you* don't find what I want. You won't be leaving Vietnam; that's a given.'

THIRTY-FIVE

Two months later—autumn in New York. Possibly the nicest time of year: cool, clear, and dry, with leaves turning gold and fluttering to the ground, reminding denizens of the city that nature still ruled the earth. Especially if you lived on the Upper East Side overlooking the treescape of Central Park—which very few people did, because very few people could afford it.

Faraday watched the limousine pull away, then picked up his flight bag, negotiated the revolving glass door, and entered the pink-and-white atrium lobby of David Goode's apartment building. A sheet of pristine water ran noiselessly down a thirty-foot wall of polished white travertine and disappeared into a narrow slit in the pale pink marble floor. Behind a large rectangular slab of emerald-green glass, two youngish men in pale grey suits watched his advance towards them with expressions of utmost neutrality.

'I'm visiting Mr David Goode.'

'Of *course* you are. And you are…?'

'Anton Faraday.'

'Welcome, Mr Faraday.'

After a whispered exchange on their telephone, he was escorted to the elevator and accompanied on its journey upwards. There were no buttons in the elevator, so he had no knowledge of the floor number when the doors opened, and he was let out into a travertine-and-marble lobby in the same colors as the main entrance. The centerpiece of the space was a life-sized sculpture of a baseball player in the style of Giacometti. A pair of ten-foot-high wooden doors opened on the far side, and he was greeted by an older man this time, in a grey striped waistcoat, dark grey trousers, and a white shirt.

'Mr Faraday! Mr Goode is aware that you've arrived and will join you in a minute. My name is Michael, and I run the house. Are you on your own? We were expecting two of you. Let me show you to your room. Can I take your bag?'

'No, thank you.'

'Anything you want, Mr Faraday, just call out. "Hey, Michael!" will always find me.'

The bag was light—the visit was to be short—but it contained a hand grenade (figuratively), so it needed to stay with him. He laid it on the bed and opened it up, checking the carefully wrapped package buried in the middle of his clean underwear and shirts. Removing the bubble wrap, he smoothed the lid of the shallow box—chocolates, or a gift, perhaps? —and laid it on the bedside table, before taking his toiletries bag to the bathroom and freshening himself up.

With clean teeth and hair almost in place, Faraday took the package and nosed around the capacious apartment until he reached the room most obviously meant for socializing. Looking down and across the park to the towers on the Upper West Side and beyond into New Jersey, he realized the heights to which serious money could elevate someone. The fact that his old school friend was that someone was sobering—depressing, even.

He heard him coming in through the wooden doors from the elevator lobby. 'Anton, you bastard, where the hell are you? There you are! I was just upstairs on a call. Where's Caroline? I'm busting to meet her!'

He bounced in on immaculate white sneakers that matched his oversized white cashmere sweater. The buddy embrace fitted the setting, but was foreign to their years of English public school friendship. Faraday cleared his throat and smiled.

'Caroline took the limo on to her parents in New Jersey. Your driver said that would be okay. You'll get to meet her before we leave.'

'I'll hold you to it, buddy. Estrella is coming in from Long Island specifically so we can make a foursome. I've told her you'll be my best man, when it happens. I need you to make that real. I did tell you, didn't I?'

'No, you didn't. No trouble. Listen, I expected to be here hours ago, but the hold-ups at the airport were insane. We had to make declarations about whether we'd been on a farm in the last two months, or handled any raw poultry, or milked a live cow—or a dead one, presumably—and then they pounced on the fact that our passports had been stamped coming out of Laos, so we had to have our temperatures checked. Thank God we didn't have stamps from Vietnam. Your immigration people have been trained by the Third Reich—not helped by the fact that they're all wearing face masks, as if that would make any difference at all in the transmission of bird flu. It's started, David. It's started. The fearmongering is being ramped up. Our campaign to expose the Paladin Foundation can't come a minute too soon.'

'Well, that gives us something to celebrate. I don't know what you told those Paladin Foundation names, but it sure as hell seems to have worked. Have you seen the pharmaceutical stocks in the last two weeks? They've fallen like a ton of bricks, and none so heavily as Anglo Swiss. In fact, the Securities Exchange Commission has started asking questions. I can't wait to hear Van Heeren's answer. You did it, buddy. You paid the bastards back where it hurts the most.'

Try as he might, Faraday could not make the cultural shift needed to meet his oldest friend on this new ground. Was it the patina of money that was so evident all around him, the experience at the airport, or the sheer foreignness of New York?

'I brought you a present,' he said, handing David the decorated box. 'This is what those twelve hundred founding members received two weeks ago, delivered by hand.'

* * * *

The lid was decorated with a painting of a dead albatross lying on a windswept seashore. The painting was drawn from Faraday's back catalogue. In bold red letters, the box was embossed with *Lift the Lid.* Was it a brand, or an instruction? Inside the box was a beautifully printed letter on unheaded, watermarked parchment paper, addressed to {Title} {Surname}, {Home Address}, and with the salutation {Dear}{Title}{Surname}.

Beneath the letter was a USB memory stick mounted on a plain black card. The letter, which David Goode immediately read out loud, required him to adopt a formal tone.

Dear {Title}{Surname},
This letter is addressed to you as a founding member of the Paladin Foundation for the Environment. Its purpose is to invite you to make a choice between the moral and the financial implications of that membership, considering the change of circumstances we are about to reveal to you.

'Moral and financial implications… Well, okay, that would get my attention. Very British, if you don't mind me saying so.

'For context, please consider the current alarm around the potential for a worldwide pandemic of the supposed bird flu virus, H5N1, being signaled by the WHO and others, and the involvement of Anglo Swiss BioLab, of which you are a shareholder, directly or indirectly, according to public records.'

David looked up. 'Were they all shareholders in Anglo Swiss, or is that a good guess? I can't remember. Anyway…

'The USB memory stick enclosed gives you exclusive (personalized) access to an encrypted site containing information about Anglo Swiss and the Paladin Foundation, involving accusations of murder and fraud, which will become available to investigative journalists, health scientists, securities exchanges,

and law enforcement authorities worldwide in twenty days' time—that is to say, at 12:00 noon GMT on November 10th, next—'

David stopped reading out loud and spun around in alarm. 'Holy shit, Anton! I thought this was all about frightening related parties into selling their shares. Don't tell me you're planning on going public with what happened in Vietnam? You'll be crucified. Their lawyers will come for you with all guns blazing. I thought you were just going to…'

'Going to what?'

'I dunno… Expose the threat of insider trading, sweetheart dealing, that sort of thing—the stuff we ran on Hercules for you. I thought it was all about naming them as members of Paladin and revealing its connection to Anglo Swiss, you know, and then maybe if they'd been diving into shares ahead of the market, and … and…' David was clearly alarmed, but who for? 'That's what I thought, Anton. Not *this.*'

Faraday walked to the window and looked out over the real estate of Manhattan. Would they come with all guns blazing and succeed in crucifying them? Or was the evidence they'd assembled and the twenty days they'd given them to think about it sufficient in the grand scheme of things to make smart and calculating people, of the caliber represented by that list, choose to distance themselves from the volcano of shit that would erupt? That was the calculation they'd had to make.

'Read on,' he said, keeping his back turned.

*   *   *   *

Kate Manning's visit to his office in August had hung like a persistent cloud over Bryan Liddell for the rest of the week, depressing him. He'd rationalized in his own mind that his decision to sit on Caroline Brinkley's story was the only option. The fact that EANA couldn't survive the court action it would trigger was academic once Karim Farzan had given advance warning to Anglo Swiss BioLab, and they'd destroyed the credibility of her affidavits in advance. But that was only part of it. What he'd realized—the cause of his depression—was that he was not free to publish the truth. Like every other media organization, he was the mouthpiece of his proprietor. If he'd skirted around that realization during his years under the ownership of Wilton McGwyer, it was only because he'd never had cause for EANA to dig deep on anything that damaged its owners' interests. Oh, sure, he'd been mindful of the risk to Caroline, to her witnesses, and even to Sinclair Baines in Hanoi, but that risk would have ended quickly once the story was made public. Bottom line: it was the risk to EANA that wouldn't have gone away, until they'd been put out of business.

'The free press,' indeed!

Nothing changed until Baines came on the phone on a Sunday night to outline the nature of what he'd uncovered from a contact in the World Health Organization. He wouldn't reveal his source, and he was cautious about the relevance of some of the material he'd looked at—mainly because it was beyond his expertise—but he was giving notice to Liddell that they would need to have a plan for how to handle it.

'I'm not a science journalist, Bryan, and I wouldn't want to be responsible for analyzing this material. What's a "chimeric virus," for instance, and a "viral spike protein"? I don't even know the difference between biosafety levels two and three, so we're going to need to pull in some trusted expertise to help unravel this stuff. For instance, there's a heap of exchanges with the Harbin Research Institute, among others, all in Mandarin. I've got someone translating those for me now, and she seems pretty good, and she tells me that the Chinese language is actually easier to work with in science than English, for those who are fluent in both—more concise yet descriptive, apparently—but I'll have to wait for her to complete it, which will take at least a week. Are you with me so far?'

Liddell had been sitting at his kitchen table at the time, toying with the tail end of a bowl of spaghetti Bolognese. Tracey was upstairs, dealing with her daughter's outrage at having to go to sleep when other people in the house were wide awake. It was not an uplifting end to the weekend, which had singularly failed to be an uplifting end to a demoralizing week. And now this.

'If I was buying the story,' he said, with a deliberate tone of skepticism in his voice, 'how would you summarize it in one line?'

'Anglo Swiss, and/or others, designed a virus in a lab, so they could spread it around and create an emergency in a soft-touch country where they could operate with impunity, before rushing out a vaccine, making a mockery of safety trials and approvals, all with the cooperation and assistance of government agencies that are in on the game.'

'Why?'

'For fuck's sake, Bryan. *Why?* Money! Power! Control! For Big Pharma and its investor sponsors and government enablers, it's a closed ecosystem with guaranteed deliverables. It's what Caroline's brother warned us was happening.'

'And who's going to stop them?'

There was a long silence, broken only by the sound of Liddell sucking the last strand of spaghetti into his mouth, then pushing his empty plate away from himself across the wooden table.

Baines sighed. 'Not us, by the sounds of it.'

* * * *

David Goode continued to read, slowly now, dwelling carefully on every word.

The site is fully encrypted, and access can only be granted using the password encoded on the attached USB stick at the Lift the Lid address, which will be automatically connected when you insert the stick into your computer, either with or without your internet browser open.

'The material on the site falls into four categories…

'Shit, Anton, it's sounding like some sort of scam. The first thing I'd say is there's no way I'm logging in to an unknown site with a password over which I have no control. If I received this, I'd throw it in the trash can.'

'No, you wouldn't. You'd read it to the end, and you'd know you have just twenty days to do something about it. So, read on.'

'FILE ONE: From the research laboratories of Nui BioLab (a subsidiary of Anglo Swiss BioLab AG), the complete genome sequencing for the combining of the avian influenza virus A (H5N1) with a zoonotic animal-to-human respiratory virus derived from secret gain-of-function work undertaken at the Harbin Research Institute in China, together with the parallel product development, human testing, and approval submissions for the vaccine VAXX-Avia conducted by Nui BioLab. For your convenience, the files are provided with a three-page layman's abstract and conclusion.

The complete files run to 0.85 GB of data and will be made available to all leading academic institutions with virology and epidemiology departments, as well as to international research foundations and the leading science journals in North America, the United Kingdom, and Europe, with free public access effective as of 12:00 noon GMT on November 10th next.

'That's a hell of a threat, Anton. You do know who controls research funding, and the science press, I presume? Do you think any of them will have the courage to break ranks?'

Without waiting for a reply, he raised his head and shouted, 'Hey, Michael! I need you.' He turned to Faraday. 'I need a fucking drink. What do you want? Beer, wine, bourbon?'

'Just a coffee.'

'Just a coffee? I need something to help me get my head around what you're doing here. Is this the stuff that what's his name—Caroline's brother—was working on? How did he get it out? Weren't they after him?'

'Tuan is his name. He had someone on the inside helping him.'

'Mr Goode…?' Michael appeared in the doorway.

'Michael, we need drinks. Two Irish coffees, please. Strong. We'll eat in tonight. Make it early. And no calls, not even Estrada. No one. *Nada. No estoy en casa.* Shit almighty… So, he's lifted the curtain, has he? Do I have to read it to know what accusations he's making?'

Faraday shook his head. 'Surely you can read between the lines? Read on.'

'FILE TWO: Evidence alleging that the epidemic of avian flu that swept through Northern Vietnam and the Guangxi and Yunnan regions of South China, affecting an estimated 15,000 people to date, was deliberately spread. Affidavits from three key witnesses (one of whom has since been murdered) name the parties responsible as the Swiss pharmaceutical giant, Anglo Swiss BioLab AG, and its Vietnam subsidiary, Nui BioLab, together with Swiss-based NGO The Paladin Foundation for the Environment, whose chairman, Charles Van Heeren, is also chairman of Anglo Swiss BioLab.

'The accusations allege that the virus was deliberately spread through the highlands and the bordering regions of South China, allowing large-scale clinical trials to be undertaken by Nui BioLab with the cooperation of local authorities and hospitals—trials that have since convinced the WHO, the United States Food and Drug Administration, and health agencies in the UK and Europe to fast-track approvals for licensing of the antiviral drug, CD8Magna, and the VAXX-Avia vaccine marketed by Anglo Swiss Biolab. These affidavits will be released to the world's news media, and charges will be laid with police authorities, with free public access effective as of 12:00 noon GMT on November 10th next.'

THIRTY-SIX

The impossible made possible, Baines had thought—that's what the tombstone should say when this story was finally laid to rest.

It had been made possible by the simple fact that Dibble did not want to go to jail. The sin that had tempted him had always had the intention of destroying him, because that was the nature of sins like that. They never went away. No matter how he repented, he would always be a recidivist. It was in his DNA. So, he hadn't tried to fight it. When he'd delivered the first tranche of the WHO's emails to Baines, he'd known it was merely a down payment on the wages of sin. More would be required, and more would follow before Dibble would be allowed to resign in ill health and quietly return to Canada, where no one knew he was a pedophile.

If any of this had troubled Baines, he only had to remember that the people he was reporting on thought nothing of human life, and they would happily kill him if they knew what he was assembling—which was nothing less than a paper trail of institutionalized corruption.

'Perhaps it is corruption,' Dibble had acknowledged, 'but some would argue that the ends justify the means, if the end is getting a vaccine into circulation quickly. They see it as providing a universal good.'

Baines had shaken his head in disbelief. It had helped that his indignation didn't need to be forced. 'Even to be able to say that,' he spluttered, 'shows you have no understanding of right and wrong, Richard. And I'm not talking about your sexual proclivities.'

'What do you intend on doing?' Dibble had asked meekly.

'I'm sending all these files to an encrypted site, where I'll get someone to work on them. What I do after that depends on what we find. If there's anything in there that involves you, and you've redacted your name or tried to hide your involvement, that'll be a sure giveaway that you're the person behind the leak. So, don't even try it. We're used to protecting whistle-blowers, as long as they do what they're told.'

Dibble looked far from reassured. 'If they trace it back to me, I'm a…'

'Yeah, say it,' Baines prompted: 'you're a dead man. But they aren't going to trace it back to you, because that isn't in my interest. My interest is in getting my hands on everything you have access to—and keeping you out of jail. Got it?'

It had been tempting to tell the man not to worry, but the truth was that it would be safer for both of them if he remained very worried.

Baines had taken the files home to go through them undisturbed. What was the premise of the story he wanted to tell? The premise was that the rules around research, testing, approval, and registration of new drugs had been broken, with the cooperation of the authorities charged with policing them. Starting with the timelines, the premise already looked clear-cut. Something that should have taken ten or twelve years had been done in less than two. The work he needed to do was to identify the parties who had participated in the process, and highlight the evidence. But it wasn't just one story, he'd realized; it was likely to prove a treasure trove of stories. That was why he'd gone out on a limb to get Caroline Brinkley. Not only was she an integral part of the story already, she had the bonus of an extra resource in her brother, Tuan.

When he came across the files in Mandarin, he felt certain that an extra dimension had been added to his starting premise. Miss Anh had told him that, in many ways, the Chinese language was better suited to science, but the WHO used English as its official language. Why had these documents not been translated, then? Or perhaps they had, but not in Dibble's office.

Realizing that Miss Anh was far too well qualified to be doing dogsbody duties in the EANA office, as Koi had suggested, he'd phoned the translating company he often used and sold them on the idea of giving her part-time work. The reports back suggested that they were mightily impressed with her. So, he had to consider: could he give sensitive documents, like the ones he'd received from Dibble, to an agency to translate, or should he take a punt on Miss Anh?

Impatient to know what those enigmatic files contained, he'd phoned his office and told them to track her down, bring a laptop, and come at once to his apartment. The thought of working with her lifted his spirits.

* * * *

The decision to meet with Bryan Liddell in person had been a difficult one for Caroline. Though she'd accepted the job as a full-time staffer at EANA, the offer had been made by Sinclair Baines in Hanoi, not by the head office in London—of which she remained suspicious, for obvious reasons. But now that he'd found a source at the WHO, Baines had persuaded her to talk with Liddell and have things out with him.

'I can't blame you for being pissed at what's happened, Caroline,' Baines said, 'but so is Bryan. Have it out with him. I need you to work on this WHO stuff with me. Whether it's tomorrow, or further down the track, it's going to go public, I swear. Find a way. Read it. Get angry. Nail the bastards. Let Bryan see who he's dealing with. I've gone out on a limb for this stuff. Even if it means quitting EANA, we can't stop now.'

She'd read enough of the file he sent her to know he was right. It needed judicious editing, but she was sure it would prove to be damning. And what sort of journalist would she have been if her willingness to investigate a story depended on a guarantee in advance that it would be published just the way she wanted? *There are two types of journalists,* her father had told her, when she'd first announced her ambition: *lapdogs and watchdogs. What do you want to be?'* The question hadn't needed an answer. She was her father's daughter. And the thing that capped it off for her and Anton was the discovery of correspondence implicating the US Embassy and Sam McAvoy, the 'information officer' who had arranged their fateful boat trip on Halong Bay.

So, mid-morning on a Wednesday, she'd caught the tube from Kensington High Street to Temple. Liddell had offered to buy her lunch, but she'd wanted a meeting behind closed doors, in an office, with no distractions from what needed to be said.

Catching the Underground proved a challenge in itself. She didn't know London, so she wasn't at ease with it: the currency, the accents, the assumption that you knew what you were doing—let alone the imagined threats that had lain beyond Anton's locked front door since the day they'd come in from Suffolk. Anton had offered to come with her, but she'd scoffed at the thought. Then she'd hit the ticket machine and the Tube map. When a manned ticket office came free, she said where she wanted to go, and was told to go back to the machine. A Muslim woman who barely spoke English did it for her.

From Temple to Wine Office Court, off Shoe Lane in Fleet Street, she followed Google Maps on her phone, arriving ten minutes later than she'd planned, but proud of herself, nonetheless.

Liddell was not at all what she'd expected. He was rumpled and thoughtful, like a slow-moving dog, wary of unnecessary action. She'd expected someone sharp and dismissive, and certainly more aloof: a hard-nosed newsroom boss.

He didn't stand up, but leaned forward to offer his hand with a welcoming smile. 'Close the door, will you, love?' His voice was as mild as his manner. 'It's good to meet you at last. I understand you're one of us now, despite the way you've been treated. Have you forgiven us for having no balls, or are you hoping to see us grow some?'

'The latter.'

He laughed softly. 'Sinclair Baines warned me. Did you know he took a pay cut to fit you into his office salary cap?'

'No.'

'Don't tell him that I told you. We live hand-to-mouth in the news business these days. It's just one of the things we have to be embarrassed about.'

'What are the others?'

He didn't laugh that time. 'Okay, let's get it out, shall we? I'm not going to release a story that will see us put out of business. That's the reality under our present structure. Unless you can find a new owner for us with bottomless pockets and no fear, my policy here has been to keep everyone employed and live to fight another day. There are lots of hills to die on in the world of journalism, but when you willingly write your own epitaph, it's the last thing you'll ever write.'

'What about this WHO story?' she asked. 'Am I wasting my time?'

'Write it.'

'It's Anglo Swiss. The same thing will happen.'

'Write it, Caroline. Write it.'

'It needs a science reporter. Haven't you got one?'

'Trust the science—is that what you're thinking?' He finally stirred himself into something resembling action, pushing himself up out of his chair and looking around for somewhere to march: a hill to climb, perhaps. 'We don't do science reporting; we're a news agency. Nobody games the publish-or-perish system like science writers. It's a set-up designed to incentivize fraud. We do the simple stuff. We lift the lid and say, "Oh, shit, what have we got here? Who'd have thought?"' He flapped his arms like a penguin, or a smoker who had lost his pack. 'The WHO leak is not one story; it's a whole string of them, is my bet. Handle it right, and it'll keep us going for months, maybe years. What it needs is a reporter with a sense of smell. That's you, according to Sinclair Baines. Is he right, or has he got you wrong?'

'What's the point if you end up being scared to publish?'

'We'll find a way. I'm working on it.'

They glared at each other. Her eyes were dark and shining, like two nuggets of polished obsidian. His were occluded, like a whale used to seeing under water. He seemed to be looking into her rather than at her. As he stood over her, she was unsure whether he was going to hit her or hug her.

Then he looked up and raised his voice. 'Megan,' he shouted, 'a minute, please.'

The woman who entered the room from the adjacent office was fiftyish, modestly dressed, and pleasant-looking, but her personality—if she had one—was almost entirely hidden from sight. *She's waiting*, Caroline thought. *Wow, how does she do that? She's mastered the art of showing nothing. Now, that's a skill.*

Caroline got to her feet and tried to do the same. It was too hard. She offered her hand instead.

'I'm Caroline Brinkley.'

'This is Megan Hastel, our financial controller and IT manager,' Liddell explained. 'She wanted to meet you.'

Megan took her hand and shook it formally. 'How do you do. I'm the person who exposed your story on Paladin to the person who gave it to Anglo Swiss BioLab. I wanted to apologize to you, and see if it's possible to set up a way of working for you that's secure to the point of being impenetrable.'

* * * *

David Goode's mood was perceptibly changing the more he read.

'Okay, let's continue.

'FILE THREE: Files released by whistle-blowers at the World Health Organization reveal that modification of the H5N1 flu virus to enhance its transmissibility to mammals was undertaken at the Harbin Research Institute, in cooperation with Nui BioLab in Hanoi, in a program funded by US and UK government agencies.

'Oh, boy!' he exclaimed. 'So, you've decided to take on the whole world.

'Correspondence to and from the WHO reveals a trail of falsified laboratory research findings, inadequate or fraudulent safety testing, and a conspiracy to green-light approvals for Nui BioLab's vaccine and anti-viral drug, involving state agencies at the very highest levels. Unredacted copies of the material obtained will be published on the Lift the Lid site at 12:00 noon GMT on November 10th next, with full open access granted to the media.'

Michael arrived bearing a tray with two cups, a plunger of black coffee, and a bottle of Baileys Irish cream liqueur.

Faraday picked up the bottle and read the label. '"Pure Irish cream and triple-distilled Irish whiskey." I can see why you drink your coffee this way. Couldn't you get a decent espresso machine, instead of this plunger crap?'

'Americans don't do coffee. Besides, I have a taste for Baileys. Since when did you become such a wowser, anyway? I've never known you to refuse a drink.'

Faraday thought about that. 'Living alone,' he said. 'Getting older. Then meeting up with Caroline. She hardly drinks a drop. It was different when we were young.'

He watched David fill his cup: half coffee, half liqueur. He already had a sinking feeling that his decision to make this trip from London had been ill thought out. The world of money was foreign to him, and no matter how careful he was, he had a suspicion that their friendship might not be enough to bridge the gap in their respective views on life, when it came to the crunch. And the crunch was coming.

'Okay,' he said, 'I'll join you. Why not? But before you continue with the letter, I want to remind you of what you supplied me from your Hercules search engine. I said I wanted to know what tied these twelve hundred people together. Why them specifically, who are they, and what did they get from it that required such secrecy? You looked at the list and guessed it was money. But you *would* say that, because that's how you think: *money*.'

David spluttered. 'Don't make it sound so dirty. That's the way the world operates. Besides, I was right.'

'Not everyone with an environmental agenda is doing it to make money. Some of them have spent years in public life speaking up for the planet.'

'At the risk of shattering your naive faith in humanity, Anton, I think I need to explain something to you. Take the history of Western wealth in the last two hundred years. First a Scotsman invented the steam engine, and then there were steam trains, and the government cleared the way to enable tracks to be laid right across the country, so railroad tycoons could make their fortunes. And in return, the tycoons decided who would be elected. Got it?'

Suddenly, a basketball appeared in his hands. Where it came from was a mystery to Faraday, but it appeared to be a device for dictating the pace of his friend's thoughts, which were accumulating rapidly. The sound of his white sneakers squealing on the pink marble floor as he twisted and jiggled in pursuit of the bouncing ball punctuated what quickly turned into a lecture.

'Then there were automobiles, right? Ford and Daimler, and whoever, and governments rushed to build roads all over the country, so car manufacturers could make their obscene fortunes—and they gave out drilling licenses, so the oil barons could make fortunes, too. And the money flowed both ways until the government and bureaucracy became essential arms of big business, each dependent on the other. Then Bill invented personal computing, and Berners-Lee invented the internet, and IT and the digital age spawned the social media oligarchs, and they've become so embedded in Washington that nobody knows who owns who. But we sure as hell know the money that's involved: it's *trillions*. Got it so far?'

He spun around and faked throwing a pass, causing Faraday to spill his coffee.

'Leave it. Michael will clean it up. Where was I…? Ah, yes… Then along comes climate change and the green agenda. Well, whoop-de-do! Do you know how many trillions in subsidies, grants, tax concessions, and bribes are being doled out by governments in this new fucking great gravy train? The clean fuel spending bonanza is so big that even the oil companies have jumped on board. And there isn't a laboratory or university department in the country that could financially survive without signing up for the doctrine that the Earth's survival depends on achieving zero carbon emissions—*no matter what the cost.*' He stopped bouncing the ball. 'Yet *you* say it isn't all about the money.'

Faraday put his coffee cup down. 'Alright,' he conceded, 'maybe I'm saying that it doesn't have to be *only* the money that motivates people. There can be other motives. To believe that it's all about money leads to an acceptance that money justifies any and all behavior.'

'I didn't say that.' David started bouncing the ball again. 'Though in some people's minds, it clearly does. People like Charles Van Heeren, for instance, who, according to you, thinks any means is justified by the ends, if it means creating a market for a vaccine. Hell, you must know that. Look at the evidence you've produced.'

Faraday walked to the window. It really was so beautiful, that park. Man and nature had got together and created a quality that neither was quite capable of alone. Or was it just mankind doing what it always seemed driven to do—manipulating everything, even beauty, to fit its own desires, not content unless it showed evidence of mankind's powers of control?

'Well, I have to hope that it isn't just the money for everyone,' he said quietly, 'because if it is, I've made a bad mistake.'

'Why? What else are you relying on? You've seen the sell-off from pharma stocks that you've triggered. That's your insiders distancing themselves in case the flack starts flying—which it definitely will, now that I see what you've released. What else are you hoping for?'

'Well...' This was the key question, and Faraday had to think carefully, because he still hadn't got it right in his mind. 'What else motivates people who are successful, and have everything that money can buy? Pride? Reputation? The respect of their family and peers? Public respect, too? Ego, maybe? You remember how I asked specifically if Hercules could identify media ownership and college grants…?'

'Yeah, and it was a hell of an ask in the time available. Those are not normal first-up search criteria for us.'

'I appreciate that, but when you read Section Four, you'll get an idea of why I felt it was so important. What the science media write, and what the research scientists endorse or deny, is driven by the source of their funding. If the leading scientists and science journals are mobilized to attack the material we're releasing, then mainstream media will follow. But if those attacks can be tied back to the individuals we've named, with Hercules's help, then it's out in the open. My hope is that they'll put their reputations first and not want that.'

David stopped dribbling the basketball, then turned and shot it to him. This time he was ready.

'Geez, I hope you're right, buddy, because you and your friends are in for the fight of your lives—and if you're wrong, I don't know who's going to help you. Now, let me finish reading this.'

THIRTY-SEVEN

Megan Hastel was not devoid of personality, despite first impressions. She simply had a manner that kept herself to herself. Whether or not her life experience had shaped her to be that way, she had evidently decided that it suited her. The contrast with Caroline could not have been greater, and no one was more aware of that than Caroline herself. So, when they were encouraged by Liddell to adjourn to Megan's office in order to discuss what could be done about safeguarding the files from Hanoi, there was an awkwardness between them, not helped by Megan's admission that she was responsible for the betrayal of confidential information to Anglo Swiss BioLab.

'Listen,' Caroline began, 'I've gotta lay it on the table. You didn't just kill a story that needs telling; you could easily have had the people risking themselves to tell that story killed as well. So, why should I give you a chance to do it again? I won't sugar-coat it. Where I come from, we are very unforgiving of traitors. Know what I mean?'

It should have been enough to make Megan shift uneasily in her chair. She didn't. She seemed unmoved. 'I do know what you mean,' she said.

Caroline waited. 'That's all?' she asked. 'That's all you want to say about it?'

'No,' Megan replied. 'I want to say what I said to Bryan.'

'Which was…?'

'I was employed by EANA's owner, Wilton McGwyer, as financial controller and IT systems manager, and part of my job description was to set up a reporting system that would allow the parent company to be copied on breaking stories, so they were informed of what was happening. That didn't seem like an unusual request to me, as they are the owner, after all. However, there was no easy way of keeping track of what was passing through the newsroom that didn't involve a lot of time-consuming work on my part. The mistake I made was in deciding that the server address used by Bryan's desktop computer was the one place where all stories ultimately landed, and this was the address that I provided as a link to Karim Farzan's office at Wilton McGwyer.'

'Without Bryan's knowledge?'

'Yes.'

Caroline clapped her hands in disbelief. 'What did he say when he found out?'

'Well, Caroline, I have to say, it was one of the worst moments of my life. He… Well, let me just say this. I have never worked in an organization where the owner did not have access to the company's information. I've worked in IT, and at a leading university, and there was always a clear distinction between someone's personal domain address and that of the employer. I was only interested in saving myself unnecessary work, and I knew that Bryan saw everything submitted for publication, so I presumed Wilton McGwyer would be entitled to it. Unfortunately, my feed picked up his personal domain correspondence as well, and what I didn't understand was the nature of journalism—how stories develop, and the need to protect confidentiality and sources. I was completely naïve.'

'Beats me why he didn't fire you on the spot,' Caroline replied. 'I would have.'

Megan smiled in agreement. There was nothing meek about her, Caroline realized. She wasn't offering excuses, but was willingly admitting that she'd screwed up.

'You ask what Bryan had to say,' she went on. 'He's a very unusual man, I have to say. He said it was his fault entirely: he's a technology dinosaur, and he brought it on himself. Then he asked me if I'd be prepared to come up with a system that could guarantee the safety and privacy of journalists' communications, which I said was easy. So, that's what I've done. But also, he said he wants us to take it to a new level, so we can offer guaranteed anonymity to secret sources, like whistle-blowers, and allow EANA to become a first choice for people wanting to anonymously leak information. He wants us to become a safer, user-friendly version of BlowSafe or GAIF— you know, the Global Alliance of Investigative Freelancers. He's really excited by the idea.'

'Wow! What does Wilton McGwyer think about that? Those sites rely on donors. EANA is a commercial agency.'

Caroline caught her thoughts and didn't like where they were heading. 'Hang on,' she objected, 'I've only just gotten a full-time contract. This could throw me back on the freelance trash heap. Does Bryan know what he's doing?'

For the first time, Megan appeared embarrassed. She pursed her lips and looked away before resolving to confront Caroline with the truth.

'That's exactly how Bryan describes EANA: "a freelance trash heap." He's not being rude about the quality of the journalists, like yourself, who work for us, but he says that's the place EANA occupies in the industry. And the industry is changing at such a rapid pace that the legacy print media will soon be dead, and hoping to make money out of running an independent news agency is what you Americans call a zero-sum game. Newspapers like *The Guardian*, *The New York Times*, and *The Washington Post* are political propaganda sheets. They peddle opinion, and pay nothing for our news stories, preferring to pick them up for free online. In the digital age, everything is ransacked free of charge. As we've found out, Wilton McGwyer didn't acquire EANA for its earnings; there aren't any. It acquired it to obtain inside knowledge of events from which it can prosper. And like all media proprietors, it controls content to suit its cause. Hence, the Anglo Swiss BioLab fiasco.'

She paused and waited. What she was saying was made more brutal by the mild manner and softness of her tone. Caroline wondered whether Liddell was using her as the messenger to soften up staff to the inevitability of the company being closed down. The case for its survival in its current form appeared to be impossible to make.

'So, where does that leave us?' Caroline asked bluntly. 'We produce stories that no one wants to buy, or that our owner wants to suppress. Is this a rehearsal for Bryan's retirement speech, or is he serious about going down the investigative journalism route and turning us into the scourge of corruption?'

Megan laughed. She was relieved that Caroline accepted the stark reality of their situation.

'"The scourge of corruption." I like that. I'm sure Bryan would like that, too.' She sat up to make herself more businesslike, hands crossed on her desktop. 'It seems that Bryan has had this idea in mind for quite some time. He and Steve Roach—who is a well-known investigative journalist, I think you could call him, and a long-standing friend—had observed the BlowSafe and GAIF models and concluded that they could be done better with some judicious twists. By "better," they meant technically more effective, and financially more rewarding. Steve Roach has donors in mind, and you and Sinclair Baines are the first to be told. My job is to convince you that we have the systems to allow stories like yours to be broadcast to the world safely. Bryan and Steve's job is to convince you that they have the backing to ensure you'll be paid.'

'And Wilton McGwyer…?'

'My interpretation of EANA's latest financial statements is that the company is insolvent and should be wound up. I doubt they will disagree when it's explained to them.'

* * * *

When Caroline described to Faraday the operating system that Megan had designed for a fully secure investigative journalism site, he recognized immediately that this was the device that would allow them to safely expose the crimes surrounding the manufacture and release of the bird flu virus, without fear of their claims being buried or subverted. The ability to receive and store encrypted information and messaging, which could only be decrypted on an air-gapped machine that never connected to any networks, was at the heart of it. But the key lay in the more than 850 investigative journalists worldwide who were members of the Global Alliance of Investigative Freelancers, and of BlowSafe, all of whom were professional, accredited journalists dedicated to exposing wrongdoing by corporations and government agencies anywhere in the world, regardless of politics. They were truth-seekers en masse, and unlike the corporate media, their drive was to expose corruption, not bury it.

'So, that's what you had in mind when you showed me your list of Paladin Foundation members in London,' David said, after Faraday explained his plan to him two months later in New York. 'You found a way of letting them know that their connection to Anglo Swiss via Paladin would have the spotlight turned on them in twenty days' time, unless they… Hang on… Unless they what…?'

'There isn't an *unless*,' Faraday replied. 'They have time to try and hide their tracks if they've been trading on privileged information. You've already seen that from the evidence of shares being dumped. But the most important outcome, from my point of view, is that the spotlight will turn on any influence they may have over media—scientific journals and academic researchers attempting to cancel or discredit the evidence. Which is compelling—compelling enough to make dedicated journos want to investigate further, and that may cause our Paladin elites to take a look at their investments that profit downstream from frauds like this, and decide whether or not they want to be seen holding them in future. And you know what they are, I don't need to tell you: the vaccine manufacturers, the medical supply companies, the hospitals, insurance companies, and medical practices. Hell, maybe they'll even be persuaded to distance themselves from the government and international agencies that are complicit in this shit. It's worth a go, David. Wouldn't you agree?'

David picked up his basketball and started bouncing it again. He wasn't sure. The ball bounced slowly, erratically, sometimes soft, sometimes hard. Did he agree, or disagree? Maybe that wasn't what he was thinking. The ball bounced faster, and his nine-hundred-dollar sneakers squeaked on the polished marble floor. He made to shoot, but didn't.

'You were always a fucking idealist, Anton,' he said, almost sadly. 'You and your sentimental soft spot for wild animals got you sucked into those Paladin people in the first place, and the money made you soft and hate yourself for not doing something better. Now here you are, twenty years later, taking on the most powerful people in the world, like you've just discovered corruption for the first time in your life, and you want to prove to your young lady that you're a fighter for justice and a selfless warrior, no matter the consequences.'

'That's what you think, is it?'

'Yes, that's what I think. And I love you for it.' With that, he shot the basketball at Faraday and got him, full frontal, in the head, which caused both of them to break out laughing and see who could hit the other hardest, like two schoolboys.

'Okay,' David said, surrendering at last, 'let's read the last bit of this goddamn letter of yours.'

*　*　*　*

FILE FOUR: This file lists the founding members of the Paladin Foundation for the Environment, of which you are one. Your major business interests and investments are detailed, including industry, political, academic, and foundation affiliations known in the public domain, which may have links, subject to further investigation, to matters referred to in Files One to Three above. This file, together with similar files for all 1200 founding members of Paladin, will be provided to the more than 850 investigative journalists worldwide who are members of the Global Alliance of Investigative Freelancers (GAIF), and of BlowSafe. Those files will be made available to them at 12:00 noon GMT on November 10th next.

Should you have additions or corrections you wish to advise to us in respect to any of the files posted on our secure site, please add these in the COMMENTS section. Your comments will be fully encrypted and unable to be read, except by the Lift the Lid site administrator, who will respond to you privately. No communication between yourself and Lift the Lid will be made public unless you request it.

Lift the Lid is a not-for-profit organization facilitating investigative journalism in a secure environment free of commercial and political bias or pressure.

DONATE

If you agree with the aims of our organization in the pursuit of unbiased truth, please support us by becoming a donor via the DONATE button in the COMMENTS section. Your donation will be anonymous, unless you elect otherwise. Thank you for your support in helping expose corruption.

'You cheeky bastard.' David chortled quietly. 'I'm surprised you didn't apologize for ruining their appetites.'

THIRTY-EIGHT

Michael was a Michelin-starred chef. Of course. And a master of wine. He'd whipped up something quick and simple, starting with white asparagus in a Hollandaise sauce with a glass of chilled Meursault. It was to be followed by a skinned and boned Atlantic salmon with a Demerara sugar glaze.

'How the hell will Estrella ever compete with this?' Faraday asked.

'She won't have to,' David responded. 'If it comes to a choice, Michael stays. Besides, being beautiful is a full-time job. Beautiful women don't cook, particularly in New York.'

'What happens when beauty fades?'

'The pre-nup kicks in.'

'Does she know that?'

'They all know that. This is America. Have you got an agreement with Caroline?'

'No. She'd rather be free to come or to go. No ties either way.'

'Get it in writing, and don't use invisible ink. Now, tell me why you came to see me four days before this story of yours goes public. Something's in play; otherwise you wouldn't have dragged yourself across the Atlantic at such an important time. What am I missing?'

Faraday took a thirsty swig of his Meursault and wiped his mouth. The sinking feeling returned. Had he thought this thing out properly?

He started slowly. 'When we became friends at boarding school, we came from very different backgrounds. You were a North London Jew, and I was a colonial from Rhodesia. But we had one thing in common: neither of us was from the Hooray Henry establishment set. We were outsiders, and our motto was "Fuck 'em!" We've stayed friends because we have that in common, even though we've barely seen each other in the last twenty years, and our lives are so different now that we might as well be aliens. You're right: I'm a sentimental fucking idealist, and you're a hard-nosed, money-making New York Jew. How could any two people be more different? But here we are.'

'Because…?'

'The more I looked at that list of plutocrats on the Paladin list, the more I came to realize that money wasn't the only scorecard they kept. Once he's got a few million dollars, the average hard-working Joe is happy to throw down his cards and walk away to an easier life. But not the plutocrat. The plutocrat wants power, prestige, and a place at the top table. Money just provides the bottom rungs of the ladder that lead him towards the top. It was that realization that led me to formulate the strategy to speak to them the way I have. Will it work? I guess we'll find out in a few days' time.'

David watched him closely. He, too, wondered whether Faraday had thought this thing out. Or maybe he was anticipating something different, and he wasn't hearing it.

'You went off-piste there, buddy, as we say in Aspen. You were waxing lyrical about how different we are, and I was waiting for you to tell me why you'd come here four days before your big unveiling. More wine?'

Michael arrived with the glazed salmon, and of course, a change of wine.

'A *Côte de Rhône*, Mr Faraday?'

'Thank you.'

Faraday picked it up, sniffed it, and put it down again. He frowned. It wasn't a *Côte de Rhône* he needed; it was clarity.

'When I looked at that list,' he continued, 'I thought of you, maybe a few years from now. I don't know what rung you're on, but looking around, I suspect it's getting up there. And your outfit, Hoffman, Latrobe, and

Goode, is certainly way up there, chasing the BlackRocks and the Morgan Stanleys in funds under management, so it was no surprise to see that your chairman was on the Paladin list, but a much bigger surprise that you never mentioned it.'

David shrugged and focused on his salmon, which he poked at without eating. He cleared his throat unnecessarily. 'A big surprise to me, as well. I mean, there isn't much that he's not hooked into: networking in Davos, the Aspen Institute, the Rockefeller Foundation… Of course, he never mentioned Paladin, because secrecy is the Paladin thing, as you keep pointing out.'

It was the response Faraday had expected. 'Anyway, that isn't why I'm here,' he continued. 'You've done me a great favor providing that Hercules research, and I wanted to thank you for that. It's the crowbar that may help to prize the lid open. I hope that doesn't put you offside with Hoffman, because it's exposed him in the process.'

David raised his glass, seemingly unconcerned. 'If he's got anything to hide, he'll know how to hide it. Look, Hercules is the best in the business, but it can only go so deep before it gets entangled in the weeds. People at the Paladin level have so many layers of beneficial owners and intermediaries that it's difficult to unravel them. That's why I told you that insider trading is so difficult to prove and prosecute. Beneficial shareholders can have their stocks held by intermediary brokers—we refer to them as shares in "street name"—where they're generally held in electronic form through a depository trust company. They may be "lent" by the brokerage firm to cover other trading activities, such as short sells, and the issuer of the stocks will have no visibility of them. Effectively, they're impossible to identify. And that's before we start looking at blind trusts, and the complexities of offshore exchanges like Frankfurt, London, and Paris, who all have different registration rules. We can get to them eventually, but it takes a lot of work.'

He put his glass down and started eating again. 'What do you think of Michael's food?'

'I hope you've got a binding pre-nup with him.'

David laughed ironically, but his eyes showed that he was still waiting for the real purpose of Faraday's trip to New York to be revealed.

'Okay, so you came all this way to thank me,' he continued. 'I hope it proves helpful and your strategy works. I have a feeling that it will. Then what? What are your plans for life after the big fraud bust? Back to painting wildlife?'

'Probably not,' Faraday replied. 'I feel it's time to move on to a different genre. As a matter of fact, there's something I was going to raise with you. You remember that guy, Lance, the neighboring farmer at Marsh Cottage, yes? Well, he rang and told me that he's putting his five hundred acres up for sale, and asked would I be interested, as he seems to think I know something about farming, I guess.'

'Well, that's true—you even know the body temperature of cows. So, what did you say?'

'I told him I'd think about it. I'm interested, but he intends on keeping his house. And that made me wonder if you'd be prepared to sell a half share in Marsh Cottage. I'd do it up—new plumbing and all that sort of thing—and you'd be able to come whenever it suits you. What do you think?'

David put down his cutlery and knocked back his wine. His expression was a mixture of surprise and relief. 'So, that's why you came over. Great! But I'll need time to think about it. This is kinda sudden.'

'Sure. There's no hurry. It was just a thought. But... Returning to this insider trading issue for a minute, do you think there's any possibility that, if I gave you two names, your people might be able to identify any trades in the last few months that could be linked to the Anglo Swiss BioLab announcements of their vaccine approvals? I know it's a big ask, but it would be the biggest favor you could do for me—before November tenth.'

'Shit! So, that's why you're here. Who are they?'

'Karim Farzan of Wilton McGwyer, and Charles Van Heeren.'

'Why?'

'Insurance. Just in case.'

'It's a big ask, Anton. It isn't like you to make big asks. In fact, until now, you've never asked me for anything in your life. If you recall, the Hercules thing was my offer to you, because you didn't even know it was possible. Now you come up with two big asks in a row. It's no problem, but it's taking me a moment to adjust, buddy.'

Faraday pushed aside his partially eaten salmon. 'I'm up against it,' he admitted, 'and I may be out of my depth. That's why I'm turning to you. Truth is, I didn't know anything about the financial world when I stumbled on this thing in Vietnam. When people said money was at the root of everything, I had only the vaguest idea of what they meant. Saying my friend David Goode is in the money business was as meaningless as saying his friend Anton Faraday was in the wildlife business. But there were some things about it that did seem obvious. For instance, when I saw the share prices of Big Pharma start to plummet after we sent out our letter from Lift the Lid, I realized that for people to be selling, someone had to be buying. I knew what the sellers knew, but what did the buyer know? Because isn't it true that in a market filled with sellers, it's the buyer that sets the price? Then someone who knows more than me said someone is shorting. So, I looked that up and learned that shorting is when you borrow stock from a broker, expecting its price to drop, then you buy it at the reduced price and deliver it back to the broker, pocketing the difference. To do that in the Big Pharma volumes being talked about in the last two weeks, you'd need to be very confident in your information.'

David held up his empty wine glass, and somehow, mysteriously, Michael appeared from the kitchen and refilled it.

'You think Wilton McGwyer and Van Heeren have been shorting?'

'No, I don't. I'm odds on certain that Karim Farzan of Wilton McGwyer used the stories EANA was preparing about the corruption at Nui BioLab in Vietnam to warn Anglo Swiss that they needed to get out front with stories of their own, and then used his inside information to dive into their shares—and other Big Pharma stocks, probably—in advance of their announcements to the market. And if I could prove it, he would be dissuaded from taking any action against EANA, and indirectly, against Caroline. The same goes for Van Heeren. That's what I mean by insurance. That's why you'd be doing me a big favor if you could get anything to back me up.'

'Okay, I've got it.' David hesitated. 'I'll see what we can do. But you do understand how difficult it is to prove these things, don't you? Particularly in the next four days.'

Faraday nodded. 'Yes, I do.'

There was a pause in the conversation while they both thought about what had been said. Faraday had lost his enthusiasm for his salmon and put down his knife and fork.

'But there are two levels of proof, aren't there?' he said, as if thinking out loud. 'There's irrefutable proof of the sort that can stand up in court, and there's the informal truth that circulates quietly in the market, because someone *knows*. Or thinks they know. Bits and pieces of that informal kind of reportage can be enough to persuade someone that a case could be built. Then, using those bits and pieces, the guilty party might be persuaded that there's more—because, of course, they know there *is* more—and that could be enough to convince them that they've been rumbled. For my purposes, that might be insurance enough on its own. At least, that's what my sharebroker contact told me.'

'I don't understand.' David seemed less than pleased. 'You mean you've asked him to find evidence on these people already, as well as now asking me?'

Faraday waved him off. 'No, he and I were talking about shorting. That's a different matter. I'm just thinking that the same theory might apply to persuading someone that you have information about their insider trading. It's the same as having information about who's shorting.'

At that point, Michael came in to clear their plates, interrupting them. He was visibly disappointed at Faraday's lack of appetite.

'Not to your liking, sir?'

'Oh, no, very much to my liking, Michael. But unfortunately, I'm on London time, which is well past midnight, and my appetite is in sleep mode. It was delicious. So was the asparagus. So is the wine.'

'Thank you. Another glass of the *Côte de Rhone,* then?'

'No, I'll sit on what I've got left, otherwise I'll nod off.'

David watched this exchange without much interest. His thoughts were elsewhere as he waited for Michael to leave the room.

'And what did he tell you about shorting,' he asked, 'this sharebroker friend of yours? And what did you call it—"the informal truth that circulates quietly in the market"? Is that a euphemism for market gossip, better known as bullshit?'

Faraday laughed. 'Better known by us Brits as tittle-tattle, in case you've forgotten. Yes, I suppose so. Isn't tittle-tattle the first place you go when you want to know something that's not public? If you wanted to know what's going on at the BBC, they used to say, ask the lady on the tea trolley. Anyway, what he said was that the volume of selling in Big Pharma stocks in the last two weeks was enormous, and the word was that someone was short-selling in New York and stood to make a fortune. So, of course, my ears perked up, wondering if one or more of my twelve hundred Paladin names had the balls to bet against his peers who were choosing to quietly sell.'

'And…?'

'"What's the word?" I asked him. "What's the tittle-tattle?"'

David leaned forward with both elbows on the table, his chin resting on his fists. 'This is turning into a shaggy dog story,' he said impatiently. 'So, what is the tittle-tattle, Anton, according to your broker friend? Who's shorting?'

'Hoffman, Latrobe, and Goode.'

The sudden silence was broken only by the scraping sound of tempered steel against polished marble as David Goode pushed back his chair and stood up. He patted his pockets briefly—in search of his cell phone, perhaps—then mumbled something vague and left the room.

Faraday poured himself a full glass of water and devoured it in one long, unbroken draught. He was parched, and he poured himself another, which he drank more slowly.

It was three or four minutes before David returned to the room. His movements were more energized, his eyes bright.

'So, you think Mark Hoffman has been shorting, do you?'

'No, I don't. I thought about it, but it wouldn't make sense for any of the named foundation members of Paladin to be engaged in anything at this time, other than quietly disposing of their interests. Assuming they take seriously the threat of the close examination that investigative journalists are going to make, it would be stupid. Hercules may be good, but eight-hundred-odd investigative journalists with the scent of blood will take it to a new dimension.'

'Who, then?'

'To be honest, David, I don't care. It's money business. In the money business, shorting is normal. Risky, yes, but not illegal—and you don't make serious money without taking risks, I'm sure you agree. My sole focus is on revealing a criminal fraud. I lost a friend in Vietnam, murdered. Caroline and I nearly lost our lives, and innocent people have been deliberately sacrificed by a conspiracy of corrupt corporations and international bureaucrats. The information we've gathered couldn't be more damning. And with your help, we're linking people to it who will, hopefully, do everything in their considerable power to try and shut it down, because they have more to lose than just money. Do you know what an antigen is?'

'Tell me.'

'It was explained to me by Caroline's brother, Tuan. The first defense against a virus is the innate immune system, which mobilizes white blood cells to recognize certain aspects of the molecular anatomy common to all viruses, managing to destroy many of the microbiological invaders, and in the process, generating molecular fragments called antigens, which other players in the immune system perceive as foreign. The second phase of defense is called the adaptive immune system, and it takes these antigens as the starting point for a much more targeted response, which can create a living memory of the microbial invaders, so they can be more easily defeated in the future. In my analogy, Anglo Swiss, its co-conspirators, and people like them are the virus. The antigen, designed to create a living memory so they can be more easily defeated in the future, is the exposure we have created through our Lift the Lid campaign. Now it's up to the integrity of the independent media, and the willingness of people to accept uncomfortable truths about the world they live in. They become the antigen.'

David clapped loudly and stamped his feet like a football fan. What had he taken when he went out of the room? It surely wasn't alcohol.

'But buddy, buddy, as much as I love your idea of creating an antigen… You're not going to stop bird flu from spreading. No matter how it was spread, it's here now and will have to be stopped with pharmaceuticals. People are still going to make money off of that.'

'At least we'll walk into that problem knowingly.'

Faraday was suddenly overwhelmed with exhaustion. The tension he'd been carrying, combined with the long flight, had finally caught up with him.

'I'm talked out. Is there anything more to say tonight?' he asked.

'Yes.' David walked around the table and stood behind him, placing his hands upon his shoulders. 'You're the crazy fucking idealist I've always loved, and always will. I really hope it works, that the antigen survives, so it's easier to defeat the virus in the future, even though we both know that the virus is human greed, and it'll never die, just mutate. You think I offered to have Hercules analyze that list of names for you so I could profit from it, because that's what I do: profit. I'm a money man. And you're right. Sure, shorting is not illegal. You acknowledge that. But don't go away thinking I need to profit if I'm ever going to help you. Money will always be secondary to our friendship.'

Faraday nodded thoughtfully. He believed him. That was a relief.

'In the meantime,' David continued, 'I've been thinking. I'd like you to own Marsh Cottage outright. You need to be connected to the land, and New York is my home now; you can see that.'

Faraday was taken off guard. 'I'm not sure I can afford to buy it outright, David.'

'Yes, you can. The price is one thousand pounds, lock, stock, and barrel. Then we're all square. Take it or leave it. And the condition is that I'll be welcome whenever I come to visit.'

THE END

APPENDIX

BIRD FLU, FEAR, AND PERVERSE INCENTIVES

By David Bell, June 10, 2024, The Brownstone Institute

A 59-year-old man unfortunately died in Mexico in late April. Having been bed-bound for weeks and suffering from type-2 diabetes and chronic renal failure, he was at high risk from respiratory virus infection.

It became newsworthy, and the World Health Organization thousands of miles distant even released a media statement, because recent advances in genetic sequencing allowed the presence of Type A (H5N2) influenza virus – a type of bird flu – to be reported in a single clinical sample a month later. Refuting the WHO's distant bureaucrats attributing mortality to the virus, Mexico's health secretary is reported as noting that it was chronic illness that caused the death.

Irrespective of cause, deaths are a tragedy for family and friends. This one made global news purely because of advances in diagnostic technology. The WHO, the media, and a growing pandemic industry had been waiting for this inevitable event, testing and screening, as it is critical to perhaps the largest business scheme in human history. There are hundreds of billions on the table, and the will and means to take it. We all need to understand why, and what is supposed to happen next.

Covid and the Resetting of Public Health

Covid-19 has proven the business case for gain-of-function research. It looks increasingly likely that some genetic fiddling really did succeed in moving a bat coronavirus into humans, where it is more amenable to monetization (there is no profit in sick bats, or fear of them). Importantly, despite the broad economic and health catastrophe that followed, those behind the program are continuing much the same work, and not being held to account. There is vast profit with little or no real risk.

However, what the Covid episode really demonstrated is the financial and political gains that can be achieved irrespective of outbreak severity. As Klaus Schwab and Thierry Malleret pointed out in mid-2020 in their book Covid-19: The Great Reset, Covid-19 can be used to subvert post-World War II concepts of democracy and human rights and return society to a corporate authoritarian model ("Stakeholder Capitalism"), even though the illness is usually mild.

What is needed is a shared narrative among those who stand to benefit; media, governments, and the corporate world. While the term "Great Reset" seems to have been discarded as unpopular, the World Economic Forum's (WEF's) stated intent to penetrate governments and change society to the benefit of their members is clearly undiminished.

Devastating mortality is not needed to drive societal change; just the fear of it. You need a test, visuals such as masks and circles on the pavement, a dependent media, and a research and health establishment whose career opportunities are dependent on compliance. The ramping up of surveillance for the vast sea of viral variants that is nature has just been officially confirmed through the adoption of amendments to the 2005 International Health Regulations at the World Health Assembly (WHA) in Geneva. Irrespective of the reality of risk or the massively disproportionate public funding required, the world is going to find a lot more potential threats, and is building a whole industry that will ensure they translate into corporate profit.

The Opportunity of Influenza

Avian influenza, or bird flu, has been around perhaps as long as birds (so was likely a dinosaur malady in Cretaceous times). Humans must have lived alongside it for over 200,000 years, and our primate ancestors far longer. Bird flu viruses are part of a range of variants of the influenza virus family that undergo regular mutation and recombination (even mixing genome from viruses that normally infect different species) that makes them appear relatively new to our immune system. This makes them more harmful and results in a new influenza outbreak almost every year, as our immunity from the last one (or from a prior influenza vaccine) only partially addresses the next.

Sometimes, recombination allows an influenza virus that is mostly confined to other animals, such as birds, to undergo a wider shift that allows it to infect other species, such as humans. This is similar to what scientists sometimes try to simulate in the lab through 'gain-of-function' research, such as modifying bat coronaviruses to become pathogenic to humans.

Humans have always lived in very close proximity with, and eaten, animals that harbor influenza viruses. The last major 'spillover' of influenza from birds to humans was the Spanish flu pandemic in 1918-19. It killed perhaps 20 to 40 million people, most probably due to secondary bacterial pneumonia as there were no modern antibiotics. In the century since, an event of this nature has not recurred, and with modern antibiotics and medical care, the mortality of the Spanish flu should now be far lower.

So, why are we seeing the current hysteria regarding bird flu, and why is the media promoting narratives such as potential mortality massively greater than the Spanish flu or any influenza outbreak in human history? The answer, presumably, lies earlier in this article. A very wealthy corporate and financial sector that is influential over governments and media that knows, and has demonstrated, that wealth can be concentrated to the tune of hundreds of billions of dollars through fear of a virus.

There is now a rapidly expanding army of virologists, 'virus hunters,' public health bureaucrats, and modelers whose sole reason for receiving funding is to find and publicize new variants of viruses. We have international public-private partnerships devoted to developing and distributing vaccines for such events, supported by taxpayer funding. We also have a draft pandemic treaty that has just been deferred by the WHA, intended to further increase public funding for this private good. From an industry viewpoint, its rapid passage in the coming months would benefit from fear and urgency.

Making Bird Flu Work

Declaration of a bird flu pandemic therefore looks almost inevitable, whether facilitated by ongoing gain-of-function research and a lab leak, or through a natural passage to humans. This inevitability is not so much because it is a real and existential threat, but rather because the industry – the financial-Pharma-media- public health complex that has arisen before and through Covid, needs it. The virus is real. The threat can also be made to appear existential. It is likely to proceed with something like the scenario below.

Traces of genome and even whole viruses can be found in raw agricultural produce. Testing these, and human sewage (contaminated with virus from birds or humans), is already underway and will demonstrate this. Genome has already been found in milk, probably because we looked for it – this has probably also happened often, undetected, before.

Extensive testing of workers on chicken farms and on farms where other infected animals are housed (e.g. dairy herds) will find people who test positive for the virus. Biology is highly variable and some people will establish short-lived mild infections. A few will become severely ill and die due to some immune deficiency or factors such as a very high infective dose. Once listed as a rare pneumonia of unknown cause, such infections can now be definitively pinned as bird flu and used very effectively by media to increase viewership. Within the public health community, these occurrences promote salary and research funding and are extremely important.

Mass killing (culling) at chicken farms. This won't halt spread, as spread mainly occurs through wild bird species. It could theoretically protect workers from the low (but not zero) risk they face. Importantly, it makes news and promotes a perception that something really bad is afoot. Those who order culls do not suffer from them, and industrial chicken producers are compensated by taxpayers, who will also pay more for eggs and chicken meat. Left unchecked, many chickens would have died in an outbreak, while some would have survived.

Mass killing of secondary hosts such as cattle. Again, a low risk to humans. It is also relatively easy to quarantine cattle herds until an outbreak has run its course. However, culling creates publicity and the impression of a dynamic, desperate response, important in creating a sense of a public health sector scrambling to save the public. It also supports a movement claiming that farming for meat should be replaced by highly processed factory-derived alternative foods, an alternative that is struggling for market share. The fake meat industry is supported by some of the same major investors as Pharma, who are very vocal in the pandemic agenda.

Modeling to demonstrate potential mass death within the population. The major modeling groups (e.g. Imperial College London, University of Washington, Gates Foundation) are funded by entities who are invested in Pharma and gained greatly from Covid-19. Modelers understand outcomes that benefit sponsors, which may have influenced the emphasis on worst-case and highly unrealistic outcomes during Covid-19.

Requirement for mass vaccination (or killing) of backyard chickens to keep the community safe. The concept of 'greater good' is the most popular of the concepts that underpin fascism, and can be used to ensure broad compliance, with vilification of non-compliers being the penalty. This was used widely by pro- corporate politicians such as Justin Trudeau to isolate and denigrate those who wanted to weigh harms against the benefits of Covid vaccines or supported the concept of bodily autonomy. The UK and Ireland recently introduced a requirement to register all backyard chickens, to facilitate this process.

Requirement for vaccination of chicken owners – owners of every farm or backyard hen. This will be sold as further protecting their neighbors and communities. Those refusing will be portrayed as 'putting their entire communities at risk', especially 'the most vulnerable.' This message, however distanced from context and reality, is very powerful and the media demonstrated during Covid how willing they are to exploit such division and scapegoating.

Lockdowns, school closures, closure of smaller workplaces. As during Covid, this will involve mainly those lacking influence at WEF and similar forums. There will be some deaths in the community, and even busy ICUs from influenza or other causes. The busy ICUs will be highlighted as unusual (which, of course, they are not) to promote a need to 'all pull together' and overcome the threat. This is a difficult message to counter, as on a superficial level such fascistic greater good claims make support for individual choice, fundamental to free societies, difficult.

Population-wide mass vaccination. Mass vaccination can be promoted as inconvenient but necessary as an all-in community safety issue. Although people may be more resistant as harms from Covid vaccination become more widely acknowledged, bird flu is already being portrayed as potentially far worse. The vaccine will be pitched as a way to get freedoms back, a form of coercion once anathema in public health but now mainstream. With hundreds of billions in Pharma sales at stake, it is an extremely hard train to stop. Billions spent on advertising, political sponsorship, and propaganda are literally minor business expenses.

The order of the above steps, and the emphasis, may change. None of the steps will stop bird flu. It spreads through wild bird species and will continue to do so. Occasionally, it will spill over into humans. Very occasionally these will cause a significant outbreak. The Spanish flu was a bad example, but life rapidly went back to normal.

Managing Perceptions

In the century since the Spanish flu, influenza outbreaks have continued to resolve naturally with little change in human behavior, but steadily building alarm. The Hong Kong flu of 1968-69 had been shrugged off as an annoyance and didn't even stop Woodstock. The SARS outbreak in 2003 (a coronavirus, not influenza) promoted widespread fear, yet killed in total the same as die every 8 hours from tuberculosis. The Swine flu outbreak of 2009, which killed less than normal seasonal influenza, precipitated an international crisis. Pandemics, though real, are mostly about perceptions. So is the response.

The pandemic industry has become far better, and more systematic, at managing perceptions. This is the whole basis on which the behavioral psychology of government 'nudge units' was based during Covid. The aim was not a calculated overall public good, but to promote a particular set of public behaviors to address a narrowly defined threat. This is now underway for bird flu. A large part of the populace will comply with increasingly strict measures, not because they have been presented accurate information in context upon which they can make rational choices, but because they are fooled, or coerced, into behaviors they would not normally follow. They will accept restrictions and interventions that they would normally resist.

Unless wider society regains control of the agenda, the Pharma industry and its investors are set to make a killing through bird flu. It will be at least as big as Covid. It will also serve an important role in further building the pandemic industry, justifying the finalization of the postponed WHO Pandemic Agreement (treaty). It is a vital cog in the Great Reset.

Outbreaks do occur and we should monitor and prepare for them. However, we have allowed the development of a system where outbreaks are almost all that matter. Perceptions of risk, and resultant funding, have become grossly disproportionate to reality. The perverse incentives driving this are obvious, as are the harms. The world will be increasingly unequal and impoverished, and sick, building on the outcomes of the Covid response. Fear promotes profit better than calmness and context. It is on us to remain calm and continually educate ourselves regarding context. No one will sell these to us.

Author: David Bell, Senior Scholar at Brownstone Institute, is a public health physician and biotech consultant in global health. He is a former medical officer and scientist at the World Health Organization (WHO), Programme Head for malaria and febrile diseases at the Foundation for Innovative New Diagnostics (FIND) in Geneva, Switzerland, and Director of Global Health Technologies at Intellectual Ventures Global Good Fund in Bellevue, WA, USA.

About the Author

A.I. Fabler is the pen name of a New Zealand-born author who has spent a large part of his working life in London, New York and Sydney, initially in journalism and advertising, holding senior international corporate roles before turning to writing full time. He is the recipient of a number of screenwriting awards, including the NY Empire Award for Drama in 2017 and the 2017 Cannes Drama Award. His political satire, "AGENDA 2060 Book One: The Future as It Happens" was published in 2021, described by Kirkus Reviews as *'A laser-focused, irresistible lampoon of woke culture'*. It was the winner of the 2022 Indie Reader Discovery Award for Popular Fiction. His 2022 novel, "The Seed of Corruption", set in Vietnam during the 2004 SARS epidemic in that country, raises questions about Big Pharma and state collusion, with timely echoes of John le Carré's "The Constant Gardener". His January 2023 novel, "A Song for Leonard", is a murder mystery set in Seventies New York.

Visit the author's website at:
http://www.aifabler.com
Contact the author at:
author@aifabler.com
Subscribe free to his Substack at:
aifabler.substack.com

ALSO BY A.I. FABLER

AGENDA 2060 Book One:
The Future as It Happens

"*A laser-focused, irresistible lampoon of woke culture.*
Like all first-rate satire, this book lets most of its subjects' own real-world excesses do the heavy lifting. Fabler's scorn is exquisitely controlled, and a great many of his jokes land. All but the most hyper-censorious readers who spend far too much time online will find the results hilarious."

— KIRKUS REVIEWS

AGENDA 2060 Book Two:
AI and The View From Space

"Fabler crafts a compelling narrative of humans fighting against AI, fake news, and governmental overreach with a satirical look at how society may look if it veers way too far to the left."

— KIRKUS REVIEWS

"Kudos to Fabler for the imaginative complexity and multiple plot threads of the worlds he created, as well as some daring points of view. In Book Two, the satire is somewhat less trenchant, yielding in places to a softer, humanistic spirituality. Loved it!"

— Greg Sapp, DISCOVERY

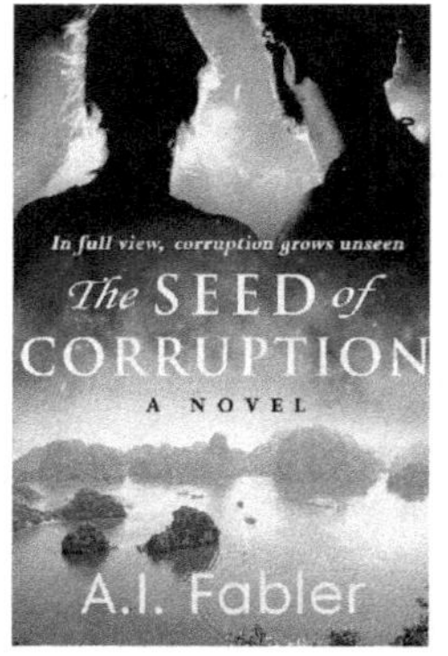

THE SEED OF CORRUPTION

"A.I. Fabler's THE SEED OF CORRUPTION is a heady stew of influences, from the travel literature of John Le Carré and Graham Greene to the dark journeys of *Apocalypse Now* and *Heart of Darkness*. Fabler's beautifully evocative, clever writing, however, transcends pastiche to emerge as a hauntingly original work."

— Edward Sung for IndieReader

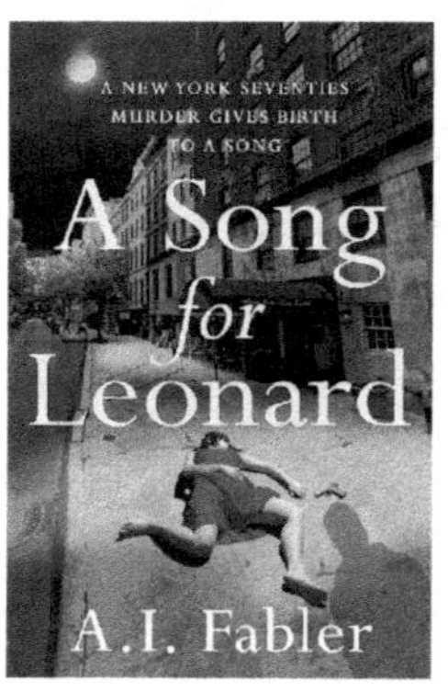

A SONG FOR LEONARD

"I had high expectations of *A Song for Leonard* and I was not disappointed at all. Fabler is a great storyteller. Books like this are what good fiction is all about - they take you off somewhere new with characters with whom you can gain an emotional response - you can recognize or dislike or root for, or other - and the events are fully realized so that your immersion in the story is complete. Fabler is definitely on my "Writers to Return to" list - a very good read indeed."

— Rachel Deeming, Reedsy Discovery

https://www.aifabler.com

www.ingramcontent.com/pod-product-compliance
Lightning Source LLC
Chambersburg PA
CBHW071422200726
48294CB00002B/487